FORGETTABLE

LISS BREWER

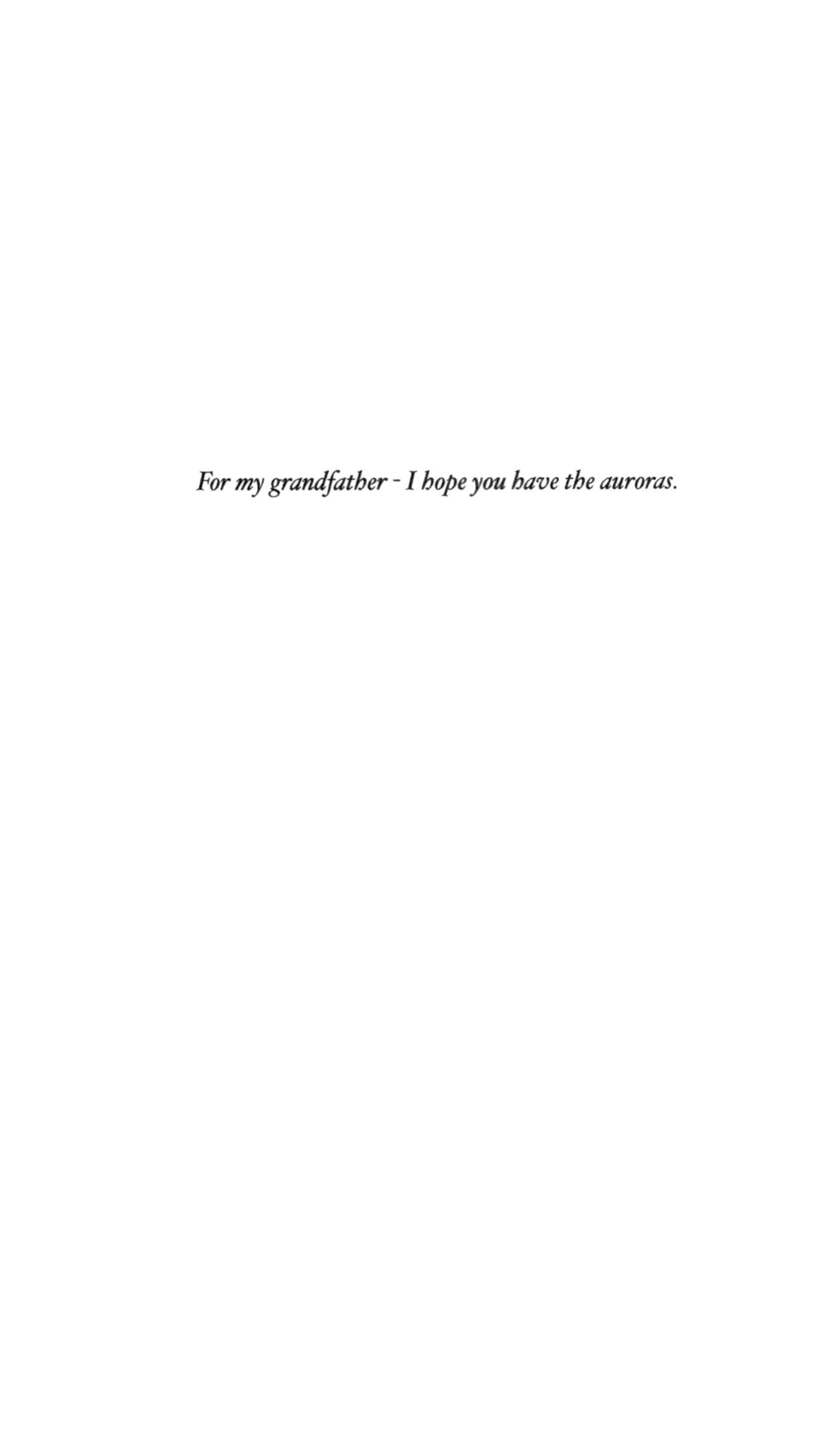

For my grandfather - I hope you have the auroras.

CONTENTS

CHAPTER 1

It began when Henry was twelve years old. A story so incredible that he never told a soul about it, except Emma, who was there and already knew. The seizures were terrifying, grand mal, his muscles contracting and releasing, and his mother screaming in horror. Then, the seizures stopped almost as suddenly as they began, and something else took their place. Like peering through a fog, the scene would come to him in flashes and pieces. At first, he shared them only with Emma, secrets about things that hadn't yet happened, soft around the edges. They left him as quickly as they arrived so that an hour later he could barely recall what he had seen, only fragments of a face, the colour of a dress. When he would try to get the words out to explain what he saw, they sounded like childish nonsense. Who was to know that when he said that he saw his father's heart like a cup dropped to the floor, it meant his father's heart would be broken - and that what *that* meant was that he would have a heart attack? His mother began to look at him with frightened eyes, suspicious, as though he wasn't really her child at all, but some kind of changeling left in Henry's place. Some time later, his father came home from hospital looking like a shadow, skin and bones, without the blustery strength that Henry remembered. So, Henry kept his own counsel, sharing only with Emma.

It would have been fine if it wasn't for what happened with Arthur. He knew that Arthur would drown. He saw it in the fog, the way his body would be pulled limp and blue from the surf. Arthur's tiny feet turned white, like the belly of a fish. Henry knew he had to tell his mother; that he must warn her that Arthur should not go swimming. They shouldn't even *take* the holiday to the seaside that she said would restore his father, as though the salt air were tonic. He tried to get the words out, the jumble that they become, but no one would listen. He decided to watch Arthur himself, and he *meant* to, but the sun was so hot, and Emma's hat had blown from her head, cartwheeling across the sand. It was only a few moments really, brief seconds of distraction where everyone's eyes were shifted to other importances. Arthur had slipped between the seam of time and into the blue and never came home. The small white casket. His mother's tight face. His father, shoulders shaking as he cried.

Emma grew used to the visions. She never tried to work out what was going to happen, accepting whatever would come. Emma - smiling at him, warm like sunshine, and saying that they could weather any storm. As the years went by, he tried to shield her from the worst of them, her empty arms and her stomach that remained girlishly flat, her breasts that would never fill with milk. But Emma knew. She always knew, seeing it in his face. She repainted the empty nursery and turned it into a sewing room, smiling at him through her tears.

When he saw the darkness in his mind and himself in the middle, lost in the mist he could not escape, he told her straight away. She cried and held him, her hands now soft and creased like tissue paper, and still the most beautiful things he had ever seen. They told each other everything, saying their goodbyes while he was still able to remember the sweetness of her face, the sound of her laugh. He could never have imagined that the small dam that separated him from the visions would break open as his memory grew more confused. The cruelty of forgetting Emma's name while seeing everything else was unimaginable. He skipped through time, like a stone upon the surface of the lake, alone, untethered, with nothing but the future stretching out in front of him.

Skip, skip, skip.

CHAPTER 2

Penny sat between two old ladies. One wore her best dress as though heading out for lunch, the other still had on a bib from the midday meal, and neither one of them seem to notice the stark differences of appearance.

"Nine," came the bingo caller's voice through the microphone. "Nine."

Penny tapped gently against the number nine on the bingo card in front of the lady in the dress, who nodded gratefully and placed her marker down. Penny looked at the clock; this would be the last game, and then she would go and check on her grandfather before she left.

Volunteering was like a strange apology to the universe. She would sit for hours each week helping with bingo, reading to those residents whose sight was failing. She would slowly push wheelchairs through the leafy gardens, avoiding the silence of her grandfather's room. Eventually, her time would draw to an end, and she would walk through the corridors, past rooms with televisions chattering and ladies sitting on the lounge until finally, Penny stopped at the door of her grandfather's room. Inside the carers might have left the tv on, or sometimes the radio was playing softly. Penny would go over and stand beside the bed, and her body would feel like it wasn't really hers anymore, like instead it was a suit and she was inside of it pulling levers and pushing buttons to make her limbs move. She would reach awkwardly for his hand, or rest hers lightly on his arm to announce her presence. At times his skin would still be warm from the sun if a carer had pushed his big fall-out chair through the garden. She had seen them huffing up their way up the hill, hoping that the sun rays might find their way inside the darkness of the Alzheimer's. She would have stilted one-way conversations with him, and he would look at her with curiosity, smiling politely. For some reason, she found it easier to sit with the people she didn't know, the dementia easier to come to terms with when you couldn't compare to the person they were before. Penny would stay fifteen minutes, watching the clock, and talking about meaningless things that drifted through ahead, before she would kiss his cheek the light stubble from his morning shave scratching against her lips. Then she would leave, ashamed by how quickly her feet moved as she hurried to her bike.

Steve kept asking her why she bothered going if it was only going to upset her. She had no idea how to explain it to Steve. Steve still had two healthy sets of grandparents, aunts and uncles in droves, and parents who were celebrating their thirtieth wedding anniversary. If she was honest with herself, his big, perfect family had been half the attraction. From the moment she stepped into his house at thirteen years old, she wanted to be a part of it. The Brents, with the Friday night board game sessions and pancakes on Saturday morning, seemed like a made-for-television family. Penny would watch them in wonder, and then go home to the small fibro house she lived in with her father. He would pull out whatever frozen dinner they were having and heat it up. They ate on trays in the lounge room in front of the television; then her father would fall asleep on the couch, and Penny would go up to her room to read until her eyelids grew heavy.

When Penny and Steve first started dating, Penny's mother had just disappeared again. Her father would bring Penny with him to the police station, where she sat in hard plastic chairs, and he begged for help. The truth was - while Charmaine Green was missing, she had never really been there in the first place. Charmaine lived in whatever world her schizophrenia took her to. After many months, her father sat her down and told her that unless Charmaine came home, or was taken to hospital where they can stabilise her mind with medication, they probably couldn't count on finding her. Penny had nodded and gone to Steve's to sit in the warm house, where mothers weren't missing, and no one even knew what microwave meals were. Her grandfather felt like her last link to her mother, the last part of her that Penny still had. Edward - Teddy to his friends - had virtually co-parented her when his daughter had left. That with his apology for her missing mother. Going to see him now was hers, for his missing daughter. Those with the things that Penny found herself unable to explain to Steve.

· · ·

She arrived at the door of Teddy's room now and stood outside for just a moment. One of the carers walked past her.

"How is he today?" Penny asked.

"He's good," he said cheerfully. "We had him outside this morning in the garden. He enjoys it out there."

Penny nodded. Teddy had always liked the gardens at his house. In the spring they would turn over the soil in the vegetable patch, planting for summer, she could almost smell the sharp freshness of the tomato plants now. If he was still at home, that's what they would be doing this month. She entered the room, Teddy was still in his big blue fall-out chair, a blanket over his legs, despite the warmth in the room. Penny resisted the urge to open a window to let out some of the stuffiness. Teddy seemed to feel cold all the time now; all the flesh had virtually melted off his bones. His room was sparse, although she had moved some of the things from his house in to help make it more familiar. On the wall were photos of the two of them, his eyes alight with laughter and lucidity. Penny found it difficult to look at them, painful reminders of all that had been taken from them both.

"Hey Papa," she said, dropping a kiss on his cheek. "How have you been?"

Teddy looked at her and smiled slightly, but no recognition was in his eyes. In the beginning, he would get her confused with her mother sometimes, although they looked nothing alike. She resembled her father mostly, dark hair and eyes, although where her father was stocky with muscles that never left from his youth, Penny felt like she was constantly doing battle with whatever diet was trending. Charmaine had dark blonde hair and blue eyes, the same as her grandfather. Both of them had lean, long limbs. Still, in the beginning, he would call her Charmaine, and then, as though he were peering at her from far away, finally recognise that it was Penny in front of him. She fussed over his blanket for something to do with her hands, adjusting it around him.

"It's a lovely day outside," she began. "The perfect weather for planting. Remember our veggie patches? We would eat the beans straight from the poles."

Teddy looked at her and said nothing.

"Work has been good," she lied. Work was never good. "I'm thinking about asking my boss to review my contract, maybe see if I can get a small pay bump. What do you think?"

He smiled. Penny looked at the clock. She glanced around the room, but there was nowhere to sit that would have her near him. She contemplated dragging the armchair to the window beside him, but it looked heavy. Penny chattered on for a while, talking about Steve and books she had read. Sometimes she made up stories that had never happened. With Teddy, she could reinvent herself however she wanted; she embellished her life to add more colour, weaving threads into her existence to make it sound more exciting. Sometimes she would read him her latest piece of writing, but nothing she wrote about Charmaine. She never mentioned her mother to him at all.

A man shuffled into the room pushing a wheelie walker. This wasn't uncommon, often the more mobile residents with dementia would wander in and out, or up and down the halls. When the mind began to fail, it seemed like they were always walking, searching for something, and never finding it.

"Hello," Penny greeted the newcomer. She didn't recognise this resident; he must be new. "I'm Penny."

He said nothing, and she bent down to look at the name card attached to his walker - Henry.

"You must be Henry," she said, straightening up.

"Henry," he mumbled.

"Right. This is my grandfather, Teddy."

Henry looked over at Teddy, who had taken the opportunity to stare out the window, ignoring his new guest.

Penny put her hand out and gently steered the walker back towards the door, "Come on, Henry, let's see if we can find you somewhere to sit. Afternoon tea will be served soon. Do you like tea?"

He allowed her to lead him from the room, down towards the lounge where three residents sat, watching the television.

She smiled at the group, "Good afternoon."

One of the ladies looked over at her, "Ahh, you've found him again. Always walking, that one."

"Yes, Henry and I have just met."

"You have met him before," the lady said.

Penny was quite sure she hadn't, but she flashed a smile, "Oh! I must have forgotten. Come on, Henry, let's take a seat over here."

Henry shuffled towards the armchair and backed in, slowly lowering himself down.

"There we go! The tea trolley will be around soon, okay?"

Penny chatted with the other residents for a moment, reluctant to go back to her grandfather. She patted Henry on the shoulder and made to go, saying goodbye.

. . .

Suddenly, Henry grabbed her arm tightly. His fingers had surprising strength. Penny gasped in shock, her instincts told her to pull away, but she pushed them aside and smiled into his face, nervous, but trying to hide it.

"That's it, Henry. Gentle. Tea is coming, alright?"

His fingers dug into her wrist, yellowed nails pinching her flesh, his eyes looked far away, and she wondered if he was having a stroke. Alarm filled her, and she looked around quickly for a carer or other staff member. Her eyes came to rest on the alarm button above the sink in the kitchenette, too far for her to reach. As she looked back at Henry, his eyes cleared, and he looked at her - *really* looked at her - with such lucidity that for a moment, Penny forgot his grip on her arm, startled.

"Henry?" She asked.

This was what she always secretly wished for with Teddy, a moment of cognition, where she could slip between the cracks and have him back, just for a second.

Henry leaned towards her, his words crisp, the voice of a younger man, "You'll slip on ice. Ice. The bear will help."

Then, as quickly has it had come, the fog fell back in front of his eyes, the clarity she saw a moment ago fading. He let go of her arm and leant back in the chair. Penny stepped quickly away. *He wasn't lucid; it was just the dementia. Ice? It was Spring.*

The tea trolley rattled down the hall. She shook her head to clear it and walked back to Teddy's room rubbing her wrist.

"I'm back, Papa," she said.

Teddy was asleep. She wouldn't rouse him, leaving Teddy to whatever peace he found in his dreams. Sighing, Penny went over to him and brushed back his hair gently, he still had most of it, although it was thinner now, and the blonde had darkened to a mousey brown since he wasn't in the sun all day. She kissed his cheek and picked up her backpack from beside the door where she had left it. Penny walked quickly back down the hall to the exit and out into the sunshine.

CHAPTER 3

Penny wandered up the path that led through the gardens to the pole where she chained her pushbike. Steve has been nagging her for years to get her driver's license; but the thought of being in charge of a tonne of metal, hurtling along the road at high speeds, filled her with dread. She simply told Steve that she enjoyed cycling, and it kept her fit. This worked well as Steve was always concerned about her weight, constantly asking her to come to the gym with him and explaining superfoods until she felt her brain actually switching off. She could never think of nothing, her mind always whirring and turning, except when Steve spoke about Spirulina or Kale. Then her mind went into a beautiful, blank, meditative space. She would sit quietly, Steve's voice becoming a background drone, and she would simply *be*.

Penny unchained the bike, dropping the chain and lock into her backpack. She clipped on her helmet, beginning the ride to the station that would take her home to the small duplex she and Steve rented from the woman next door. They had moved in six years ago when both Penny and Steve were just nineteen, and Steve was looking for a place closer to the university. They had both enrolled, Steve studying physiotherapy and Penny studying journalism, but she had quickly dropped out after the first trimester, unable to manage the study-load and also work part-time. Steve's parents paid his half of the rent, but Penny had to work to pay her half, her father unable to help her, and her unwilling to ask, knowing the pain it would cause him to say no. When she was offered full-time receptionist work, she took it. Linda, the landlord, loved Steve, always complimenting him on his appearance, gushing to her friends about the clever man next door, and finding an excuse to wander outdoors when Steve mowed the lawns. Linda viewed Penny with vague suspicion, as though she wasn't quite sure why Penny was there at all.

Penny thumped down the gutter and peddled along the street, passing afternoon walkers out with their dogs. She smiled and inclined her head in greeting. She steeled herself for the ride past the pub, where the tradesmen gathered in the afternoons for a knock off beer before going home. Usually, they ignored her, but occasionally they would whistle or whoop as she went past and she would peddle faster, trying to escape their gaze. She rode towards it now and just as she caught sight of the hi-vis workwear shirts, she felt the bike slide out from underneath her. Flying through the air, she landed hard on the bitumen, scrapping the palms of her hands and her right shoulder as she skidded along the road.

. . .

Penny lay there dazed for a moment, brought back to reality by the stinging of her shoulder and pain blooming in her knees. Shouts of alarm came from the pub. Sitting up, she took stock of her injuries. Her backpack had fallen off, ripping open and it's contents were scattered along the road. One of the tradesmen came running over to her and knelt beside her. His face was weather-lined from decades spent in the sun, but his blue eyes were kind.

"You've done a good job on yourself, love," he remarked, helping her to her feet.

Penny nodded dumbly.

"Anything broken?" He asked. He scanned her, wincing at the gravel caught in her knees. "Bet that hurts like buggery, hey?"

"Yes," she said, through gritted teeth. He put his arm around her to take some of her weight as they limped back to her bike.

"Here, let's get you inside and cleaned up. Dean will have a first aid kit inside; god knows enough drunks fall down needing it. I'll come back for the bike."

Penny looked at her backpack, "My things..."

The tradesman leant her against one of the cars in front of the pub and quickly dashed around picking up items. He shoved them back in her bag, handing it to her and steering her towards the entrance of the pub. Penny allowed herself to be herded inside, the yeasty smell of beer filling her nostrils. People looked over at her as she came in, and she felt her face flush in embarrassment.

"Dean!" The tradesman called. "You got a first aid kit for the lady?"

They reached the bar, and the young man behind the counter turned to look at them. His smile immediately turned to concern, and he motioned them through to a back room and had Penny sit in a chair.

"I'll be right back," Dean said.

The tradesman patted Penny's shoulder, "Dean will look after you. I'll go grab that bike and come back to check on you."

Penny looked down at her knees, encrusted with blood and debris, and moaned. She felt woozy and vaguely sick at the sight of them. The room spun, and she closed her eyes and leaned back in the chair.

"Hey, hey," Dean said, coming back in with a box. "You aren't going to faint on me, are you?"

"Maybe," Penny admitted. "Quite possibly."

He knelt in front of her, "Please don't do that. I know I seem capable, but I'm actually really bad in a crisis."

Penny looked into his face, noticing for the first time his smile, slightly lopsided and startlingly beautiful. He tilted his head to the side as though he could hear her thoughts and Penny looked away hurriedly.

"I'm sorry. I just really can't stand blood."

"Who can? It's revolting - and yet, I am going to clean it off of you. How nice am I?"

He began to unpack the box, pulling out gauze and saline while he talked, and pulling on gloves.

"What's your name?" He asked.

"Penny."

"Like the song?"

"What?"

Dean dabbed gently at the gravel embedded in her knee, and she winced.

"Sorry," he said, looking at her. "You want me to call an ambulance and get a professional to do this instead of a bartender?"

Penny shook her head, "No. It's okay. Thank you."

He continued, "So Penny, what do you do when you aren't crashing bikes in front of my pub?"

"I work as a receptionist for a book company. We publish academic texts, like textbooks for universities. Ouch!"

"Sorry, sorry!"

"No, it's me. I'm a big baby."

"How did you fall anyway?" He asked.

"I don't know, I was riding fine, and then the tyres just skidded out. It felt like a slip and slide."

"A what?"

"A slip and slide. You know, those things when you were a kid? Like a big sheet of plastic with sprinklers attached and you would slide on your stomach down them. The neighbour's kids and I would put dishwashing liquid on ours, and we would slide so fast we would launch off the end and on to the grass. You never use one when you were a kid?"

Dean laughed, "No, I did. I just needed you distracted so I could clean the other knee."

He placed a large square adhesive bandage on her knee, and she looked down in surprise to see them both clean and neat.

"That was fast," she said.

"I'm very experienced. People are always falling over in bars."

"I suppose they would."

"Now for your hands," he said apologetically.

Penny held them out towards him, looking at his face so she didn't have to watch as he cleaned them.

"Your eyes are different colours," Penny blurted out.

Dean burst into laughter, "Wow. You're right. Most people don't notice. One is blue, and the other is green. I got one from each parent."

He cleaned her palms swiftly, then looked at them with a frown, "I don't think I can bandage these. Unless I wrap them totally. But the grazes aren't deep."

"They'll be okay," she said, sliding off the chair. "Thank you so much."

"You want me to call your fiancé?" Dean asked, pulling off the gloves and washing his hands in the little sink on the wall.

Penny stared at him with her mouth open.

"How-"

"You have an engagement ring on. I noticed when I was cleaning your hands."

"Oh. No. Steve would be at work. I'll be okay to ride. I only need to get to the station; I can walk the bike home from there, it isn't far."

Dean grabbed some paper towels and dried his hands, eyeing her sceptically, "Why don't I drive you?"

"No, I couldn't! You have customers."

He shrugged, "It's up to you. I wouldn't want to be peddling with those knees."

"I'll be okay," she insisted.

He opened the door for her and led her back into the pub. The tradesman was standing by the bar with her bike.

"How did you go?" He asked.

"She was a trouper," Dean said.

"Well," the tradesman said, as Penny took the bike from him. "It's no wonder you slipped; there was oil on the road. It would have been as slick as ice."

Penny felt her heart skip, "What?"

"Yep. Oil. The road was so slippery I damn near fell over myself. You got some sand or something I can put on it, Dean?"

"Why would I have sand?"

The tradesman shrugged.

Penny barely heard them. *Ice. Henry. What had he said?*

"Kitty litter will work too," the tradesman said.

"Do you think I keep cats in the bar?"

You'll slip on ice. Ice. The bear will help.

Penny eyed Dean and the tradesman. Neither looked much like a bear, although the tradesman's arms were heavily covered in hair.

Dean looked at her curiously, "Are you sure you're okay?"

Penny shook herself back to reality, "Fine. I'm fine. Thank you again."

She stuck out her hand, and Dean looked at it dubiously, "If it's all the same, I think I won't shake."

Penny looked down and remembered the grazes on her palms, "Oh! Yes. Well..." She trailed off, before shrugging and giving him a thumbs-up. "Thank you."

Dean gave her a thumbs-up back, "It was my pleasure, Penny."

Penny turned to the tradesman, "I don't even know your name?"

"Ray," he said.

"Thank you, Ray."

"No worries, love. Go home and rest. Dean will pour me a beer for my heroics, I reckon."

Dean rolled his eyes and went behind the bar where a line had begun forming.

"Do you reckon we could use sugar to soak up the oil?" Ray asked Dean, sliding on to a barstool.

Penny wheeled her bike out of the pub. The cool air of the afternoon kissed her face, and she climbed on to the seat tentatively, placing her foot on the peddle. She decided she would ride down the footpath for a while, in case there was more oil nearby. She pedalled slowly past the cars that lined the street, utes filled with ladders and toolboxes that must belong to the patrons at the pub. Suddenly, she pulled up sharply, to her right was a dirty blue ute, covered in dust from the day. The signage on the side had been splashed by a kind of muck at some point, and one letter was half-covered. Penny climbed off and walked her bike over to the side of the tray, picking at it until she uncovered the letter.

Ray Bean Constructions.

She let out a breath and laughed at herself.

For a second, she could have sworn it said Ray Bear Constructions.

The new job is going well, I think. I hope. I still feel strange when I'm getting ready for work in the morning - like I'm putting on someone else's life while I am putting on my blouse. I imagine this 'other me' as having it together - she probably pays her bills in advance. I make my lunch, and double-check I have my house keys and walk to the train station. In the mornings, I seem to be focused. But in the afternoons, I daydream as I come home. I think about Penny and Lloyd, and what I might make for dinner when I go over on the weekend. I have all these conversations with them in my head, and in my daydreams, we are always happy and smiling, like an intro to an 80's sitcom. On the walk home, there is always a raven that hops along behind me. I fed him one time, and I think he remembers who I am and hopes he might persuade me to give him more food. I like ravens in general; they're clever creatures. But this one bothers me with the way he follows me from tree to tree and stalks along behind me as I walk along the footpath. My grand-mother used to say that to see one of them meant sorrow. I'm happy now; things are going well. But in the back of my mind, I always keep waiting for the other shoe to drop. Like sorrow is just following me around. Waiting.

CHAPTER 4

Penny opened the door and wheeled her bike into the entry hall, leaning it up against the wall. She put her backpack on the floor and hobbled into the lounge where Steve was watching television. He held weights in his hands and was alternately curling each arm while staring at the screen.

"Hey," he said. "You forgot to take the bin out this morning. We missed the garbage truck."

Penny rolled her eyes, "Yes, I'm fine, thank you for asking."

Steve said nothing, and began a new set, lifting the weights above his head.

Penny walked into the bathroom and began to strip off her clothes, wincing as she lifted her shirt over her head. She turned to her side to the mirror and twisted her head to inspect her shoulder - no broken skin, but already a nice sized bruise coming up. She gingerly peeled off the dressings Dean had placed on her knees, figuring she had better give them a proper washing out in the shower. Turning on the spray, she waited for it to warm before stepping in and winced as the water flowed over her grazes. Her knees had begun to feel stiff after sitting on the train, and the short walk home had been excruciating. She almost regretted declining Dean's offer to drive her home.

She tilted her head back to the spray of the shower and closed her eyes. For Penny, showers were like meditation. She would stand there for as long as the hot water lasted, decompressing, allowing the day to flow through her mind and disappear. She was naturally frugal, the product of growing up without money. Penny didn't buy branded items at the supermarket, she pieced together her wardrobe from clothing she found at op shops, she never paid full price for anything. The hot water bill was her luxury, she paid it without apology, treating it the same way other women she knew treated hairdressing appointments or gym memberships.

In the beginning, when she and Steve first moved in together, he would slide back the shower door and join her. They would stand under the water kissing and washing each other's hair, drunk on the freedom of life outside their parent's houses, giddy on young love. She wondered when that stopped. Was this just what happened to love? At work, Sarah and the other women would talk about their partners and how they would get angry if they didn't arrive home when they said they would. Penny couldn't remember ever getting mad at Steve for being late - Steve was home, or he wasn't. Sarah said that Penny was 'independent' - and Penny wasn't sure she meant it as a compliment. It was true that Penny was never bored, she always found something she could do; she had been amusing herself since she was a child, her father had little time for play. Penny would read, or write, she would take a bike ride, or lay outside and stare at the clouds. A dreamer, her father called her, and she liked that expression more.

Sometimes, when Steve was home, Penny found herself vaguely irritated by his presence. He expected her to talk to him, watch a movie, go to lunch - it seemed like he was intruding on her life. That happened less often now. Steve went to the gym or work, then he came home and mixed smoothies or shakes. They both read, but different genres. It seemed like they lived two lives, side by side, close - but never touching. Yet, the thought of not being with Steve was such a strange concept that Penny couldn't even contemplate what that would look like. Steve had been her constant since they were thirteen years old. At twenty-six, she had lived just as long with him as she had without him. *Everyone feels like this*, she told herself, *after so long together*.

Steve knocked on the door, "Hey," he called. "It's your night to cook. You want to do that chicken in the fridge? We could steam some veggies?"

Penny sighed, "Do you mind if we order in? I'm pretty exhausted. I had an accident on the way home."

"What kind of accident?" Steve asked, he walked in and opened the door, inspecting her.

"I fell off my bike."

"Christ, Penny. Your knees look like minced meat."

"A beautiful analogy," she snorted.

"An accurate one. Is it just grazes or do you think you've done some muscle damage?"

Great, Penny thought, *I've become a patient*. She turned the shower off and motioned for him to pass her a towel.

"I'm okay," she said, drying her face. "I'm just sore and feeling sorry for myself."

Steve stepped back so she could get out of the shower and finish drying off.

"Yeah, okay," Steve walked out the door. "I'll grab you some pyjamas."

He stuck his head back in, "Or do you want a nightie?"

"Either one is fine," Penny said, as towelled off her hair.

Steve nodded and padded up the hall.

"Thank you!" She called after him, as an afterthought.

Sometimes Steve was alright, she thought.

They sat down a little while later to pizza.

"This is actually disgusting," Steve said, wrinkling his nose.

"You said 'delicious' wrong," Penny lifted a slice to her mouth and took a large bite.

"I can hear my arteries clogging up," Steve complained.

Penny asked him how his workday was so he would stop ruining pizza for her, and Steve launched into a blow by blow description of the day, allowing her to drift in and out of the conversation.

"How was yours?" Steve asked. He was on his fourth slice, Penny noted, despite his harsh critique on the food.

"Well, work was work, but it was half-day Friday, so that is always good. Then I went to the nursing home after lunch to see Papa. Actually, it was really weird. Another resident walked in, Henry - he's new," Penny recounted what had happened with Henry, her fall and oil on the road, and Ray Bean looking like Ray Bear.

"Pretty weird, hey?" she said. "Almost like Henry predicted it. Maybe he's psychic."

"It sounds like dementia to me. If he was a psychic, why didn't he just say 'Penny, watch out for oil on the road. Also, you will meet a guy called Ray.' That would have been more helpful."

Steve shut the pizza box and leaned back in the chair, "I already feel like crap. I'm bloated. Maybe I am gluten intolerant."

"Maybe," Penny said, cheerfully, reopening the box and taking the last slice.

Steve yawned, "I'm going to go read in bed. I need an early night, I was going to go running at five tomorrow morning."

"Ugh! Why?" Penny asked.

"I like to go before it gets hot."

"Okay. Well, don't wake me. I'm planning a big day of getting up late and loafing around the house."

Steve got up and wandered down the hall to brush his teeth before going to bed.

With Steve gone, Penny switched off the television and retrieved her backpack from the front hall, wincing as she walked. She sat back on the couch and removed the contents that had been haphazardly shoved in by Ray. The bag was trashed, she would need a new one. She pulled out pieces of paper and flattened them as best she could. Penny had a habit of writing down what she called 'snippets' - phrases or memories that popped into her head. She wrote them on whatever was handy at the time, the backs of envelopes, sticky notes, napkins. When she had time, she would transcribe them into her journal, kept tucked away in a drawer in the room. Eventually, she hoped, she would string them all together like beads on a necklace and have something that was complete. She showed no one this work-in-progress, guarding it and tending it like her own secret garden. She wrote about the disappearance of her mother, about her grandfather's dementia - and more recently, about the emails she had been receiving.

The first one arrived on Penny's twenty-fifth birthday. It was a Sunday. Steve had gone to the gym, and Penny had been lying in bed, contemplating getting up and riding to the cafe down the street for cake. It was perfectly acceptable to eat cake for breakfast on one's birthday, she had rationalised. She picked up her phone and checked her emails. She was marvelling at how every store you had ever purchased anything from seemed to email you on your birthday when she had gasped and shot straight up in bed. There was an email from her mother.

Penny had dropped her phone, and it had skittered under the bed, forcing her to get down on her hands and knees, grasping wildly in the dark. She had pulled out three odd socks and a dust bunny before brushing her hand against her phone and pulling it out. Shaking, she sat on the floor and opened the email.

Happy birthday, it read. Penny read the email quickly and then, confused, read it again. *Happy birthday, my darling. Today you are thirteen.* What? Her mother went on to tell her how proud of her she was, that she was sorry she wasn't always around. She talked candidly about her mental illness and trying harder to manage it. She spoke about a new unit she had rented and how it had a bedroom for Penny. It was exactly as though Charmaine had written it twelve years beforehand. Penny scanned it again. Right there, at the top of the email, was the date - the date of Penny's birthday the year she turned thirteen. It didn't make sense. She knew that posted letters could sometimes be delayed, once she had ordered a book that had been lost and turned up five months later, the package battered and scuffed. But email? Was it even possible?

Steve had come in then, covered in sweat, his shirt clinging to his chest.

"What are you doing on the floor?" He had asked.

Penny had stared at him, her mouth opening and closing like a fish out of water.

"Well, get up. I'm taking you to breakfast. One of the guys at the gym knows this vegan cafe in the city," he had held up his hands in mock surrender. "I know, I know. It *is* vegan - but he assures me they sell delicious baked goods. We'll find you a muffin or something and shove a candle in it."

He had left the room to shower, Penny staring after him. In the end, she hadn't told him. It was some kind of glitch, an accident. What was there to say?

Then the next week, there was another - week after week for nine months, email after email. Sometimes, her mother talked about her new job at the pharmacy, where she had worked as a dispensary assistant. Sometimes she recounted a visit with Penny. Increasingly, though, the emails began to curate her mother's spiral into her delusions.

Lloyd is seeing that woman again, she wrote.

She talked about Penny's father having an affair, saying that she had seen him with someone else. Lloyd and Charmaine had never had an easy relationship, more often than not Charmaine had lived alone, Penny living with her father. Sometimes Charmaine would come and live with them for a few months, but she preferred her own space. Still, she knew her father loved her mother. Once she had asked him why he didn't get a divorce, and he had shrugged.

"She is the love of my life. I know she doesn't need me, she lives so much in her own head, but she loves us as best she can. I just live for whatever parts of her she will let me have. That's enough," he had said.

The thought of him having an affair was unthinkable.

Then, Charmaine began to talk about being watched. She felt like someone was following her. She spoke of things in her unit being moved, of laundry going missing. Paranoia. Penny could barely stand to read them, it was what she and her father had always suspected, that she had gone off her meds and been carried off by her delusions. Here was the answer for why Charmaine had left, given to Penny through some cyber glitch. She wondered how different the situation would have been if she had have received them when they were written; if she and Lloyd had known. Then suddenly, they had stopped.

Penny had contemplated going to Lloyd and showing him, but when she thought of those times at the police station, of hearing him cry at night when he thought she was asleep, she couldn't. It was better to let sleeping dogs lie. She might have told her grandfather if he had been himself, but he had already begun to fade, the Alzheimer's had him firmly in grasp. Instead, she began to write it down. The way the letters had shown up, her feelings watching from afar as her mother described the confusion in her own brain, and of course, the last remaining question.

Where was her mother now?

CHAPTER 5

Penny walked through the door of the pub, with flowers in each arm. Over the tops of the blooms, she could see Dean leaning against the bar, grinning.

"Well, if it isn't Penny, my favourite patient. Who's the lucky recipient of those flowers?"

"You are," she said, putting the bouquets down on the bar top, she glanced around. "Well, you and Ray. Is he around?"

"Should be any time now," Dean said, he picked up a bunch of flowers and eyed them. "I've never been given flowers before."

Penny slid onto a stool, "I thought about buying you both a bottle of whiskey, but it seemed a bit strange to be bringing booze to a pub."

"Good point."

"I wanted to thank both of you for helping me out last week. I would have come sooner, but I couldn't ride until now. Plus Friday is my half-day."

Dean peered over the bar at her knees, still thickly

encrusted with scabs, "I'm terribly sorry, Penny. Those knees are absolutely revolting."

"Thank you," Penny said, cheerfully, not insulted at all.

"Let's get you a drink on the house. What would you like?"

Penny thought, "Cider, maybe? Thank you."

"Excellent choice. I've got one on tap here that you'll love."

Dean poured her a drink and slid it in front of her, "I see your palms are looking much better, though."

Penny looked down at them, most of the grazing had been superficial, the scabs already peeling off in places, leaving behind pink, new skin.

Voices boomed behind them as a group of tradesmen entered the pub.

"Here he is," Dean said.

Penny turned and spotted Ray, giving him a wave.

"Hello, lass. Did you ride here today, or fly in again?" Ray said.

"I took the more conventional way," Penny replied. She held out the flowers, "These are for you."

Ray went a startling shade of red as he took them from her, "Christ. I've never gotten flowers before."

"That's what I said," Dean remarked.

"Well, you both deserve them," Penny said.

"Thank you, love. I'll take them home and give them to my wife. Except since it's not Mother's Day or her birthday, she'll think I've gotten myself into trouble and am trying to soften her up."

Penny laughed, "I'm sure she'll love them."

Dean poured rounds of beer for the tradesmen, who took them outside to their regular tables.

He turned to her, "Did you end up getting home okay, last week?"

Penny nodded, sipping her cider. Dean was right, it was delicious.

"There is pomegranate in it," he said.

"What?"

"The cider."

Suddenly, he jumped, "I almost forgot."

He reached under the bar and pulled out a wrinkled sheet of paper, water-stained, and slightly dirty. He handed it to her.

"Is this yours?"

She looked down at it, and her face flushed, "Where..."

"I found it outside in the bushes as I was clearing tables. Ray had said your stuff went all over the road. I thought it might have blown there. I knew it couldn't be any of theirs because...well..." He looked embarrassed. "Sorry, I feel really guilty. I read it. I had to, to see whether it was rubbish. But then, I realised it wasn't, and I didn't want to throw it out. I wasn't sure if it was your only copy."

Penny traced the words, "It is. Thank you for saving it. It's okay if you read it."

She read it to herself now, one of her snippets she had saved to copy into her journal.

"When I visit my grandfather, there is a strange invisible wall between us. He is right there, but his mind is far away. I want to liken him to a time traveller, but that is not what it is. It is an absence. A distance.

In the dementia unit, I hold long conversations with old men who believe they are still young men, who believe they still need to find enough work to support their families. They hold out their hands, gnarled and withered, and they see only the strength that was in them decades before. With them, I talk about a time that existed before I did, as though it were happening today. My grandfather is not like that. He doesn't skip through the years. He simply floats on the surface of this one, like oil on water. He is beyond time.

I wish he would talk to me. I would be anyone he wanted me to be. He could forget my name and think I am a stranger, and I think it would be better than the silence.

He curls into his bed, he is a lump under the blankets. It always disturbed me as a child to see adults sleeping. I felt as though they must always be awake when I was. It felt wrong to be in the world, conscious and aware, when they were not. I have an urge to climb into the bed beside him and lie there. I would talk about my day, my life, my work.

I want to lie beside him with a photo album and point out all the people we know. I want to watch television there, or we could read the newspaper, and we would both be there together. Him, silent. Me, chattering. But instead, I stand awkwardly by the bed. There is nowhere to sit. I cannot think of a single thing I have done to tell him. My memory is a blank as his. Both of us spinning through the emptiness, never touching.

Where are you? I need to know.

His eyes are blue. They remind me of a cloudless sky, endless, empty, forgettable.

They say that love is the last thing to go. Long after you forget your children, your wife, your own name - you remember love. You know that you love the person in the room, even if you don't know who they are. I picture it like a light... flickering, once and then again. Then gone.

I wonder if I will know when you forget that you love me."

"Your grandfather is in the home up the road, I'm guessing?" Dean asked, breaking Penny from her thoughts.

Penny nodded, "For almost two years now. I go to see

him a few times a week, usually. I volunteer up there too. I haven't been this week because of my knees. He doesn't notice if I'm not there, of course...but I know."

Dean looked at her sympathetically, "That must be hard."

"It is. It would be harder to not go, though. Or maybe not. I don't know."

"What do you mean when you say that he has forgettable eyes?" Dean asked.

Penny laughed, "Wow. You really read it, hey?"

"Once or twice."

"I guess I just mean the colour they are. They're blue, like the sky when it's cloudless, but there is no other way to describe it. When the sky is stormy, you can spend ages writing about the texture of it, the variation of colours. When it's sunrise or sunset, it's the same. But that clear, clean blue? It's forgettable. You see it and move on. I feel a bit that way myself most of the time."

"Forgettable?"

"Just... ordinary, you know? Like I could slip in and out of a room, and no one would ever know I was there."

"Unless you come in bleeding all over their bar. That tends to be a showstopper."

"Exactly."

A patron walked up to the bar, and Dean took the order, waiting until they had left before turning back to Penny, "So, you're a writer, huh?"

Penny ducked her head, "Oh, no. Not really. I just write down bits and pieces of things I think, sometimes. My grandfather and my mum. You're actually the first person who has ever read anything I have written. Sometimes I read parts to my grandfather, but, well..."

"What about your fiancé?"

"Nope. He doesn't know. Steve wouldn't be interested in what I write, he reads different things. Health books, some war novels, that kind of thing."

Dean smiled at her, "In that case, I am honoured to be your first reader."

Penny finished her drink and stood up, "I should be going. It's my night to cook. Thank you again for your help last week."

Dean took her glass and upended it on a rack, wiping the counter down with a rag, "It was nothing. Thanks for the flowers. Come in next time you see your grandfather, I'll shout you a drink."

Penny went to decline politely but found herself saying she would. She reached the door when Dean called out to her, "Penny!"

She turned, he was leaning on the counter, flashing her that smile again.

"Yes?"

"You're not forgettable."

She stared at him for a moment, then flushed, before rushing out the door to where she had chained her bike, surprised to find her hands were shaking.

Penny got home before Steve. Usually, on a Friday, she would have gone to the nursing home to volunteer, but she had rung in sick this week, letting herself heal. All week she had been hobbling around, feeling as though she was eighty-five years old. Avoiding the bike, she had taken the train to work, her shoulder had felt so stiff from the fall, she could barely move her arm in front of herself at all. Finally, she had asked

Steve to check it, fearing she had done serious damage, but after he prodded and poked her, he proclaimed her clumsy, but healthy.

"I'm not clumsy!" She had protested. "There was oil on the road. Anyone would have fallen over!"

"Whatever you say, Humpty Dumpty."

She went into the kitchen now and opened the fridge and pantry, looking for snacks. Penny picked up one of Steve's protein bars and eyed it suspiciously. *Chocolate. Well, that can't be too bad*, she thought. Opening the top, she sniffed and then took a tentative bite.

"Ugh!" She exclaimed, spitting it back into her hand. "Oh, god. That's revolting. Why? Why would someone do this to food?"

She disposed of the contents in the bin and washed her hands. Peering around the corner, to be sure Steve wasn't coming in, she opened the pantry again and climbed the step ladder to the top shelf, pushing aside reusable bags until her fingertips grazed the edge of a box.

"Pop tarts, my forbidden love," she said to them. "Come. Let us run away with each other."

She ripped open the foil and took a bite. Sighing, she leaned against the kitchen bench, blissful.

The front door opened, and Steve called out a greeting from down the hall.

"Shit!" Penny muttered under her breath, hastily shoving the box in one of the drawers. She stared helplessly at the pop tart in her hand.

Steve wandered into the kitchen in his gym clothes, scratching his chest, and looked at her critically. He took a bottle of water from the fridge and chugged half of it down, his Adam's apple bobbing with each swallow.

Nothing for it then, Penny thought and took another bite.

Steve frowned. "Do you really need to be eating that? God, Penny. It isn't even real food." He left the room without waiting for a response.

Penny swallowed. "Do you really need to be eating that?" she mimicked, flipping the bird at the empty doorway.

"Huh? Did you say something?" Steve called out.

"Nope," Penny called back. "Nothing."

She sighed. "Asshole," she muttered under her breath. Penny looked down at the pop tart in her hand, "Don't you listen to him. I still love you."

"What?" Steve yelled.

"Nothing! I'm talking to myself."

"You've lost the plot, Penny," he called back. "I'm taking a shower okay? Can you start dinner? Not pasta! I've gone gluten-free. We can make spaghetti with zucchini."

Penny rolled her eyes to the ceiling, "Okay!"

She peeled back the foil from the last of her pop tart, "I may have to eat your friends later."

She popped the last of it in her mouth.

CHAPTER 6

Penny sat at her desk at work, clicking her pen. It was a quiet day. There hadn't been many phone calls, and the emails were all up to date. Grant, her boss, had given her a text to edit and she had flown through it and was now sitting, with nothing to do. Through the glass in front of her she watched the cars go by, and thought longingly of lunch, even though it was barely eleven o'clock. She took a deep breath. *Okay, just get up and do it*, she thought, *come on. Up you get*. She stayed sitting. Sarah came out of her office and walked to the water cooler, filling her cup.

"God, I need to stretch my legs more often," she complained. "I think I'm getting varicose veins." She turned and pointed to the backs of her knees, "Can you see them?"

"No," Penny said.

"Well, they're there."

Sarah came over and leant on Penny's desk, "What are you doing anyway?"

"Nothing. Slow day."

"Well, go ask Grant for another text to edit. There is

more than enough. God knows I can't do it all myself, Anne is on holidays until next week, and Steph called in... sick." The way Sarah said it implied heavily that she believed Steph was not sick.

Penny sighed, "He doesn't like me to edit too much."

"Well, he's a dickhead, then. You're good at editing. How long have you been here for?"

"Seven years."

"Seven! Shit, Penny. We need another editor. Speak to Grant."

Penny nodded so Sarah would drop the topic, and smiled at her as she went back into her office. The truth was, Penny had been working up the courage to ask Grant to give her an editor position for over a year now. She just couldn't find the right moment. Taking a deep breath, she went and tentatively knocked on his door.

"Yep?" Came the voice from inside.

Penny opened it reluctantly, she always felt apologetic whenever she entered anyone's office, as though she was disturbing something very important.

"Are you busy?" She asked.

"Yes."

"Oh. I can come back," Penny turned to go when Grant sighed heavily.

"You may as well come in now, Penny."

He leaned back in his chair and crossed his arms, his brown eyes looking at her expectantly.

"I was wondering... well... I saw that you had advertised for another editor. I was wondering, could I maybe not be considered for that role? Rather than hiring outside, I mean." She faltered at the beginning and then blurted out the end. Her heart raced, and her palms felt sweaty.

"Penny," Grant began, "It's not that I don't appreciate the work you do to help out. We just really need someone with a bachelor degree. We are editing and publishing academic texts, how would it look if the person editing them only held a high school certificate?"

Penny flushed, "I know. I understand, but we hired Steph when she was a first-year uni student. How is that different? Also, I edit all the time when we have too much work. I edited today."

Grant sat up and picked up his pen, "I'm sorry, Penny. The answer is no. If you want to go back to uni, I can look at our options then."

"I can't afford to go back, Grant."

"Well, it is what it is."

He put his glasses back on and looked at his screen, indicating that the conversation was over.

Penny turned and walked out, feeling tears welling.

Sarah stood outside, "Well?"

Penny shook her head.

"Ugh. He's an idiot. You would be better than Steph never-turns-up."

"It is what it is," Penny said.

After work, Penny decided to ride by her father's house. *Sometimes,* she thought, *you just needed the comfort of home.* She pedalled along the bike path that ran through the park that bordered the back of her father's street. Hoping off she wheeled the bike over the grass and through the gate that led into the backyard. Lloyd was standing by the hose, turning it off after watering the garden.

"Well, hello there, stranger. I wondered who was coming through the gate, I nearly sicced my guard dog on you."

His guard dog was actually a cat, and at that moment lying in the sun, soaking up the last of the day's rays.

Penny reached down to scratch the old tom under the chin, "Hey there, Buttercup. You wouldn't eat me, would you?"

"I wouldn't be so sure, cats have no loyalty. If I ever collapse in the house and no one feeds him for a couple of days, you would come in and find him munching on me."

"Dad!" Penny laughed.

The went inside, and Lloyd poured her a glass of juice, placing an umbrella in the top, a habit he had gotten into when she was little.

"Your cocktail, miss," he said in mock seriousness.

"Thank you."

Growing up, she had felt like it would have been easier for Lloyd if she had been a boy. She could remember her father, his big calloused hands awkwardly clasped in front of him in the lingerie store when she was thirteen and needed a bra. His neck had flushed red as he stared at his work boots as though he were trying not to make eye contact with the mannequins. The first time she had gotten her period, they had both sat down with the packet in front of them, Lloyd squinting at the directions on how to use a tampon before she had taken pity on him and gone to figure it out herself. He had tried his best to be both a father and a mother for her. She blew gently on the umbrella, making it turn circles in her glass.

. . .

Lloyd leaned back against the kitchen counter and looked at Penny expectantly.

"What?" She said.

"Wondering to what I owe the pleasure of your company?"

"I can't just come see you?"

"You can. You do. But generally, when you show up out of the blue, you are looking for a listening ear."

Penny sighed and plucked the umbrella out of her drink, twirling it in between her fingers. She looked up at her father, who raised one eyebrow.

"I don't think there is anywhere for me to go with my job. I think I'm going to end up sitting at the desk when I'm fifty, answering phones and emails." She looked guiltily at Lloyd who was still dressed in his workwear, his boots scuffed and battered, crusted with dirt and debris from his construction job.

"I know I should be grateful for any job," she said hurriedly. "Lots of people would love mine... it's just... I don't."

Penny filled him in on the conversation between her and Grant at work and how trapped she felt.

"I can't go back to uni because I can't afford to work part-time and still make enough to cover the bills. It feels like a puzzle I can't work out. I need to go to uni to get a better job, but I can't afford uni without a better job first. It's like the whole system is set up for people who already start out ahead."

Lloyd nodded in appreciation.

"I just feel so stuck. Everything in me is always screaming 'not this', but I don't know how to change it."

Lloyd came and sat down across from her, "There isn't a

thing wrong with answering phones if you don't mind doing it and you're happy. The real problem is that you aren't happy. Telling yourself to be grateful for something you don't want is likely to be a fool's errand. If 'not this' then what? What will make you happy, Penny?"

Penny sat there, mute. *What would make me happy?*

"I don't know," she finally answered.

"Then that is what you need to figure out. Life is a blank page, kid. You can write whatever you like on it."

Penny finished her juice and went outside to help her dad hang his washing on the line, watching him through the gaps in the sheets.

Is he happy? she wondered. *Is happiness something we are even owed?* She put another peg on the sheet and picked a wet one up from the basket, draping it over the line. She wasn't *unhappy*, she knew that - she just felt... discontent somehow. As though she were constantly waiting for something to happen that would make everything click into place.

"You know what?" Lloyd said.

"Hmm?" Penny pegged the last sheet.

"Part of your problem has always been you let everyone else tell you what you are worth. You wait for someone else to notice you're clever or kind. Then, if they say you are, you believe them. You tend not to believe in yourself until someone else says it first."

Penny picked up her backpack and got her bike from where she had left them, "Oh, I don't think that's true. I asked for the promotion, didn't I?"

Lloyd waved a hand, dismissively, "I'm not just talking

about the job. What did Steve say about you wanting to go to editor? Or about not being able to go back to school?"

Penny flushed, "I haven't told him."

"Well, you would think if he got his head out of his own abs for five seconds, he would see you aren't happy. You supported the household bills while he was at uni, aside from his rent. I'm just wondering why he hasn't offered the same to you now that he is working?"

"I guess he hasn't thought about that. I hadn't either."

This wasn't entirely true. Penny had considered the possibility that Steve might be able to tip their household financial scales so she could go back to uni, but she wasn't sure she could manage back at school. What if she went back and failed?

"Are you still hiding pop tarts?" Lloyd asked.

"Maybe."

Lloyd made a *tsk tsk* noise of disapproval.

"He doesn't like unhealthy food," Penny protested.

"Well, he isn't eating them, is he?"

"Dad, Steve isn't that bad."

Lloyd snorted, "Well, he might not be that bad, but I'll tell you this much for free - he isn't that great, either."

Penny laughed in spite of herself and embraced her father, "I love you, Dad."

"I love you too, kid. Now, get outta here."

That evening Penny picked at her salad, her father's words in her head.

"Steve?"

"Yeah?"

He had a book on raw foods open at the table and was reading while they ate. Penny stole a glance, noticed a photo of kale, and wrinkled her nose.

"I was thinking about going back to uni."

He speared a forkful of greens and put them in his mouth, "I thought you said you couldn't afford to go back?"

Penny watched the salad being chewed as he talked and was momentarily sidetracked from her train of thought.

"Penny?" he prompted.

"Yeah?"

"I thought you said you couldn't afford to go back to uni?"

"I can't," she said.

"Well, then. How is that going to work?"

"I thought maybe you could cover the bills, I would still work part-time. Then after I've been back a while, Grant might put me on as editor."

Steve closed the book and leaned back in his chair. He scratched his face and looked out the window.

"Well, we could... but what about setting a date to get married?"

Penny was stunned into silence, Steve had been putting off setting a date for two years. From the moment he proposed she had begun looking at dresses and venues. Steve always had a reason for why they needed to wait, more money, more stability in his job. Penny had stopped bringing it up a year ago, right around her birthday when she had begun receiving the emails from her mother and gotten sidetracked. Steve had never seemed to notice.

"You... want to set a date?" she asked.

"Sure. I mean, if we set a date and got married, you said you wanted to start a family. How would that work with uni?

You could be right in the middle of it and pregnant. Or even if it didn't happen right away, you would have just started a career and then need to put it on hold to raise the children. Right?"

Penny ached a little at the thought of children. For as long as she could remember, she wanted two things - to write, and to be a mother. Her eyes were drawn to babies in prams, their chubby little fists waving, the way they kicked their legs in delight. For so long Steve had refused to discuss trying for a child, and now here it was, dangling in front of her like a carrot on a stick.

"So, if I stay at this job, we can set a date? We can talk about children?" Penny asked.

"Sure," Steve said, stabbing a tomato with his fork.

Penny stood up from the table, taking her plate to the bin and scraping her uneaten food into the trash.

"I'll think about it," she said. "But Steve, if I decide I want to go back to uni first, that's still an option, right?"

She turned around, but Steve was on his phone, putting the meal's calories into his fitness app. Sighing, she left the room to have a shower.

CHAPTER 7

Penny spent the next two days turning what Steve had said over in her head. The truth was, that while she still wanted to be a mother, the thought of getting married didn't give her butterflies the way it once had. On Wednesday, at lunch time, she walked through the city and stopped in front of a bridal shop. She looked through the glass to the mannequins in the window, yards of satin and tulle.

Impulsively, she walked inside, a bell tinkling as the door opened. Two women stood fussing over a young, pretty woman who stood on a box in front of the mirror dressed in a gown and veil. An older lady, Penny assumed the bride's mother, stood nearby taking photos on her phone, her eyes misted with tears. No one looked over at Penny. She walked aimlessly past racks of dresses, her hand brushing against the cool fabrics as she passed. She stopped in front of one of the dresses on display. It was still there. She had gone looking at dresses when she and Steve first got engaged, and this one had been in the window then. On lunch breaks, she would come down and stand in front of it, imagining herself trying it on. It had a sweetheart neckline and a small train. The bodice was beaded with hundreds of tiny seed pearls.

"Can I help you?"

Penny whirled around. One of the saleswomen was standing there, smiling at her. She was tiny and impeccably put together, her foiled hair sat without a strand out of place, a perfect helmet. Penny felt strangely unkempt by comparison and glanced down at her blouse, which bore a mayonnaise stain from the sandwich she had eaten earlier.

She swallowed, "I would like to try on this dress." She said it with a slight challenge in her voice, as though she expected to be thrown out at any moment.

The saleswoman was unflustered, however, "Of course."

She pulled the dress down from the rack and ushered Penny to a change room, where she carefully hung the dress, unzipping it from its clear protective bag and asking Penny questions about her plans for veils and tiaras. The woman was a whirlwind of positivity, and by the time Penny shut the door, she collapsed on the small sofa inside, exhausted. The change room was enormous. An entire bridal party could have fit inside, and she wondered if that was what it was for; brides with sisters and friends who would all come in to help do up buttons and zips, clucking like hens.

She stood and removed her clothing, careful not to look at herself in the mirror. Pulling the dress from the hanger, she stepped into it with some awkwardness, losing her feet amongst the piles of fabric that had pooled on the ground. As she pulled the bodice up, she called out to the saleswoman to help her with the zip, and Penny stepped outside the room. The other woman joined them and helped place a veil in Penny's hair, one of them sweeping it up with a practised hand, and slipping in bobby pins to hold it in place. The women stepped back, smiling and clasping their hands to their chests proudly, as though Penny were their own sister.

"Go and take a look," one of the women said, gesturing to the box the other bride had been on before.

Penny swished her way to the box, stepping on to it, like an athlete taking the podium.

She barely recognised herself. The Penny in the mirror had shiny, dark hair that had been pulled off her neck and a veil drifted dreamily around her bare shoulders, offsetting the olive of her skin. The bodice nipped in at her waist, the seed pearls glinting in the light that shone through the window. She was beautiful.

"What is your fiancé's name?" One of the women asked.

"What?" Penny asked.

"The groom?"

Penny glanced back at the mirror. Her reflection in the mirror stared back, coolly.

"Penny," she answered.

The woman looked flustered, "Oh! Of course. Another bride, lovely. And will she be coming to look for a dress too?"

This isn't me, she thought. *I don't belong in this dress.*

She stepped off the box and turned around.

"No. I don't think she will."

She walked back to the change room and shut the door, and struggling with the zip, she pulled the dress off, as though escaping from a straitjacket. She picked up her blouse with the mayonnaise stain and slipped back into herself.

Penny walked back to the office and stopped out front. Inside, her desk was waiting for her, piles of editing that Grant had dropped to her sat untouched beside the phone. She sighed and opened the door. Sarah came out of her office and began doing lunges across the reception area.

"Ugh. I need a standing desk. My ass is numb," she rubbed her behind absently and looked over at Penny, concern crossing her face. "Are you okay? You look like shit."

"Thanks," Penny replied, rolling her eyes. "I feel a bit weird, actually. Just... strange."

Sarah crossed to her and lay a hand against Penny's forehead.

"No fever," she stepped back, assessing. Penny felt oddly like she was back on the box in the bridal shop.

"You should go home," Sarah decided.

"What? No! Grant would flip out."

"Screw Grant. Who gives a shit?"

Penny looked at her pile of editing.

Sarah followed her gaze, "Oh, *hell* no. That isn't even your job. No. I'm telling Grant you're going home."

Sarah strode to Grant's door, Penny hissing at her to come back. Sarah stuck her tongue out at Penny and flung open Grant's door without knocking.

"Penny's sick. She's going home," She announced, then shut it again as Grant began to protest.

She turned to Penny and raised an eyebrow, waving her hands at Penny to shoo her out. Penny rushed to grab her backpack and hurried out the door before Grant could come out and argue.

Penny rode through the streets, unsure what to do with herself. She had never taken a sick day before, especially when she wasn't actually sick. She just felt... unsettled. Something about seeing herself in that dress had been jarring. It was beautiful, it was perfect. It fit like a glove. It just didn't *fit*, somehow. Without realising where she was going, she rode towards the facility where Teddy lived. She hadn't seen her grandfather since the Friday before last, and she suddenly missed him with a keenness that almost hurt.

Inside the facility, nothing had changed. It bustled with the usual activity of carers, cleaners, and lifestyle officers. She spotted Brooke, one of the lifestyle assistants, and waved to her. Brooke smiled warmly, her blonde hair pulled back into a ponytail that bounced as she walked over to Penny.

"Hey stranger," Brooke said. "I wasn't expecting to see you until Friday."

"I have the afternoon off," Penny replied. "How is Papa?"

"He's good. He's been listening to some music this morning. He's outside on the verandah right now, enjoying the sunshine."

Penny thanked Brooke and went out to the back verandah, where Teddy sat in his fall-out chair, a blanket tucked around his skinny legs. Orange socks with non-slip bottoms poked out the end. Nearby, a staff member sat with another resident, chatting to them while they painted. Penny pulled up a chair and moved it beside Teddy, dropping a kiss on his cheek.

They sat companionably, neither one talking, watching the birds dart from tree to tree, in the garden in front of them. The painters went inside, leaving their work to dry on the easel. Penny looked over at Teddy, who had shut his eyes and was sleeping, his mouth slack. She took his hand and gently lifted it to her face, resting it against her cheek.

One time, when she was seven, she had been reading a mystery novel and decided to practise her detective skills by fingerprinting the whole family. Charmaine had been around then, and she and Teddy were sitting in the patio, drinking coffee. Lloyd was at work. Penny didn't have any ink, so she coloured their fingertips with permanent marker and printed them on to a piece of paper. It wasn't difficult to get the marker off. A little soap and water and it disappeared – but on Papa's fingers, it had sunk into the whorls and loops, staining them. He stomped around the house, scrubbing at them, cross that the ink wouldn't come away. His hands were work-roughened, that was why the dye stuck the way it did. Charmaine and Penny had soft fingers, and so the stain hadn't set the way it had on him. She thought about that sometimes. The way his hands were so strong and rough from work. She thought if she did it again now, the dye would come right off, his hands felt smooth and fragile in hers. His grip was still strong, though. Sometimes he would hold tightly to her hand, clutching at it. It was as though he wants to tether himself to her, despite not being able to express the words. Just that tight grip, holding on. She wished she still had those fingerprints.

Two carers walked towards the verandah, their chatter startling Penny back into the moment.

"The new resident? Henry?" one said.

"Yep. He said to me, 'You'll find the Queen on the street'. Then I went out to lunch and found a five-dollar note," the other carer held up the note, tapping the Queen's face on the front. "I mean, he wasn't *wrong*."

The carers caught sight of Penny and Teddy and waved. She waved back, thinking about Henry and his strange warning to her about the ice that was really oil.

The carers went to go inside when the second one spoke again, "And Donna said that he told her that her 'house was in the river'. She went home, and the pipe had burst in the bathroom. She had two inches of water in the living room."

The carers disappeared inside. Inside her chest, Penny's heart was thumping. Could Henry really be seeing things?

Brooke came outside, pushing an elderly lady in a wheelchair and was followed by a beautiful woman with a shock of long red hair.

"Hi Penny," Brooke said. "I wanted to introduce you to one of our new residents. This is June Parker, and this is her granddaughter Rosie."

Penny got to her feet and shook both of their hands, introducing Teddy to them.

"I'm sorry he's asleep right now," she said.

She didn't add that it wouldn't have made a difference had he been awake.

"Would you like to sit out here for a while, Grandma?" Rosie asked.

"I'd like to sit in my *own* garden," June retorted.

Rosie stared helplessly at Brooke and Penny.

Penny turned her seat around and sat down in front of June, "Do you have a garden at your house? My Papa had a beautiful garden, he and I would spend all spring and summer out in it."

"Vegetable or ornamental?" June asked.

"Both," Penny replied. "How about you?"

June launched into a description of her garden beds, and Rosie looked at Penny with gratitude. Brooke smiled and waved goodbye, quietly walking back inside while the women chatted about roses and lavender.

Later, Rosie and Penny wheeled their grandparents to the lounge room for tea, where June made fast friends with some of the other women on the Wattle wing, where she would be staying.

"Thank you for spending the afternoon with us," Rosie said.

Penny shrugged, "It's hard for everyone when their family moves into care. June will be fine here once she settles in. The staff are really wonderful, and I volunteer on Fridays so I can come spend some time with her."

Rosie's phone beeped in her pocket, and she looked

apologetically at Penny, "That will be my mother. I've got to go. I might see you on Friday, then?"

Penny nodded, and Rosie went back to June to kiss her goodbye before leaving.

Penny went up to Teddy's room to check his toiletries before she left, in case she needed to put anything on the shopping list. She jotted some items he needed on a scrap of paper from her backpack and was zipping up her bag when Henry walked in.

"Oh! Henry!" She said. "Good grief, you gave me a fright."

Henry looked at her, "Emma?"

"Uhh. No. I'm Penny. We met the other day?"

Henry nodded slowly.

Penny looked at him, he didn't look like a... psychic. He looked like an ordinary elderly man, dressed in long pants and a plaid button-up shirt.

"Hey, Henry," Penny began, "I actually... the other day you gave me a warning about some ice? And I did actually slip. It wasn't ice, it was oil. But I guess I should have paid more attention, hey?"

"They happen," he said.

Penny shifted her weight, awkwardly, readjusting her backpack on her shoulders, "Right. Well..."

She couldn't say what made her do it. Maybe just a strange compulsion to see if it would happen again. Slowly, she reached out to him and took his hand. Penny scanned his face, waiting to see if it would clear again, the way it had last time. Henry blinked at her like an old owl. She let go, feeling stupid. The sound of the tea trolley made Penny jump.

"Let's go, Henry," she slipped past him and beckoned him to follow, but he stopped in the doorway.

"You'll find her," he said. His eyes shone with a clarity, "The grass lady. The one with the cloudless eyes."

Penny's heartbeat roared in her ears, and she felt her knees go weak.

"The grass lady? Grass... do you mean green? Green? Henry?"

Henry looked at her, "Green. Green grass."

The fog rolled over his eyes. He was gone again. *Green. Charmaine Green?* Could he mean her mother? Penny backed away quickly, tearing down the hallway, breaking into a run as she left the building.

CHAPTER 8

Penny pulled her bike up in front of the pub and chained it to the post outside. Her hands were shaking, and she found her whole body was intermittently shivering, despite the warmth of the day.

Striding inside, she called out, "I need a drink."

Dean turned around, a glass in his hand, and eyed her quizzically. Penny sat down on one of the stools.

"Seriously," she said.

"Okay," Dean said. "What sort of drink? Another cider?"

Penny snorted, "I think I need something stronger."

"Rum? Vodka? Scotch?"

Penny looked at him and bit her lip.

"Tequila?" he suggested.

"Can I be honest with you?" Penny asked.

Dean raised an eyebrow.

"I don't actually drink spirits," Penny confessed.

"Right... Shall we just stick with the cider then?"

"Please."

Dean poured her drink and placed it in front of her.

Penny pulled it in front of her and twirled it around. Dean busied himself with odd jobs around the pub, wiping down tables and pushing chairs in while Penny sipped at the cider and steadied herself. She didn't know what to make of what Henry had said. It seemed as though he had some kind of precognition, but the words came out jumbled. *Maybe because of the dementia*, she thought. Or, it could just be the strange things that come out of the mouths of confused people, and all be a coincidence.

Dean came back behind the bar and hovered nearby.

"So," he asked, "do you want to talk about it, or just pretend it didn't happen?"

"What?" Penny asked.

"Whatever it is that made you blow in here on a Wednesday afternoon asking for spirits that you don't drink."

Penny took a deep breath and closed her eyes. Where would she even begin? Back in the bridal shop when she realised she didn't want to get married anymore? When she slipped on the road after an elderly man warned her cryptically about ice? Or years ago, when Charmaine first went missing? She opened her eyes, and Dean was still in front of her, his strange mismatched eyes looking back at her warmly. The corner of his mouth pulled up in a smile.

"You know the other week when I fell over?" Penny began.

"Of course. Your knees were so gross that I thought I was going to puke all over you."

Penny rolled her eyes, "Thanks."

"I'm sure they're beautiful knees when they haven't been ground off on the bitumen though," he added.

Penny laughed, "Yeah, okay. Well, anyway, that day I went to see my grandfather and before I left one of the other residents warned me that I would slip over and told me I would be helped. That's weird, right?"

Dean leant back against the back of the bar and crossed his arms, considering, "Well, yeah. He told you that you would fall off your bike?"

"Not exactly. What he said was that I would slip on ice and that a bear would help."

"Ice?"

"Yes."

"But you slipped on oil."

"I know," Penny said. "But when Ray came in he said the road was *as slick as ice.*"

Dean nodded slowly, "Okay. I can see where you're going with this."

"I thought the bear part didn't make sense, but then when I was leaving I saw the signage on Ray's ute, and it said Ray Bean, except there was mud over the 'n' and it looked like an 'r'."

"Plus he has those hairy arms," Dean added. "Completely bear-like."

"Do you think I'm crazy?" Penny asked.

"No. This has been bothering you since you slipped over?"

"Well, no. It was just that some other people have had him say things to them too. And then today he told me something else."

Penny told Dean about what had happened in Teddy's room with Henry.

"My mother has been gone for thirteen years. Her last name is Green. And her eyes..."

"Cloudless," Dean said. "Forgettable."

"Exactly."

"So, you think this old guy was saying that you are going to find your mum?"

"I don't know."

"When Mum was first gone, at first it was no big deal, it happened often. She would leave for a while and then show up out of the blue. The medication made her feel bad, and sometimes she would forget or deliberately not take it. But she always came back. She always came home."

Penny told Dean about her parent's strange relationship, married but living separately for much of the time. It was easier on Charmaine and Lloyd to have separate spaces.

"The thing was," Penny continued, "even when she was gone, she always called. She let us know where she was, or she checked in to see how I was going and how Teddy was. This time it was radio silence, and that's what made Dad so worried."

He had gone to the police and filed a missing person report. Penny had found herself looking in crowds as she walked through the city, trying to find her mother's blonde hair, the way she walked with her arms holding each other as if she were trying to put a shield between herself and the world. Eventually, she and her father had gone to her mother's unit and boxed up all her things, Lloyd couldn't afford the rent on it, and Charmaine had stopped paying and received an eviction notice. Penny had slipped her mother's clothes into the cardboard box, running her hands over cotton and silk, the threadbare heels of her socks, her hairbrush and comb, golden hairs still caught in their teeth. Little had been missing from the unit, just a duffle bag and a few pieces of clothing, her mother's handbag and a photo of Penny and Charmaine that had sat on her dresser.

"Then, a year ago, I started getting emails from her," Penny said.

"She contacted you?" Dean asked.

"No," Penny said. "That's the thing. They were from just before she disappeared. She wrote the first one on my thirteenth birthday. They started out kind of normal, she was talking about everyday things. Then, the paranoia started. She accused my dad of having an affair. She began talking about someone moving things in her house, that she could smell them when she came inside after work and knew someone had been there. It was devastating and sad. Like I was watching her slip down a rabbit hole and couldn't help her because it had already happened years ago. Then one day, they just stopped. I kept hoping in one of the last ones she would write and tell me where she was going, but there was nothing there. I was just as clueless as beforehand."

"God, Penny. I'm so sorry," Dean's eyes were filled with sympathy. "I can see how what happened today would have affected you."

Penny nodded. She picked at the edge of a coaster absently, lost in her thoughts.

"You want to get something to eat?" Dean asked suddenly.

Penny looked up, surprised, "Here?"

"God, no. There is a burger place down by the water."

"Don't you have work?"

She glanced around at the bar, which was slowly filling with people now that it was nearing dinner time.

"My shift ended thirty minutes ago. Jono is just out back talking crap to the chef."

"Oh."

Penny looked at her watch, Steve would be at the gym. She found she *was* hungry, ravenous, in fact.

"Okay," she agreed.

Dean smiled, his face lighting up, and Penny found she had butterflies in her stomach. She felt oddly guilty, as though she were doing something wrong. *It's just a burger*, she told herself, *it's not a date*.

Dean went out the back to collect his things, and Penny sent Steve a text to say she was eating out. When Dean came outside, he helped Penny put her bike into the back of his old station wagon. She slipped into the passenger seat, and Dean started the car.

"It's old," he said, referring to the car. "But it still runs. Plus it only cost me three hundred bucks."

They drove in silence down to the burger place, Penny lost in her thoughts. Dean sang to himself quietly, a song Penny hadn't heard before, slow and bluesy.

"That's very beautiful," she said when he finished.

He chuckled, "I've been working on it in my spare time."

"You *wrote* it?" She asked in surprise.

Dean shrugged, "Sometimes it feels easier to play music instead of talking about your feelings. Plus, I can't afford therapy."

He looked over to her and winked.

. . .

They pulled up in front of a small shop, across from the water. The sea breeze brushed stray hairs across Penny's face, and she realised her hair was still done up from when she was in the bridal shop. She touched it self-consciously. *How is it that at lunchtime I was standing in a wedding dress and now I am here*, she wondered. The burger place was done up like a beach shack in blues and sandy yellows.

"What will you have?" Dean asked her as they stood in front of the menu.

Oh carbs, Penny thought, *blessed carbs. Not a zucchini in sight.*

"Whatever is the most deluxe gluten-filled burger they have," she answered.

"Well, alright, then."

Dean placed their orders, and they found a table outside underneath an outdoor heater. Fairy lights twinkled in strands that crisscrossed along the garden.

"It's nice here," Penny observed.

"Wait until you taste the burgers. If God himself wanted a burger, he would eat here."

They chatted about easy things while they waited. Penny told him about her job and her rejected promotion; Dean spoke about his music and friends at an arts group he goes to.

"It's hosted at a different house each week, and anyone is welcome. Some people will come along and paint, a few of us will play music. There are even some people there that fire-twirl. You should come one time, we have other writers there."

"Oh, I couldn't! My writing is... no. It's not really anything. It's just scribbles. A journal more than anything."

Penny imagined standing up and reading some of the

things she had written about her mother and blushed. It would feel as though she were naked. Also, she couldn't help but feel she would be out of place. In her mind, there was a group of people that probably had dreadlocks and a favourite tattooist, and there she would be... just Penny, in her sensible black flats and floral blouse, bringing the vibe down.

Their food arrived, and they ate in silence. Generally, Penny felt she needed to constantly fill the quiet spaces with words, but right now with Dean, she just felt comfortable. Penny looked at him from under her lashes as she ate, she had told him more about herself than she could remember ever telling anyone. He knew about Charmaine, her crazy encounters with Henry... he had read her writing. *Maybe it's a bartender thing*, Penny mused. *People probably told them things they usually wouldn't all the time.*

Penny sat back halfway through.

"I can't go on," she said, staring at the half-finished burger.

"I know," Dean agreed. "I'm going to burst. I feel like a barrel. You'll have to roll me back to the car."

"It's such a shame. We will have to split one next time," Penny said, sliding back her chair and standing up.

Dean smiled at her, "Yes. Next time."

He dropped her back to her unit, lifting her bike from the back of the car, and waving to her as she wheeled it up the path. Penny noticed Linda, the landlord, peeking out from between her curtains. She scowled at Penny as she went past.

"God, what is her *problem*," Penny muttered under her breath.

She got to the door and unlocked it with her key, turning and waving goodbye to Dean, who was insisting on waiting until she had gotten inside.

"See you later," she called.

"Goodbye, Miss Lane!" he called back.

"What?"

He grinned, "Like the song."

He got into his car and shut the door, driving away, and leaving Penny staring after him.

CHARMAINE'S JOURNALS

Mr. Johnson lets me take time off for my appointments with the psychologist. He is a good man. He never makes me feel like it's a burden, even though I know he doesn't have the staff to cover me when I'm gone and runs both the dispensary and the counter while I'm gone. There are a lot of people who don't understand or who treat you differently when they find out, but there are also a lot of good people out there. I hope that Penny meets a lot of good people in her life. When I was pregnant with her, I used to read her fairytales because I had heard somewhere that babies can hear in the womb. I remember sitting down by the riverside, on one of those beautiful clear days that you can barely believe are real. I was reading a fairytale where a baby was given blessings, and because it was a fairytale, the blessings were all things like beauty and grace. I thought if I could bless Penny with anything I would want it to be good people who love her. Right then, as I was thinking it, I felt her move for the first time. Like a fish flicking its tail as she swam around inside. I never knew my own mother, but right then I felt such a deep connection to her and all the women that had come before me - like they were all there with me, welcoming this new branch on our family tree. I never knew how much you could love someone that you hadn't even met yet.

CHAPTER 9

It was like she was thirteen again. As she rode to work, she looked for her mother. She spent her lunch walking through the city, watching the faces of women who passed her. Would she even recognise Charmaine after all this time? Would she see those eyes and know it was her? She took her time riding home, pedalling past Charmaine's old unit in Clayton Hills. She stopped out the front and looked at it, the geraniums that spilt from a large terracotta pot beside the front door, the mailbox stuffed with pamphlets the tenant hadn't collected yet. Across the road, a woman peered at her through a security screen, her face pinched and suspicious. Penny rode on.

In the northern suburbs, not far from where Lloyd lived, there was a river that Charmaine had liked to sit beside in the afternoons. When Penny was little, and Charmaine had lived with them, she used to take Penny down there for picnics. Charmaine would pack a big blanket and peanut butter sandwiches, and Penny would scribble in colouring books while Charmaine would write in her journal. She had asked Charmaine what she was writing one time, climbing into her mother's lap and tracing the words written in her loopy script. They reminded Penny of the passionfruit vines that grew in Papa's yard, tangled chaos that he tamed to the fence with string and poles.

"I'm writing about everything," Charmaine had said.

"Why?" Penny had asked.

"So I don't forget. We like to think we remember everything, but we don't."

"What are you remembering today?" Penny looked up at her mother, whose mouth had curved into a smile. Her cheeks were pink, flushed from the heat of the day. The sunlight had caught her hair and lit it up, as though it were a halo.

"I'm remembering you," Charmaine had said. "I'm writing about your long eyelashes and your tiny half-moon fingernails. I'm writing about the little scrape on your knee from where you fell off your tricycle yesterday."

Penny had looked down at the scab on her knee. It seemed a silly thing to want to remember, she had thought.

"Do you want to remember other things too?"

"Everything," her mother had said. "I want to remember everything."

Penny pulled up at the riverside. She wheeled her bike over to the spot her mother use to like to sit and watched the river gently glide by. Dragonflies lit on the water, darting about on their business. The sun caught the ripples, and the surface of the water glittered like fools gold. It was beautiful here. Quiet. She remembered her mother's journals, she had covered them in pieces of fabric she collected. The covers were memories too. One made from a worn-out dress of Penny's, blue and yellow flowers on a cream background. Another, an old tablecloth that Lloyd had been wanting to throw away after he scorched it with an iron.

It wasn't until Penny was older and began to write herself that she understood why her mother was drawn to the details. Remembering happens in broad strokes, the small pieces of a moment get lost to time. When her mother had vanished, she found she couldn't remember exactly the way Charmaine had laughed. Was it sudden, like a summer storm? Or tinkling, like a bell? She had asked Lloyd, and he had shrugged.

"It sounds like a laugh," he had said.

But Penny needed the details. She needed to remember. So, she had begun to keep a journal herself. Inside she wrote her snippets, thoughts that floated through her head. She wrote details about her day, the small things that she was likely to forget.

The white ghost of the moon in the morning sky.

The smell of hardwood burning in Lloyd's fire pit, embers dancing upwards like fairies.

The sandpaper feel of a man's cheek against her lips.

Warm eyes, one blue and one green, crinkling on the sides as he smiled.

The way her mother had looked that afternoon, her forgettable eyes like a clear blue sky.

On Friday Penny came into work to find a young man behind her desk.

"Umm, excuse me," she said.

He looked up at her, expectantly, "How can I help you?"

"That's my desk," She pointed to the photo of her and Lloyd that sat beside a potted succulent.

The young man looked down at the image and back to Penny. Flushing a bright scarlet, he stood up, "Right, sorry. I'm Jensen. I'm just hanging out for a moment while Grant gets off the phone and then I'll go to my office."

"Your office?"

The bell above the door tinkled, and Sarah came in, a stack of papers tucked under one arm and a takeaway coffee in her other hand.

"Who the hell are you?" she asked Jensen.

Penny felt her face go hot, even after four years of working with Sarah, she had never gotten used to how abrupt she was.

"This is Jensen," Penny answered.

"What is he doing here? He looks like he's twelve," Sarah eyed Jensen disdainfully.

"I'm actually eighteen," Jensen said. "Nineteen next month."

Grant's door swung open, and he strode into the room, clapping Jensen on the back.

"Ladies! This is Jensen, he's our new editor."

Penny felt her stomach drop. *The new editor? He looks barely old enough to vote.* She felt oddly ashamed, as though she had been foolish to think she was smart enough to take on the position of editor if Grant had been willing to hire someone barely out of high school over her.

Grant ushered Jensen up the hall and into the spare office, closing the door.

Sarah looked at Penny and raised one eyebrow, "He cannot be fucking serious. Not only is this insulting to you, but it's also insulting to me. I didn't bust my ass for years, eating ramen in a share house infested with roaches, so I could work for the same pay as someone who probably still raises his hand to ask to go to the bathroom."

Penny ducked her head and went and sat behind her desk, rearranging papers to keep her hands busy.

"Anne comes back next week," Penny said. "At least between Jensen and her, you will have some of the pressure taken off you."

Grant came back out, and Sarah pounced on him, "Grant, you have to stop hiring first-years. Especially if you aren't willing to put Penny on. She has been doing the work of an editor for years and would have far more experience than Jensen-can't-grow-a-beard in there. Either you're fine with training people, or you aren't."

Sarah and Grant argued all the way into his office before shutting the door, muting the sounds. Penny was grateful for the quiet.

"Just get through until lunch time," she said aloud. "Blessed half-day Friday."

The morning went by quickly. Sarah had stormed out of Grant's office swearing, and then none of them had left their offices for the remainder of the morning, avoiding each other. Since Grant had shuffled her editing pile to Jensen, Penny easily got through all of the paperwork, filing and responding to emails with time to spare.

She was standing by her desk, with her backpack and helmet and still two minutes to go until midday, watching the clock tick down when the door up the hall cracked open, and Jensen peeked out at her.

So close, Penny thought with a sigh. *Another two minutes and I would have been gone.*

She hoped he wouldn't want to talk to her.

He did.

He scurried down the hallway, looking around him as though he were a rabbit in a field, watching for predators. He looked so nervous that Penny felt sorry for him. Stopping in front of her, he ran a hand through his hair.

"I wanted to say sorry," he blurted. "I... well, I overheard Sarah and Grant. I feel like I've taken your job. I didn't know. I'm sorry."

His eyes were filled with embarrassment and his neck flushed red. Penny sighed. She'd really wanted to hate him. Damn it.

"It's okay, Jensen. It was never going to be my job," She looked over at the clock. Twelve. Finally. Penny turned back to him and patted his arm in a motherly fashion. "I'm sure you'll be a great editor. I've got to go. I'll see you Monday, okay?"

She fled without waiting for a response.

Penny rode towards the nursing home, avoiding pedestrians who insisted on walking in the bike lane. As she passed by them, she kept apologising, as though she were a great inconvenience. All of them were men, she noticed. When she passed by women, they both apologised to each other. *Why do women do that? Apologise for simply occupying space?* She wondered. The next time she passed by a man walking in the bike lane, she consciously clamped her mouth shut.

She pulled up at the nursing home and chained her bike to the pole, slinging her backpack over her shoulder. On the verandah, easels were set up, and a half a dozen residents were painting at them, a vase of flowers stood on a table in front, clearly the object of their art. Inside, she could hear music playing from the hall at the end, she veered towards it and found Brooke handing out cups of soft drink to seated residents who were watching a man play his guitar and sing for them.

Penny spotted June and Rosie at the end and waved to them. June was tapping her foot and smiling. *Looks like she is settling in*, Penny thought gratefully. Penny assisted Brooke with handing out refreshments and walked around greeting the residents, busying herself. Two of the residents got up and danced at the front of the crowd, surprisingly fleet of foot and graceful.

"It's a lost art, really," Brooke said to her, tilting her head towards the dancers. "These folks came of age going to Cloudland. We grew up heading to Mary Street for dollar drinks. The only thing I learnt was how to walk up the hill to the station in heels and not fall on my butt."

Penny had never gone to a nightclub but nodded absently.

The concert concluded with rounds of applause and Penny wandered over to Rosie and June to say hello before heading down the hall to see Teddy. She found him sitting outside in the garden in his fall out chair. He was in the shade of a jacaranda tree, the fading sunlight warming his face. Nearby a small group of residents and a carer were watering the vegetable patch.

"Hello, Papa," Penny said. She picked up his hand and held it, warm and dry. Teddy blinked at her and opened his mouth as if to say something. Penny leaned forward eagerly, not wanting to miss anything. His mouth moved as if he were speaking, but nothing came out, as though the words were trapped inside. *What could it be? What might he have said?*

"Well, it looks like you have one of the best seats in the garden. Look at all those blooms! We have some on the street where Steve and I live, remember? But they're scrawny compared to this one. Steve complains that they leave their flowers all over his car, but I like them."

Penny had become good at drawing out the most simple of statements into paragraphs. She talked for both of them. The gardening residents began to pack up to go inside, and the carer looked at Penny questioning, asking if she wanted him to bring Teddy in too. She shook her head and smiled, she would wheel him back in shortly. The wind picked up, and jacaranda blooms rained down on them. Teddy laughed, startling Penny so much that she dropped his hand. It had been so long since she had heard it, that she had nearly forgotten what it sounded like. He pointed a gnarled finger towards her head. She reached up and felt blossoms. He was laughing at the flowers in her hair. Tears filled her eyes, and she laughed herself as she pulled them out. Such a simple gift. Interaction.

"I guess I look pretty ridiculous, huh? Alright, let's wheel you back inside. They'll be doing dinner soon."

Penny pushed Teddy back inside and down to the dining room, where Rosie was helping June up to the table.

"Bring Lucy next time," June demanded.

"I will, Grandma."

Rosie looked at Penny and rolled her eyes. Henry was coming up behind Rosie with his wheelie walker, and Rosie stepped quickly out of his way, as he continued his path to an empty chair. He sat down carefully, eyes vacant and unseeing. Penny watched him as she pushed Teddy to an open spot in the room and pulled a portable table over to him. Henry seemed like every other resident there, he didn't look like someone you would expect to be a psychic or seer.

Henry pulled the salt shaker towards him, and picking it up, he dropped it neatly into his drink as though it belonged there.

"Oh!" Rosie said and moved towards him. "Here let me help you with that."

She reached for his cup and went to turn back to the kitchenette to fetch a new one when Henry grabbed her by the arm. Watching it as an outsider, Penny was fascinated.

Rosie's expression was similar to what Penny imagined her own expression had been, the first time Henry had touched her. She watched as Henry's eyes focused clearly on Rosie. *I wonder what he's going to tell her*, Penny thought. *A lottery win? A flat tyre?*

But Henry's eyes swivelled from Rosie and found Penny across the room, boring holes into her. Her heart thumped in her chest. Rosie looked at Penny bewildered.

"A house in a field with one tree. And you. And she."

He looked back at Rosie, "And you."

Henry let go of her arm and pulled the pepper towards him. A carer reached over and plucked it away before he could upend it.

"Not the pepper again, Henry."

The carer took the glass from Rosie's hand with the salt shaker still inside and went to the kitchenette.

Rosie looked at Penny questioningly. Penny kissed Teddy goodbye and started quickly up the hall with Rosie jogging to catch up.

"What was that?" Rosie asked breathlessly.

"What?"

"That thing that happened back there."

Penny shook her head, "It's just dementia. They say weird things sometimes."

"You looked kind of freaked out," Rosie said.

"So did you," Penny retorted.

Rosie reached out and pulled on Penny's arm to stop her from walking, "Can we just stop for a minute. You walk really, really fast."

Rosie doubled over and put her hands on her knees, catching her breath. She stood up and pulled her curls into a messy bun and fanned the back of her neck.

"God. See? This is why I don't run. There is too much sweat involved."

Penny smiled despite herself.

"Now," Rosie began, "can we talk about the weirdness back there? Because it felt like you and he were having a conversation, and I walked in halfway through. Are you... did you know him?"

Penny looked at Rosie, assessing. How could she begin to explain this? She would sound crazy, and she barely knew this woman. She shook her head and forced a smile on to her face.

"No, he's just said a couple of weird things before. It's nothing really. But I do have to go. I'll see you next week, okay?"

Without waiting for a response, Penny jogged off waving, leaving Rosie staring after her.

CHAPTER 10

Penny waved to Ray as she walked up to the pub. It was busier than usual today, and as she entered through the doors, she noticed a large party – clearly, it was someone's birthday - taking up almost half of the room. Dean looked rushed off his feet. She nearly turned to walk out, she didn't want to disturb him while he was busy, but his eyes found her across the room, and his face lit at the sight of her. He smiled and gave her a wink. Penny felt butterflies burst to life in her stomach, her skin prickled all the way to her fingertips. Self consciously, she made her way to the bar and found an empty seat away from the party. She watched Dean as he worked, rushing back and forth, but never with impatience. Even while he chatted to a customer, his hands moved at a task, seemingly without instruction. She found herself drawn to his hands, there was a strength in them, and yet, they were quick, dexterous, musician's hands with long graceful fingers. They made her wish she could draw, to try to capture the lines, the way the tiny hairs on the back of his hands caught the light, the scar on his right index finger's knuckle. She took her pen from her shirt pocket and pulled a napkin towards her, writing down the word 'hands' on it. She slipped the napkin into her pocket; she would write in her journal later.

Across the bar, a small group of women about Penny's age were giggling like teenagers, she followed their eyes and realised they were talking about Dean. Unsurprising, Penny thought. His white shirt clung to him, he looked like... christ, she was staring too. She ducked her head to her lap and pretended to be absorbed in her phone.

"Your usual, Miss Lane?"

She looked up to find Dean smiling at her. He placed a cider on the coaster in front of her.

"Thank you. You seem busy tonight?" She fumbled with her purse to retrieve her card to pay for the drink.

Dean waved her card away, "Don't even think about giving me that. I got this one."

"Dean, I've been in this bar several times now and not once paid for a drink. Let me at least pretend I'm a customer."

He shook his head, "You can pay me in company. I'm off in thirty minutes. Will you wait for me?"

Penny looked over at the women, who were looking at Dean, who was looking at her. What was happening here? She looked up at him and swallowed.

"Yes," she answered. "I think I'll wait outside, though."

Dean glanced over his shoulder, "Because of those women? Penny, you don't have to wait outside. They've had four drinks apiece. They hit on Ray before."

Penny flushed, realising he knew why she was uncomfortable. She wasn't his girlfriend, it shouldn't have mattered even if they had been interested in him.

"You're so pretty when you blush," Dean teased.

"Shut up," Penny laughed. "I'm going to wait outside with Ray. I'll see you in half an hour."

Ray and his friends were surprisingly charming. She had expected them to be rough and crude, but they had welcomed her into their circle and included her in the conversation like she had known them for years. It felt like she was sitting around with seven different versions of her father.

"Well, your boss sounds like he doesn't appreciate you, love," Ray had said after Penny told them about Grant and Jensen.

The circle of men nodded and muttered in agreement. She wasn't sure why she had ended up telling this group of perfect strangers about her work troubles, but the words had just poured out of her. By the time Dean came out, swinging his bag over his shoulder, she was almost reluctant to leave the group of men she had just come to know. Penny pushed back her chair and thanked them for the chat.

"You're taking away our beautiful companion then, Dean?" one of the tradesmen said.

"Afraid so."

"Alright then, lass. Go be with your man," Ray said.

Penny didn't correct him.

Dean placed his hand on the small of her back to guide her to his car, warming her skin with his touch.

· · ·

"Where are we going?" Penny asked once they had loaded her bike into the back and started driving.

"Wherever you want to go," Dean answered.

"Maybe we could just go down to the waterfront?" Penny suggested.

The drive was short, they grabbed some hot chips from the burger place and found a spot sheltered from the wind where they could watch the moonlight on the water. Dean grabbed a jacket from his car to give to Penny to keep the chill away. They spoke about their day, and Penny told him about the new editor and her conversation with Steve about going back to uni.

"Do you want to go back?"

Penny shrugged, "Honestly? I'm not sure. I don't really know what I want. I know I really hate that job."

They finished the chips and leaned back, watching the water without talking.

"Henry said something else today," Penny began. She told him about the latest of Henry's jumbled predictions - if that was what it was.

"This is crazy, right?" she said, looking over at him.

"Do you believe him? That he really is *seeing* something?" Dean asked her.

Penny thought about it. It wasn't rational, psychics weren't real, they were people who were good at reading the signs other people put out. The white tan-line of a missing wedding band. The way someone would lean forward subconsciously when you said something that resonated for them. Psychics didn't exist. And yet... she *did* think Henry was seeing something. Or knew something.

"I do," she admitted.

"Then, so do I," Dean replied. "So, I guess now we just have to find the field with the one tree in it?"

"Well, that should be simple," Penny snorted.

"Penny, if you believe Henry is telling the truth, and he said you will find your mother, then you have to believe you will. Which means, maybe, finding this field will be easier than you think. Right?"

Not entirely illogical when you put it that way, Penny thought.

Dean stood up and stretched, "You feel like going somewhere else? It's arts night. You could come along and check it out. If you would rather not, I can drop you home on my way."

"Go along to your arts club?"

"Sure. I'm going to play that piece I sang the other day."

Penny looked down at her clothes, she wasn't dressed to go out.

"You look fine," Dean said, reading her mind. "I smell like a brewery. Trust me, no one is going to be bothered by what you are wearing."

"Okay," Penny agreed.

The arts night was hosted at a share house in the inner city suburbs. The house was an old Queenslander and in desperate need of some attention. The verandah sloped alarmingly to the left, not helped by the fact that it was housing a small army of plants. They hung from macrame hangers, spilt out of pots and containers of every kind. Fairy lights wound up the poles and lanterns hung from the rafters.

"This is Aberdeen's house," Dean said. "Well, hers and

her housemates. But she is hosting it tonight. She's a sculptor."

Dean led Penny around the side of the verandah, and down a set of stairs at the back towards the noise of the party. And a party is what it was. There were probably fifty people in the backyard, scattered around in smaller groups. Music was drifting through the night from one corner of the backyard where someone was playing the violin. There was a fire pit in the centre of the yard, and nearby two women were fire twirling. Sticks spun in the air, illuminating the faces of the women while people stood nearby entranced by the dancing flames. A woman was sculpting up on the verandah chatting with a small group of people as she worked, moulding clay with her hands. Aberdeen, Penny assumed.

Dean led her to a table holding large jars filled with sangria and poured them both a cup. They wandered through people in the yard, Dean introducing her as he greeted friends and acquaintances. Penny nodded shyly, sipping at her drink. Soon, Dean worked his way over to a group of people sitting on what appeared to be bales of hay covered by blankets and an odd assortment of fold-out chairs. Penny stood out of the circle, watching him as he talked for a while, before picking up his guitar and strumming it a few times. He made a few adjustments and then began to play. It was the same song he had sung in the car, but the guitar gave soul to the lyrics that it hadn't had before. His words vibrated within her, making her chest ache and her skin break out in goosebumps. His fingers moved over the strings as though the guitar were an extension of himself; it was beautiful, as though they were dancing. He finished before Penny realised what was happening and took an odd little bow. He met her eye and flashed her a grin before he was caught up in conversation with another man. *Something was happening here.*

Penny stepped back and went to the table where the drinks were to pour another for something to do. She didn't know this man. Not really. And yet she had somehow ended up sharing the darkest parts of herself with him. *Something is happening here*, she thought again. *And I'm not sure whether I want it to stop.* Guilt bloomed inside her and she took another sip of her drink to quell it. Topping up her cup, she moved back into the guests, occasionally stopping to admire an artist at work, steering clear of the fire twirling which, while beautiful, filled her with anxiety.

Penny gravitated towards a small circle of people who were reading their writing. She found a place just outside the ring, trying to be unobtrusive. The sangria was deliciously fruity, and she took another sip. *I'm slightly drunk*, she thought. Penny did not get drunk, but tonight seemed like it didn't belong to her. It was something else, a time outside of time. A beautiful man with olive skin and dreadlocks was reciting a piece he had written.

I knew there would be dreadlocks, Penny thought and smiled to herself.

His voice was like a balm on her jagged edges. The night was scented with candles and woodsmoke, she took a deep breath and felt something inside her unwind. He was speaking about mental illness she realised, a deep darkness that the subject was wrestling with. It was beautiful and sad and somehow strong. When he finished, Penny felt bereft, wishing she could sit there and listen to him talk for days until she felt like all the broken parts of her had been stuck back together. His eyes met hers across the circle, and he smiled at her so warmly that it was as though he had been reading just for her.

"I'm Leif," he said.

Faces turned to her and Penny blushed. She greeted them shyly. She expected to feel on display, but she didn't. She felt welcomed and accepted. Aberdeen had wandered over to listen at some point during Leif's reading and turned to Penny. Clay speckled her arms, her dark hair shone in the firelight, and Penny felt a strange kinship suddenly to these people. *Everyone is a little broken*, she thought.

"Would you like to share something?" Aberdeen asked.

Penny was about to say no, but something about the way Leif had laid himself bare had loosened her tongue. Or maybe it was the sangria. Either way, she stood, the firelight warming her face. She closed her eyes, she didn't need a piece of paper to read from. This snippet was inscribed on her heart. As she spoke, the grief wrenched free and tumbled forth into the listeners waiting hands. She spoke from a place inside herself that she had kept hidden.

"There is a place you cannot comfort me.

They call it an ache, but that is only because it runs so deeply under the surface like a bruise.

But it's sharper than a bruise.

It sits within me, somewhere dark.

Hidden.

Blackest black.

Infinite.

Small.

I wish it away.

And yet...

It is almost precious to me, for if I release it and it left, I would have nothing.

It feels solid when I bump against it unexpectedly, as though I could build a city upon its foundation, but I pass through it like fog.

You cannot comfort me here.

I must walk it alone.

My steps disappearing behind me into the inky depths.

Grief.

Never, never. Always, forever.

Never.

Always.

You cannot comfort me here.

I taste it. Just the tiniest sip of drowning.

And then I lock it away.

Never, never.

Always."

She opened her eyes. Faces beamed back at her, some people clapped. Aberdeen thanked her, and another woman stood to read a piece she had written. Penny slipped back into the shadows, her hands trembling. A hand touched her gently on the shoulder. She turned around and looked up into Dean's face.

"Your mother?" He asked.

"Yes."

The firelight danced on his skin, his eyes glittered blue and green before her. Unthinking, she nearly lifted her hand to touch his face, before realising what she was doing and dropping it to her side.

"I'll help you find her," Dean said.

It was a simple statement, casually given. It was an impossible task, to think after all these years, they might find Charmaine after she and her father had failed. That she and a bartender she barely knew might take the tiny clues given by an old man and stumble across a field with a single tree and there she would find her mother, as though she had been waiting for her all these years. For some reason, she believed him. She believed Henry. She nodded.

"Come on," Dean said. "I'll take you home."

An hour later, Dean dropped Penny at the unit. Penny opened the door and put her bag down in the hall. The television was off, and she could hear Steve brushing his teeth in the bathroom. Penny went up to the bedroom to gather her pyjamas and took them to the bathroom where Steve was finishing up.

"Where have you been?" He asked, wiping his mouth on his towel.

"I went to an arts night."

"An arts night? Like a gallery?"

Penny leaned past him to turn on the water and let it heat up, "No. it was in someone's backyard. People turn up and either show pieces they've been working on, or they do their art in groups. It was amazing, actually."

Steve wrinkled his nose, "You smell revolting."

"That's probably the smoke from the fire pits."

Penny began to strip off, she smelled her shirt, it did smell like smoke, a not entirely pleasant smell but one she didn't mind as it felt almost like the night was still on her somehow. She lifted her hair to her nose and inhaled. She would have to wash her hair too.

"Well, I'm going to bed," Steve said, leaving the room and padding up the hall to the bedroom.

Penny shut the door behind him, allowing the room to fill with steam that billowed out of the shower. The haze softened her reflection in the mirror, fogging the glass until she could only see the bare outlines of her body. She could be almost anyone. She stepped into the spray and tilted her head back, imagining the scents of the night washing away.

CHAPTER 11

The next morning, Penny woke early for once. She and Dean had decided to spend the day driving around in search of the field Henry had spoken about. They decided they would start on north side out near Heathmont, a little town on the outskirts, about thirty-five minutes from the CBD. Heathmont had once been farmland, but parts of it had been divided into new estates with five-acre plots of land and brand new houses built on it. Pseudo farm life, Dean had called it. People from the city who wanted to pretend they had a little slice of the country while still being able to commute to their office jobs. Penny herself had not been out to Heathmont in years but remembered it as a charming little village with rolling paddocks of land dotted with grazing cows.

"It's changed a lot in the town," Dean said. "But the surrounding farms are still out there. It's probably as good a place to start as any."

Penny slipped out of bed and pulled on jeans and a t-shirt. She felt hopeful and apprehensive at the same time. It was impossible to think that they might actually find her mother, but some small flame of hope had reignited in her. She had to look.

Steve was in the kitchen, pouring a dubious-looking concoction from the blender into a glass.

"You're up early," he remarked.

"I'm going out driving today. Well, a friend is driving. I'm the passenger."

Steve cocked his head, "What friend?"

"Dean. He's a bartender."

Penny braced herself for a barrage of questions and was unsurprised when they came. She filled Steve in on the conversations with Henry, about Dean and Ray and how she had been calling into the pub after visits with Teddy.

"You cannot be serious?" Steve asked incredulously.

His smoothie sat untouched on the bench where it had begun to separate, pale green liquid floating on top of dense pulp. Penny's stomach rolled looking at it.

"I am serious. I have to look for her. I can't just ignore it."

"Penny, the man has dementia! He isn't a seer. As far as I can tell, he hasn't said anything that would lead you to believe you will find your mum. It's all nonsense!"

"I can't explain it, Steve. His eyes... they actually *clear* when he says it. He looks lucid. I *do* believe him. And he was right about my accident."

"No, he wasn't! You heard what you wanted to hear. That's what people do with fortune-tellers - oh, you will have a win at work - and then you look for that win. And this guy is not a fortune-teller, he is just an old man speaking crap!"

"Can you stir that drink?"

"What?"

"Your drink is separated, it's really grossing me out."

"I don't give a shit about the drink. I care that you are driving around with a guy you met three seconds ago, looking for your mother who has been gone for years and - I'm sorry to say it Penny, but likely doesn't want to be found - all on the advice of an old dude whose brain is swiss cheese! You're fucking insane!"

Steve upended the cup in the sink and stalked out of the room swearing, grabbing his keys from the hall table and slamming the front door.

Penny sighed and rubbed her face. She picked the cup up and washed it, putting it neatly into the dish rack. Maybe Steve was right. All of this was insane. She should call Dean and cancel. She opened her phone and pulled up his number, staring at it for a few moments. Is that what Steve really thought? That her mother didn't want to be found? That didn't track with what she remembered of Charmaine. She had her own demons, sure. But she loved Penny and Lloyd. She wouldn't just leave them and not ever mean to come back. She had always called. Always. She couldn't stop looking. Not until she knew.

Never, never.

Always.

She shut her phone and went to grab her backpack from beside the door. She would wait for Dean outside.

They drove towards Heathmont in silence, Penny still stewing over Steve's words. Dean seemed to pick up on her mood and stayed quiet. The radio played softly, and he occasionally sang along with the words. The highway wound up beside the state forest and led them past hills patchworked by the greens and golds of the grass. Now and then Penny spied a herd of cows moving slowly across a paddock.

"They always seem to be in a line," she said, breaking the silence.

"What?"

"The cows. It's like one gets up suddenly and begins a pilgrimage, and the rest all come along for the journey. I wonder if the one at the back even knows where she is going? Maybe she just didn't want to be left alone."

Dean smiled.

"Why do you think my mother left?" Penny asked suddenly.

Dean looked over at her, "Hmm. I'm not sure I would want to guess. That's what we will find out, I suppose... when we find her."

"You really think we will find her?"

"Henry said so. And I can tell looking is important to you, so by extension, it's important to me. That's what friends do for each other."

"We are friends?"

"Of course. Since the moment you bled all over me. Blood seals the deal. Everyone knows that," he grinned at her and dropped her a wink. "What was she like?"

Penny leaned back and closed her eyes, the sun was warm on her skin. Dean's car's air conditioner had broken, and they drove with the windows down, her hair whipping across her face. *The country has a smell*, she thought. *Earthy and pure.*

"She was... complicated. She had layers. She was beautiful, I'm not just saying that. Everyone thought so. My dad is indigenous, and he is quite tall, very muscular, even now he is older. Back then, he was what he has termed 'a ladies man'. He was on a date with another woman when he saw Charmaine enter the cafe they were at," Penny closed her eyes, hearing her father's words.

"She came in and ordered a hot chocolate. Her hair was long then, down to her waist. She had these jeans that made her butt-"

Charmaine had swatted him, "Stop it! You'll scar the child!" But her face was flushed with pleasure and Lloyd had grinned at her, tenderness in his eyes.

"Anyway," Lloyd had continued, "she stuck what must have been sixty-seven sugars in her mug."

"It was four!" Charmaine protested.

"Fourteen, maybe."

"Four," she said decisively.

"And right then I knew I was in love. My date went to go to the bathroom, and by the time she got back, we were gone."

"Dad!" Penny had exclaimed, scandalised at the thought of the poor woman coming back to find herself abandoned.

"I paid the bill before I left!" he protested.

"That's awful!" Penny had said.

"It was a bit awful," Charmaine admitted.

Lloyd had shrugged, "I couldn't help it. I was bewitched. Enchanted."

"They were engaged before the end of the month and married by the end of the year. I was born nine months later. She didn't always live with us, she needed space - more space than I think most mother's need. But she always came over or called. She wrote too. She kept journals with bits and pieces of her day or things she didn't want to forget. She would cover them with pieces of fabric that she salvaged from old clothes and sheets. They were missing, actually. When we went to pack up the unit after... She was a good mum. She was."

"She sounds like quite the woman," Dean said.

They pulled into the town of Heathmont, small shopfronts that had been renovated to look like they had back when they had been built, with the modern conveniences of air conditioning and refrigeration.

"I thought we would start out by heading left at the end of the main street, there are older farms out this way that might fit the description we are looking for."

Penny nodded, and they started out, both of them scanning the countryside. They chatted about their families as they went. Penny learned that Dean had five sisters, he was the youngest of all the children.

"So, obviously I grew used to having cold showers because by the time they were all finished washing their hair and shaving their legs, the hot water system was exhausted. Christmas is chaotic, I have *fifteen* nieces and nephews. *Fifteen*, Penny! I have to start buying gifts in September because otherwise I'd be living on crackers and baked beans for the whole of December. It's very expensive to have such adorable relatives."

"Yes, I imagine it's a great suffering."

"Definitely. Anyway, one sister still lives at home with Mum and is - blessedly – child-free at the moment. We made a rule years ago that we would only buy for the kids, but I sneak Dee a gift anyway, because she has no children she's forcing me to buy Tonka Trucks for."

"Do you want kids?" Penny asked suddenly.

Dean gave her a look, and Penny blushed.

"I'm sorry," she said hurriedly. "That was too personal. You don't have to answer."

"No, it's fine. I just don't think anyone has ever asked me that before," he mulled over the question for a few moments silently before answering. "I mean... short answer would be yes. Long answer would be that I feel like I do not have myself together in any way, shape, or form to be parenting a child. But Dee reckons everyone feels like that."

"I thought she didn't have kids?"

"She doesn't. She just has very strong opinions about parenthood." He grinned while watching the road, and Penny imagined what his house must have been like with so many siblings. She felt a keen sense of loss for something she had never had. The same way she felt when she had been at Steve's house when she was younger. There was a bond between siblings that she couldn't seem to understand. She always felt like she was standing on the outside looking in. As though everyone was in on a private joke that she was missing the punchline for. It wasn't just that she didn't have brothers or sisters, it was - Penny realised now - that she didn't really have any friends before Dean. She had a father, a missing mother, a grandfather who couldn't remember her and Steve. She shook herself free of her thoughts and turned to Dean.

"Can I ask you another really personal question and you have to promise not to be mad?"

Dean cut eyes at her, "Ooookay."

"Your mum named two of her kids Dee and Dean?"

Dean burst out laughing, "Well, yes and no. Dee is actually Deanna, and she is the second youngest. My dad's name was Dean. Mum really wanted to name a kid after him, so she named Dee for him thinking it might be her last chance. But then, I surprised her a few years later, and she finally had a boy and named me after him too."

"Deanna and Dean."

"Yep. Anyway, I think Mum regretted it because Dad ended up running off to a commune down in New South Wales with a woman named Moonbeam when I was three."

"That's awful!" Penny exclaimed.

"I know, right? Who would ever call themselves Moonbeam?"

Penny snorted, "That's not what I meant."

"I know. But life's better if you laugh about it."

By dusk, they had travelled every main road and back road of Heathmont and come up empty-handed. They saw paddocks with no trees, paddocks with several trees and paddocks dotted with bushes but none with just one tree. They stopped for lunch at a small pub in the middle of Heathmont, where they ended up chatting to several of the patrons. Dean played pool with a pair of local cattle farmers, and Penny sipped a beer and watched him as he delicately extracted clues on other places to search without giving out information about why they were looking. By the time they left, Dean had organised a music gig at the pub for next month and had a pocket full of phone numbers from his newly found friends.

"Sorry to pull you away from your new besties back there," Penny joked.

"What can I say? People like me."

They spent the afternoon checking out the new leads Dean had discovered while blasting 90's music from his half-broken stereo where the sound cut in and out every few minutes. Dean sang extra loud during the gaps, insisting Penny sing back up. By the time Dean drove Penny home with promises that they would go out again, she had almost forgotten that they were on a mission and not just a day out.

"We'll head up towards the coast next time," he said. "Or maybe over the south side."

"Okay," Penny said.

"Penny? I don't want you to feel bad because we didn't find anything today. We will find her."

"I know," Penny replied. She smiled at him and thanked him. Stepping out of the car, she walked up towards the front door feeling lighter than she had in a long time.

CHAPTER 12

On Sunday, Dean had sent Penny a text saying he had someone that he would like her to meet. Penny had barely seen Steve since their argument Saturday morning and reading the message she looked around the empty unit and felt unsettled. She had washing to do, and the floors needed a vacuum. *I should probably stay home and try to sort things out with Steve also*, she thought. Before she could respond to the message and decline, her phone vibrated again. She looked down at the text message. Steve.

Going out to play golf with the boys this afternoon. Be home late.

She sighed and sent Dean a message back, asking what time he wanted to meet.

Dean picked her up at lunchtime and drove towards the city, parking the car in an alley behind a cafe that was owned by a friend of his. They walked to the restaurant located down a skinny side street, the tables spilling outside of the establishment and into the sunshine. Penny picked a table outside and took a seat next to Dean. On the drive, Dean had told Penny about his friend, who he said had a business tracking down information on people. The way he said 'business' made Penny think it was not exactly registered with the taxation office.

"What? Is she like a private eye? Are they even a thing? Or is that just in spy movies?" Penny asked.

Dean laughed, "They are a thing, but no. She's not an investigator. Mae is... something else. She just knows people, what makes them tick. She knows if they're hiding something."

Penny thought for a moment, "Can I be honest? She sounds a little terrifying."

"I wouldn't put you in any danger. I've known Mae for a long time. We don't have to involve her, but she might be able to help you. She usually charges a fee, off the books, cash. But she would do me a favour, she owes me one."

They waited for a while, browsing the menu until a woman walked towards them and Dean stood up to greet her. Penny had been nursing visions of a supermodel, maybe someone Dean had had a romance with long ago, but Mae was in fact, perfectly average. She was average height, her hair was dark blonde, her eyes were a deep blue. She was pretty, but not remarkable. In fact, she was almost so unremarkable that Penny would have found it difficult to describe her to some-one, as though the moment you left her, you forgot what she looked like. Yet there was also something familiar about her, like Penny had met her before.

· · ·

Mae weaved between people, to get to their table.

"Dean!" she crowed. "The man himself!"

He grinned at her and pulled out a chair across from himself and Penny.

Penny stuck out her hand, "Hello, I'm Penny."

Mae looked at her hand but didn't reach for it, "I'm Mae."

Penny put her hand down, feeling slighted. Dean noticed and said, "It's nothing personal. Mae doesn't touch people if she can help it."

"Oh, I see," Penny said, although she *didn't* see. She wondered if Mae might have a fear of germs, but then Mae promptly licked her finger and began turning pages in the menu.

"I'm starved," she announced. "What's good here?"

"All the burgers are excellent," Dean said. "But the pasta is good too."

"I'll have both."

The waiter came to the table and took their orders, returning with drinks and promising a short wait.

"So," Mae began, "what can I help you with?"

Dean began to fill Mae in on the disappearance of Penny's mother, starting at the beginning and ending with the clues given to them by Henry.

"And we have started looking for the field described by Henry, but it's a bit of a needle in a haystack," Penny said.

The waiter came back with their meals, and they stopped the conversation until he left. Mae lifted a forkful of carbonara to her mouth and chewed thoughtfully.

"We were wondering if maybe you could... talk to some

people," Dean said. "You might be able to find out if there was anyone that knew where she might have gone. Maybe she had told someone something that might help."

Mae took a sip of her drink, "You know I'm in town at the moment for business. I'm kind of in the middle of something of my own."

"You always are," Dean said.

A look passed between the two of them which was full of unspoken words, heavy with meaning. Penny felt vaguely like she shouldn't be there. There was some kind of history here that she didn't know. Mae looked from Dean to Penny, as though she was assessing them. Suddenly, she stuck her hand across the table to Penny, offering her to take it. Penny looked at Dean curiously, and then tentatively reached over and placed her hand in Mae's. Mae closed her eyes for a second and opened them, a small smile on her lips. She let go and sat back in her seat.

"Okay," she said and picked her fork up again.

"Okay?" Penny asked.

"Yep. I'll do it."

Dean shot Penny a grin, and she smiled back, although she had no idea what was going on.

"I thought you didn't touch people," she asked Mae, popping a chip in her mouth.

Mae swallowed and reached across and took a chip from Dean's plate, "Oh, I don't, not usually. I just wanted to see who you really were, Penny. Hot damn, girl. You are one wild ride."

Dean chuckled and took a sip of his beer.

Later that afternoon, Penny and Dean walked Mae to her car

and waved goodbye. They walked back the way they had come, towards the cafe where Dean had parked his car.

"So, that was Mae," Penny remarked.

"The one and only," Dean said. "Thank god. The world couldn't handle two of her."

"How did you meet?" Penny asked.

"She stole my car."

Penny stopped in her tracks, "What?"

Dean laughed and pulled at her hand to get her to keep walking, "We were young, I was only seventeen, barely had my license for two months, and I parked it out the front of a mate's place while I was inside visiting. A little while later, I hear my car start up, and we ran out the front to see it driving up the road. I was just about to chase after it when it did this weird little stutter and stopped. It broke down, about ten houses up. We run down there, and Mae gets out. She tells me my car was a piece of crap. She wasn't wrong, I swapped it for a case of beer - I'm surprised it even lasted long enough for me to get it out of the guy's driveway. We invited her back to the house for a drink to commiserate. I've known her ever since."

"You're still friends, even though she tried to steal your car?"

Dean shrugged, "Well, it wasn't a very good car."

They reached the car and Dean unlocked it and opened the door for Penny.

He dropped Penny back and her unit, and she went inside. The sun was still high in the sky, and the unit was filled with light and warmth from the spring afternoon, but it felt somehow gloomy and cold to Penny. She held up her hand that Mae had taken and looked at it, running her fingers over the creases in her palm. She had felt nothing when Mae had touched her and yet, it was almost as though she had seen her naked, exposed. It was... supernatural almost. Penny shivered and went to the bedroom where she pulled her journal from one of the drawers in her bedside table and set it out before her. Her writing was messy, and she had considered switching to writing on a laptop awhile back, but there was something about handwriting that she found soothing. The journals that her mother used to write in had been like little pieces of her that could be held and touched. Suddenly, she wanted to see them desperately. She had avoided the boxes of her mother's things for years; when she and Lloyd had packed up the unit, she had been sullen and quiet. He had done most of the work himself, dry-eyed and matter of fact, stopping every now and then to say, "We'll just keep these for her until she comes back" or "Your mother will want this when she returns". Penny had never answered him as he pottered back and forth, collecting, sorting and discarding pieces of her mother's life. He had taken the boxes back to their house and put them in the spare room there, shutting the door with a click that sounded oddly final. Penny put her journal back and hurried to the hall, collecting her backpack and helmet and heading out the door with her bike to ride back to Lloyd's.

She knew. Even as she was riding, her heart thumping in her chest, she had a suspicion. She flew past Lloyd in the garden with little more than a hello and a quick kiss on the cheek, barrelling into the house as though she were being chased. The hall was dark, her eyes hadn't yet adjusted to the dimness inside, and she stumbled to the door of the spare room by touch. The handle was cold under her hand, the one they never turned. Inside the boxes were covered with a thick layer of dust, Penny's hands leaving prints on them where she touched them to open the lids. She rifled through one after another, clothing and shoes. Jewellery and handbags. Books and more books. Lloyd came to stand in the doorway, looking at her with a mixture of concern and something that bordered on fear.

"Are you okay, kid?"

Penny looked up at him, "The journals are gone."

Lloyd scratched his head, his brow furrowing, "The books your mum had?"

"Yes! They were covered in fabric, remember? She would write everything in them," Penny reopened a box she had already gone through and looked again.

"I guess she took them with her," Lloyd said, shrugging.

Penny leaned back against the wall and closed her eyes. There was something so logical about her taking the journals that hurt the very core of her. She had taken nothing really, a few clothes, a photo, her handbag. They were things that Penny thought someone might take even if they were confused. The photo itself even wasn't that strange, it was a small oval frame, and Charmaine would take it even if she were just staying away somewhere for a night. But the journals were a choice. They were bulky and heavy. If Charmaine had taken them, it was because they felt so important to her that she couldn't bear to leave them behind. But...

"She left me behind," Penny whispered.

Lloyd knelt beside her and took her in his arms, leaning Penny towards him so that her cheek rested on the rough fabric of his shirt, letting her cry as he held her.

"I know, kid," he said, his voice thick with emotion. He pulled back and tilted her chin so that she was looking at him, "Penny? *I* will never leave you behind, okay? I will always want you. I will *never* leave you behind."

"Never is a big promise, Dad."

"Yeah, well... I'm good at keeping promises."

CHARMAINE'S JOURNALS

When I came home last night after work, I felt like I'd stepped into a house that wasn't my own. Everything looked the same, but it seemed different somehow. Like when you sit down on a train seat that someone has just vacated and it still feels warm from the body that was there beforehand – like they had left something of themselves behind. I walked through all the rooms, and no one was there, but it just felt off. I began to berate myself for being paranoid, everything was exactly where I left it. Still. When I went into the bathroom, I swear it smelled differently. Like a man's cologne. I thought maybe Lloyd had been by – he has a key – but he never wears cologne, and he would have told me if he had stopped by. Sometimes, I feel like my mind is made of spiderwebbing, delicate strands that anyone can push through and destroy. I go about my day, and I feel like I am normal – going to work, buying groceries, finding Penny sparkly hair clips. And then something like this happens, and I feel so fragile; like at any moment I may crack and all the dark parts of me that I hold back will come tumbling out.

CHAPTER 13

Mae walked through the station to get on the train, placing her hand out casually, lightly brushing the man who walked past her. Her fingertips grazed over the back of his hand, warm to the touch. He was scrolling through his phone with the other hand and didn't even notice. Mae closed her eyes for a brief second and continued on. The man had a girl-friend he was going to propose to, he worked in accounting and had some very kinky fetishes. *And good for him*, Mae thought. Sometimes she did that still, just brushed past to see. She never knew what chance touch might lead to the person she needed to find. Mostly though, she tried to keep her hands to herself. People don't realise how often they touch strangers, bumping against them in shops, hands lightly touching as change is dropped into an open palm.

She had gotten the basic details from Penny and Dean on Charmaine before she disappeared, the unit she had lived in, the place where she worked and anywhere she frequently went where people may have seen her. She had already seen into Penny, and what she knew, so she didn't really need to ask, she mostly did it for show. If you don't ask enough questions people tend to get really creeped out, really quick, she had discovered. She figured the best place to start would be down in Clayton Hills at the unit Charmaine had lived in.

Mae got on the train and found an empty spot away from other people. From her seat, she watched a couple with a small son pointing out the window. They were showing him pieces of scenery as the train passed by. The little boy was delighted, his laughter infectious and soon half the train was smiling into their newspapers and phones, pretending not to listen but caught up in his joy. The woman leaned her head against her partner's shoulder. Mae sighed and looked away. She didn't try to wonder what that would be like. It was depressing. People like to say they have no secrets from their significant others, but everyone does. *It's necessary*, she thought, *to hold something of yourself back*. What they mean, she had come to realise, was that they told each other the big things. They just kept the little things hidden. They didn't come home and talk about how they checked out a hot woman on the bus. They didn't talk about missing their ex sometimes. These were secrets they kept out of love, knowing they would cause more trouble than the honesty was worth. Any partner of Mae's wouldn't have that privacy, she knew everything, which made her an excellent lover – and a really awful girlfriend.

The train pulled up at Clayton Hills, and both the couple

with the son and Mae departed. She didn't pull out her phone to check on how to get to the unit Charmaine had lived in, she knew the way by heart. Calling this particular area Clayton Hills was kind. It was on the fringes of the suburb, dotted with housing commission houses that hadn't been renovated in decades. The yards were large though, and the streets wide. She came up on Drayton Street and walked along it once, surveying the unit from the other side of the road. No one that lived in Charmaine's old unit now would be able to help her, having obviously arrived after she went missing. The neighbours might be useful though, but thirteen years was a long time, and it was possible that there might be no one living here now that had also been around when Charmaine was.

The unit Charmaine had lived in was the bottom right of a set of four, two up, two down. A path wound down each side to lead to the communal backyard. The units themselves seemed well maintained, the grass neatly clipped. A border of hedges grew below the windows down the side of the unit. A wind chime tinkled from above the door. Mae was considering knocking on the doors of the other units when a man wheeling his bin out to the road came down the driveway of the house next door. He was an older gentleman with a stooped posture, shuffling his feet carefully along the uneven surface of his driveway. Mae looked both ways and crossed the road, fixing a wide smile on her face.

"Hello!" she called out.

The man raised his hand in greeting and waited beside his bin for her to get to him.

"What can I do you for?" he asked, pleasantly.

That phrase had always irritated Mae. She smiled wider.

"I'm a real estate agent from Stephen Bower realty, I'm just coming by today to see if you might be looking at selling in the future?" Mae fished in her pocket and pulled out a business card, offering it to the man. He looked at it but didn't reach for it. *Take it*, Mae thought, *Just take it to be polite.*

"I'm not interested in selling, love. I'm quite happy here."

"Maybe you might be able to pass this on to someone else in the area?" She asked. She could always reach out and just touch him, but that tended to freak people out. It was better if it was an incidental touch that they didn't realise had happened.

The old man fixed her with an eye so discerning that for a second Mae felt as though he could read her thoughts. Still, he reached out slowly and took the card from her, his fingertips grazing hers as he did so. He flashed before her eyes, fragments of life rushing into her, all the things that made him who he was. She pushed through them, searching for the information she needed.

"Thank you," she said as she turned to leave.

"Have a good day," he called to her.

"You too, Jim," she crossed the road.

He had nothing useful about Charmaine, he had moved to the area only six years ago, purchasing a smaller property after his wife died. Still, it wasn't a total loss. She now knew that the other tenants in the units had all moved in after that date. No one in the building would know Charmaine or remember her. She also knew that the house across the road housed a woman who, according to Jim's memory, had lived there for at least as long as he had. She might be a start.

Mae walked up the small path that led to the doorway of the woman. The yard there was overgrown and in desperate need of a mow. A lemon tree brushed up against the house, laden with fruit, some of which had ripened and fell to the ground, littering the area around the tree with decaying yellow citrus. A cat ripped out of the cat door and bolted across the yard. It brushed Mae's legs as it did, but she saw nothing. It didn't work with animals. They were the only living things she could touch side-effect free. One day, when she was done, she would settle down and get a dog. Or two. Or three.

Mae climbed the three concrete steps to a small porch and knocked on the security screen at the front of the house. She heard shuffling inside, and the curtain in the window beside the door twitched as the occupant peeked out at her. Finally, the wooden door opened, and a woman that seemed to be in her fifties looked at Mae through the screen.

"Hi!" Mae said brightly. She gave the woman the same spiel she had given Jim across the road and held up a card.

"I'm not selling," the woman said and went to shut the door.

"Wait!" Mae said. "Maybe you know someone who is? You could give them this card for me."

"Nope. I don't know anyone," the woman shut the door firmly.

Mae sighed.

. . .

She went house by house, up one side of the street and down the other. Few homes had anyone that lived in them thirteen years ago, and those that did knew nothing. The only thing she had learnt was that the woman with the psycho cat had definitely lived there for at least eighteen years, and no one in the street seemed to like her very much. One resident was considering complaining to the council about the state of the yard. Her mind was full of suburban dramas as she made her way back to the train station, her feet sore and her head thumping. *Too many reads*, she thought, rubbing her temples. She wanted nothing more than to go back to her hotel room and take a long hot shower, but she rolled her shoulders and cracked the kinks out of her neck. She had her own business to take care of tonight. Charmaine would have to wait until tomorrow.

<h1 style="text-align:center">CHAPTER 14</h1>

Penny had just chained up her bike and was just about to go into work when her phone rang, and Dean's name popped up on the screen.

"What are you doing today?" he asked after she answered.

Penny looked through the glass into the office to where Grant and Jensen were standing behind her desk, engaged in conversation. Anne should be back today. The thought should have pleased her, it had been weeks since they had had a full staff, instead, it made her feel claustrophobic.

"It's a work day. I'm going to work."

"Argh! Of course! Sorry, I tend to forget people have normal weekday jobs and don't come home smelling like beer."

Penny wondered if Steph was back from being 'sick'.

"Why?" she asked. "Did you need help with something?"

"No. I was just thinking about driving around some more to look for the field."

Penny felt a tugging in her stomach. She looked in the

window at Jensen and Grant laughing at the door to Grant's office.

"I'll go."

"What about work?"

"They can get by without me."

It felt scandalous. Penny the reliable. Penny the responsible. Ditching work like a teenager skipping school so she could go driving. For years, she had gone in to work without thinking much about it. *No one really likes their jobs,* she rationalised, *it's just something you have to do*. And she had. It was only that lately, it hadn't been so easy to step into the door and sit at her desk and pretend she didn't hate every minute of it. In the mornings, as she opened her eyes, an overwhelming feeling of dread came washing over her as she lay there. She had been relaying this to Dean as they drove out towards the south side of the city. The windows were down, and Penny breathed in the sun-soaked air, the sweet smell of the wattle that lined the highway. She sneezed violently three times and wound up the window.

"Allergies," she said apologetically.

Dean reached across and popped the glove box, handing her a small packet of tissues.

"Thank you," Penny said, blowing her nose. She cast her eyes about for somewhere to stick the tissue and settled on shoving it in the front pocket of her backpack to dispose of later.

"So," Dean began, "What do you want to do?"

"Pardon?"

"If you weren't going to be a receptionist, I mean. If you could be anything."

Penny sat back and thought for a moment, "I want to write."

The words tumbled free before she realised she was saying them. She felt foolish and exposed, as though she had just told him she wanted to be a princess.

"Then write."

"I can't. I don't know how. I started going to university, to study journalism–"

Dean looked over at her, "You wanted to be a journalist?"

"Well… no. I don't know. I think I just wanted to write, and that seemed like a job that would allow me to do it. It seemed more respectable somehow. A serious writer job."

"You don't need to have a degree to write, Penny. You already write."

It was the validation, she realised. As if, unless someone else agreed that she could, she felt like she was playing pretend. She was reminded of her conversation with Lloyd where he said that she always waited for someone else to tell her what she was worth before she could believe it herself. She imagined sitting down and really writing, committing to something. A book. Her book. Something more than just scribbles on a napkin.

"What if I suck?" she asked.

"So what if you do? Artists don't make art because they want other people to like it. Artists make art because they have to. It's how they figure out the world. Write for yourself. Everyone else can figure themselves out. I don't play music for other people. I play it for me. They just listen."

"What would I do for money?"

"Whatever you like. You could work at a bar," he gave her a grin. "Look, the thing is, people get too attached to their job as an identity. You aren't a receptionist. That's your job. I'm not a bartender, it's just what I do to get money. It's weird that people try to neatly put themselves in a box. People are messy and complicated. You're Penny, funny, smart, clever, beautiful. You like burgers with pickles. You're empathetic. You bite your lower lip when you're thinking about something. You write. You happen to work as a receptionist. All those things can be true at the same time. You want to be a writer? You already are. You just need to claim that part of yourself."

Penny's heart raced at his words. He said them casually, off-hand. Pieces of her that he had collected and remembered. It seemed intimate. She wondered what pieces of herself Steve had collected. What would he say if he was describing her to someone?

Dean pulled up in front of a field. It was a wide expanse of grass, knee high, surrounded by a barbed-wire fence that was held up by old posts that leaned to and fro. There was a platform with a long-forgotten purpose standing nearby, and a single tree grew almost on top of it, long roots reaching down to the soil, like tentacles.

"How did it get there?" Penny wondered allowed.

A house stood back from the road, an old Queenslander on stilts, clearly abandoned and with no discernible stairs that Penny could see.

"What do you think?" Dean asked. "It's worth a look. It's the only field we have seen so far with a single tree in it."

They got out of the car and walked over to the fence.

"What if we get in trouble?" Penny asked. She glanced

anxiously up and down the road for passing cars, as though at any moment one might pull up and the occupants demand to know what they were doing trespassing.

"We might," Dean agreed. "But I doubt anyone is going to come along. We can just say you were taking a leak."

He grinned at her mischievously, and she blushed. They got through the fence with some difficulty. The wire was strung too closely together to easily slide through, and Dean had to pull tightly on it to allow enough room for Penny to squeeze through, with her repeating the process for him once she was on the other side. The grass was long but sparse and dry, the ground hard and compacted from lack of rain. Penny heard a rustling in the grass nearby and jumped, fearing snakes.

"They'll avoid you if they can," Dean said.

"What will?"

"Snakes."

"How did you know I was worrying about snakes?" she asked.

"Because *I'm* worrying about snakes. I'm trying to reassure myself," he laughed, eyes anxiously scanning the ground.

They picked their way across the field to the house and found a stack of wood at the back that they could stand on to pull themselves up to the verandah. Dean picked up a stick and bashed at the pile of wood to alert any reptiles of their intention before they climbed up it. By the time Penny stood on the verandah, she was panting and covered in sweat. She surveyed her work pants and blouse, now covered in dirt and other unidentifiable debris and sighed.

"I didn't really dress for this," she mused.

· · ·

The house was unlocked, which was unsurprising considering the location and lack of accessibility. The windows were so dirty that the light inside had a muted quality to it, and it smelled of dust and disuse. No one had lived here for a long time. Still, it was sparsely furnished, with old couches and tables. There were books on dust-covered shelves, but no linen on the beds or clothing in the drawers. A calendar on the wall was set to August 1991.

They separated and combed through the rooms, looking for any sign that her mother had been there. Penny went into the bathroom. The tub was pink and dirt had blown into it from the open window above. A mouse lay dead near the drain, it's head half stuck down the plug. She shuddered.

"Poor thing," Dean said, coming up behind her. "It must have been looking for water."

Penny turned to him, "There is nothing here."

"I know."

"I don't know why I feel so let down. There must be hundreds of places that fit. She could be anywhere. It's stupid to think I might find her with the first one."

They went and sat on the couches, Dean handing Penny a water bottle he had taken with them. She drank deeply and gave it back. She felt separated from reality, as though here in the abandoned house, time had stopped and wasn't a part of the world outside. Dean looked at her quizzically.

"What's on your mind?" he asked.

She looked over at him, his dark shirt was covered in a fine spray of cobwebs over the shoulder, and he had a smudge of dust or dirt on his cheek. She wanted to reach out and wipe it away, but it felt too intimate, so she left it be. Surely he had better things to do on his day off then drive around backroads and wander through snake-infested fields. He smiled at her, his eyes crinkling at the sides in a way that was startlingly beautiful.

"Why do you believe in it?" she asked him. "What Henry says? Most people would think it's crazy."

Dean took a swallow from the bottle and leaned back into the couch. He opened his mouth and shut it again, as though he were deciding whether or not to tell her something.

"I've just had my own experiences with crazy, I guess," he said, finally.

"Like what?"

He waved a hand, "The usual. Seeing things out of the corner of your eye. Having a sudden compulsion to do some-thing out of your usual routine that ends up averting danger."

He hesitated and ran a hand over his face. "And Mae."

Penny looked over at him. He swallowed, his Adam's apple bobbing. He looked nervous and the hairs on her arms prickled.

"What about Mae?" she asked.

She knew there was something a bit different about her. It was odd, almost like meeting someone you had met before, but not being able to place them. After they had met, Penny had spent the afternoon trying to think who it was that Mae reminded her of, but it didn't seem to be one specific person. It felt oddly like she reminded Penny of...

everyone. Dean took a deep breath, and Penny understood on some level that he was trusting her with a secret.

"Well, Mae is different, which you might have guessed. I told you about how we met. After that, we stayed good friends. She lived nearby at the time, in a share house with a few other people. She was rude, loud, and unpleasant most of the time. Still is, actually," Dean chuckled. "But I liked her. And she seemed to always know what people really thought. She was wildly good at cards - always knew when anyone was cheating. Sometimes, we would play that drinking game 'Never Have I Ever' and she always knew when people were bullshitting. She ended up moving away, she never stayed anywhere for long, but I always called to check in on her, see how she was going."

Penny felt her heart lurch a little at that. She glanced over at him, wondering if Mae was the one that got away for him. But Dean didn't have that wistful look that people tended to get when talking about someone they used to love - and still did, somewhere deep inside.

"One day she turned up at my place, out of the blue. She looked... god. I've never seen anything like it. I barely recognised her, she had dyed her hair blonde, and she was half-dressed, a big shirt that didn't fit her covered in dirt and torn and no... no pants. Her hands were covered in scratches and grazes, the knuckles were all busted up. Her nose was broken, and one eye was black. And more than that, she looked... haunted. I took her inside and put her in a shower. I had to literally wash her, she just stood there, staring. Kind of catatonic, almost. I wanted to shake her and ask what happened, but I was too scared to."

"Oh my god," Penny breathed. "What had happened to her?"

"She had been down in Melbourne, and she had brushed against someone in a crowd. She saw... inside him. When she touches people, she can see inside their mind. Their memories, who they are, what they like, what they know."

Penny thought of Mae reaching out for her hand. *Mae doesn't touch people*, Dean had said. It was impossible. But Penny believed it.

"She sees inside," Penny repeated.

You are one wild ride.

"Yes. And she brushed against someone in the crowd and saw something bad. Evil. He had hurt people. Only Mae said, when she touched him, it wasn't just her looking in. He was looking back. He could see inside her too. He was like her, I guess. She said she could feel him grinning at her as she saw what he had done. And she wanted to stop him. So, she hunted him with the things she had seen inside his head."

"Did she find him?"

"She did. Or rather, he found her. She got away, but so did he. She's still looking."

"So, that's why she is in town?"

"That's why she's in town. She's looking for her monster."

———

Penny was showering when Steve came home. He wandered into the bathroom and surveyed her discarded clothing on the floor, covered in bits of cobweb, dust and cobbler's pegs from her trek through the field.

"What have you been doing? Did you fall off your bike again?"

"What?" Penny asked. She was washing the shampoo out of her hair, and the water had run into her ears, muffling his words. She wiped her eyes and looked out of the glass where Steve was picking up her shirt and holding it at arm's length.

"Oh," she said. "No. I didn't actually go to work today. I called in and took the day off."

She braced herself mentally for the questions she was certain would follow, but Steve merely looked up at her coolly.

"You were with the bartender," he stated.

"Yes."

She waited, counting the seconds. There was something in his eyes, an emotion she hadn't seen there before.

"You're becoming obsessive, Penny. This thing with your mother? I don't know who you are anymore. Calling in sick to work, hanging out with people you don't even know."

"I just... I feel like I'm right on the edge of finding her, Steve. I can't explain it. I just know that somehow the answer is right there in front of me."

She covered her breasts with her arms, feeling oddly self-conscious suddenly. Steam billowed over to where he stood, muting his features.

"You know that feeling you get when you just know something?" she asked, trying again to explain it.

He snorted and looked off to the side, "Yeah. I know. I know exactly what you mean."

"What are you talking about?"

Steve shook his head, "Never mind. Listen, I've got a work trip, training down in Sydney?"

Penny shook her head, "I don't think you told me."

"I did, you probably just didn't listen."

She bit back a retort and settled for raising an eyebrow.

"So, I'll be gone tomorrow morning, and I'll be back on Thursday night. Maybe you could just spend a bit of time actually thinking about all of this, okay? Because here is the thing, Penny - your mum may be gone, and I know that sucks, and it's hard. But there are people right here in front of you. And it just feels like maybe you've forgotten that."

He turned and walked out of the room, the steam drifting like fog over where he had stood, as though he had never been there at all.

CHAPTER 15

When she woke the next morning, Penny called in sick to work again. She had spent the night awake, tossing and turning, hearing Steve's words in her head. *You've changed*, Steve had said. And Penny supposed he was right. She had changed. She could feel it like static electricity, raising the hairs on her arms. It reminded her of the mornings she would wake in late spring and could smell the heat of summer in the air and would know the season was about to turn. She *was* different. Before, she had felt like a mouse. She would walk through the shopping centre and feel like no one had even noticed she was there. She had been a ghost, a wraith, an invisible girl. People would bump into her and then look startled, as though suddenly realising she was there, as though she had materialised before them. And she would apologise to them, never sure why. For taking up space, she supposed. For being inconvenient. She could never seem to find the place where she fit in. She was always too loud, too quiet, too cheerful, too sombre. She could never figure out how she was supposed to be. Now, she was realising she was getting tired of trying to figure out how she fit in with everyone else. She was wondering why no one had ever just made space for her. A Penny-sized space where she could just *be*. Sighing, she rolled over and went back to sleep.

Sarah had called her at midday, waking Penny from a nap where her dreams had been disjointed and confusing. Penny had answered the phone reluctantly, her voice husky with sleep.

"Are you okay?" she had demanded.

"No. Yes. I don't know. I'll be in tomorrow. I just needed..."

What? What do I need?

She fumbled out an excuse about a headache and tiredness, and Sarah had told her to rest up and get better. Penny had hung up the phone and stared at the ceiling, watching the fan turn lazy circles above her. At Papa's house, she had a room where she sometimes stayed on weekends. He had hung curled pieces of coloured paper from it, and they would turn the fan on low and watch them spin around like pieces of seaweed. He would read to her, stories of pirates and treasure, of family and women who wore long dresses and longed for the same freedoms she took for granted. Penny would drift off to sleep to the soft lull of his voice, feeling safe and secure and loved. She missed her grandfather.

After she got dressed, she grabbed her things and wheeled her bike to the front door, opening it. It was bright outside, the sun was shining, and she could hear the thrumming of bees in the bottlebrush by the gate. Taking a deep breath, she smelled the earth baking in the heat of the day and the softer sweet smell of the clover by the garden. The season was changing.

Penny chained up her bike and went up the path that lead to the facility. Inside, she made her way through the halls to Teddy's room, greeting people as she went. Music played softly from a small stereo in the corner. His mouth hung open slightly in his sleep, and part of his hair was sticking up like chicken fluff. Penny smoothed it down, and his eyes opened.

"Hello, Papa," she said.

He nodded at her in greeting.

"How have you been? You have any wild parties while I've been gone?"

He looked at her with interest but not recognition. Where did the memories go? Were they still there, trapped and inaccessible as though someone had locked them away? Or were they erased? Loneliness crushed her.

"Papa? Do you know who I am? It's me, Penny."

He said her name then, softly. His voice cracked with disuse. Penny. That one word. She had never realised it before, the way that when people say your name, it is laden with all their thoughts of you. An intimacy as they spoke that made the word heavy with meaning. When Teddy said it just now, it was hollow and empty.

· · ·

There had been a day when he first moved into the facility where something of him remained. He was confused, unsure why he was there as she patiently explained it to him over and again.

Finally, he had said, "It's for the best."

Part of her had ached at his acceptance, his surrender to the passing of time and the loss of his own independence. He knew her name. He knew where he was and why. It was the closest thing she was going to get. She had said goodbye. She couldn't have said what had made her do it, that day especially. But the day she said goodbye was a good day and she wasn't sure how many of them she had left.

"Papa, I want you to know that I love you so much," she had begun.

"No, you don't," he had smiled at her, embarrassed and touched by such an open display of affection from his grand-daughter.

"I do," Penny had said, firmly. She had squeezed his hand and looked deep into the blue depths off his eyes, as though she were trying to imprint this somewhere inside him. He had squeezed back, his hand warm.

"And I want you to know that I will miss you so much," her voice had wavered. She had kissed him on the cheek, and as she walked out, she did not look back. She made it all the way to the nurse's station before she broke down. Raw sobs of grief that shook her shoulders. The RN had come out of the room and without a word, she had folded Penny into her arms and Penny had leant against her - holding on to some-thing stable that could tether her to this world when it felt as though she might fall apart. One of the residents had come up and placed a soft hand on Penny's back, and she had glanced over at the tiny woman before her. She had softly curled hair around her face and huge round glasses. Her face was smiling with warmth and sympathy.

"He will be alright, love," she had said.

And taking Penny's hand, the older lady had slowly walked Penny around the facility, taking her on a tour and chattering away until her tears had stopped. The next time Penny had gone back to see Teddy, he was gone. He had never been lucid again like he was that day, and she knew she had been lucky to slip in between the fracture of time that allowed her to say goodbye. It was just that one moment. That one day. An ordinary day, a good day, a heartbreaking day, a lucky day. The day she had said goodbye.

⁂

After she left Teddy, Penny walked to the vending machines near the front door to buy a coke. A man was standing in front of it, counting coins in his hand. He turned to her.

"It keeps spitting out my fifty-cent pieces," he said. He smiled ruefully, his brown eyes warm and friendly.

"It does that. It is easier if you swipe your card. Here, I'll buy us both one, and you can give me the change. I accept all fifty-cent coins," she joked.

She purchased their drinks and handed him his. He dropped his change in her hand.

"I'm Jaxon," he said, holding out his hand.

She shook it, "I'm Penny. Are you visiting someone?"

"Yeah. My uncle moved in a little while ago. My aunt comes up a couple of times a week, but she has a cold and didn't want to make him sick. I said I would go check in on him."

"What's your uncle's name?" Penny asked.

"Henry."

She felt her heart thump, and her feelings must have shown on her face because Jaxon immediately began to chuckle.

"You've met him, I guess. He's told you a riddle that sounds like a clue to a cryptic crossword and then later you've realised he was predicting the future in the most irritating way possible?"

Penny swallowed, "Something like that."

"Well, I hope it was something good. When I was nine, he told me 'mangoes would make the chalk break'. I spent a whole week during summer staring suspiciously at mangoes and wondering what the chalk was. Then, I was climbing a mango tree when the branch snapped, and I broke my arm. The doctor said it had snapped like a stick of chalk. Henry told me he had warned me and I asked him, how come you couldn't just tell me not to climb the tree or I would break my arm? But it doesn't work that way. He can't get the words out."

"I thought maybe that the riddles were part of the dementia," Penny said. "They came out confused because his mind was confused."

"Oh, no. They have always been like that. Henry told me that it came over him like a fog. He would see it drifting past, he would try to tell people, but it never came out right. But it always comes true."

"What if you figured it out? The riddle. Maybe you could change it. If you had of known what he meant by the tree, maybe you wouldn't have climbed it."

"Maybe. But I think it's more like, whatever he sees, that's how it is. You can't change the future any more than you can change the past. Whatever happens, was always going to happen. A lot of my family is scared of him. My brother hasn't seen my aunt and uncle in years now. But I like Henry. It's not his fault."

"No. I guess it isn't."

Jaxon tilted his head, assessing her, "So, what did he tell you?"

Penny hesitated, not wanting to discuss her mother and unsure how to even begin explaining to a stranger.

"He said I would fall over. Which I did," she said finally.

"Sorry to hear it."

Penny nodded and looked up the hallway to where Henry's room was.

"You can go see him, you know. If there is something else he has said that you feel you want to talk about with him."

"Are you psychic too?" Penny asked.

Jaxon shrugged, "If I were, I'd be driving a much nicer car."

He checked his watch, "I've got to go. I'll see you around, Penny. Thanks for the drink."

Penny stood there for a moment after he left, considering. Then she started back the hall towards Henry's room. Maybe there would be something else he could tell her that would narrow down their search for Charmaine. It couldn't hurt to try. He was sitting in a chair by his window, looking out at the trees, his eyes unfocused and unblinking.

"Hello," she had said. She sat down in the chair opposite him, the sunlight warming the side of her face.

He had looked at her and then slowly, he had reached out his hand, almost in invitation. She reached out and took it.

Penny felt like she was walking blind as she stumbled through the hallway. Tripping over her own feet, she dropped her phone and bent to retrieve it, the world tilting alarmingly. Penny fled towards the exit, pushing through the doors and into the air, gulping down lungfuls of it, like she had been suffocating. She ran to the pole, past carers who were watering the garden with residents, past the jacaranda tree where Teddy had laughed at the blooms in her hair, to where she had chained her bike and leaned her head against the cool metal, closing her eyes for a moment. She unlocked her bike and put on her helmet and rode as fast as she could, flying past the pub without glancing towards it. She rode until she reached the river where she had sat with her mother and collapsed on the sunbleached grass, it's roughness prickling the backs of her legs. The sun was fading, glinting off the river. Birds flew overhead, seeking their way home before dark fell. The air was humid and thick, but despite the warmth, Penny shivered.

When she had touched Henry, he hadn't said a thing. She sat there beside him for so long, her hand resting in his that she began to feel foolish. He had a clock in his room that ticked almost comically loud, counting down the seconds. Finally, she had risen, disappointment settling within her. She had been foolish to come; moreover, she felt guilty. She didn't know Henry at all, she wasn't visiting him. She was... using him, for his gift, for what he could do for her. She felt embarrassed and disgusted by herself. She had reached his door and was stepping into the hall when she heard his wheelie walker moving behind her. Overcome with sadness, she had turned to him.

"I'm sorry, Henry. I shouldn't have... well. Have a good evening, okay?"

But as the words had tumbled from her mouth, she had noticed that Henry was not himself. His eyes were clear again, whatever fog trapped him inside his own mind had once again lifted. More than that, his eyes were filled with a deep sympathy that made Penny's heart immediately catch in her chest. This wasn't just an old man delivering a message. This was a man who was about to give her bad news. She knew it. He had been wrong. She wouldn't find her mother. Charmaine was gone, and this was a wild goose chase that she had lead herself, Dean, and Mae on. Henry had reached for her, grasping her hand in his and squeezing gently. It was sympathy.

He had opened his mouth, and his expression was concentrated, as though he were picking his words, trying to find the right ones.

"Your father's daughter," he said.

"Yes?"

"She's dying. Your father's daughter will die."

Penny had felt her mouth go dry.

"I don't understand, Henry. How? I... is it an accident?"

Penny thought of the oil on the road, of cars that came to close to her when riding. Men who leered. Dark alleys. Suddenly, the world was full of danger.

Henry shook his head, "No. No. Bad blood. Dying."

"I'm sick?"

Penny watched as the fog began to fall in front of his eyes.

"No! Henry!" She squeezed his hand back, the way he

had squeezed hers, trying to hold him to her, but he slipped away, back beyond the veil that held him.

Her father's daughter was dying.

And Penny was an only child.

CHAPTER 16

She couldn't stay by the riverside forever. Eventually, the mosquitos began swarming around her, heedless of her anguish, and Penny had been driven away, slowly riding the streets until she got back to the unit. It was full dark when she arrived home, no light shone in the window, and she fumbled with her key to open the door, dropping and retrieving it, unable to stop her hands from shaking, feeling as though she were chilled to the bone. Seeking warmth, Penny had stripped off and taken a long hot shower. There, she had found herself inspecting her body, looking for lumps and bumps, signs that something was wrong with her, something unseen. She imagined the sickness waiting inside her like a time bomb, set to go off at any moment. She would have to go to the doctor, she thought. But what would she even say? She didn't feel physically unwell, they couldn't test everything. *It always comes true*, Jaxon had said. Before she met him, she could have pushed aside the other things Henry said as coincidence. Strange little phrases, given up by a man who was lost inside his own mind. She kept seeing

Henry's face in her mind as he told her. He wasn't just lucid, he was... sympathetic. She could see him struggling to the surface, trying to piece together the words to warn her. Henry had said she would die.

Penny tucked herself up in bed, unable to stop shivering. She kept waiting for Steve to come home, and belatedly remembered that he was away on his work trip. The house felt empty. Was this going to be her life? For the rest of the days left to her was she going to eat zucchini and watch Steve curl weights, work in her job that she hated and just slip away unnoticed from the world? She hadn't done anything! She wasn't ready. The arts night floated into her mind, the fire and words drifting on the night air. That had been living. A strange temporary connection to people she didn't know but who she bared her soul to. She had felt... seen. Finally. Briefly, she had felt seen by people. Dean. Ray. Rosie. Henry. Even Mae. She didn't want to go out like a dying flame, leaving nothing but ashes and dust. She wanted to leave a mark on this world. Exhausted, she slipped into sleep.

Riding to work the next morning, she was amazed to find the world had continued on as usual. It seemed like everything should stop somehow. It reminded her of when her mother went missing, and Penny had spent the evening with Lloyd at the police station, standing there in his navy blue work shirt, worn soft with washing, explaining in soft tones he thought Penny couldn't hear about his missing wife. She thought the world would stop, but the next day she had gone to school, and the teacher had slid a test across the table, and she had stared at the maths problems in front of her wondering how it was possible that something as mundane as algebra could exist in the same world as one where a woman was missing.

She chained her bike up and went inside the building, where everything was absurdly normal. She could hear Grant in his office on a phone call. She booted up the computer and sat back. *What if it isn't a sickness*, she wondered. *Maybe I'm just going to have a sudden stroke and die right here at my desk.* She shuddered. Sarah came in and gave her a grunt of acknowledgement before heading to the kitchen to make coffee. Penny tapped her pen against the table. Her chair didn't feel right. She adjusted it up and down, trying to make it fit her. Anne and Steph came in, followed by Jensen, who ducked his head and went straight to his office.

The clock ticked loudly on the wall. Penny opened the inbox for the emails and stared at them but didn't open any of them. This wasn't right. She had woken this morning different, unable to fit into the life she had made. The phone rang, and she didn't answer it. It rang again. Sarah stuck her head out and gave Penny a curious look.

"Dude? You doing okay? Do you need to go home?"

Penny stood abruptly, her chair rolling backwards on the carpet. She swallowed and went to the door to Grant's office and flung the door wide without knocking. He looked up at her and did a double-take.

"Penny?"

"I quit."

The words tumbled free before she could think twice about them, slipping off her tongue and into the room. Her heart thumped in her chest, and she expected to feel terrified, but she only felt relieved. Grant began to protest, but Penny could no longer hear the words over the roaring of her own blood rushing in her ears. She collected her bag from under the desk and picked up her succulent from her desk, pressing it into Sarah's hands, who stood silently, her mouth dropped open.

Stepping outside, she breathed in the air, heavy with heat and the promise of summer. A man walked towards her on the footpath, staring down at his phone. Penny had always moved over, Penny had always apologised. But she stood there, waiting, still, allowing him to bump into her, where he looked up shocked. She stared back at him, her mouth closed in a firm line.

"Sorry," he muttered.

"I will not apologise one more time for taking up space. I will *not*."

He scurried off.

"I will not," she said to the empty air.

By the time she had ridden home, she was furious. A rational part of her mind told her it was part of the grieving process. The angry part of her mind told the rational part to sit down and shut up. She ripped open the mailbox and checked inside.

"Junk mail!" She announced. "Which is typical. It's not

like there is a sign that specifically says I don't want junk mail or anything."

She waved her offending brochures at a man walking his dog on the street, who looked at her with concern and hurried on. Linda looked up from her pruning of the hibiscus and glared at her. Penny's eyes narrowed. Stomping across the lawn, she stopped in front of Linda.

"What is your problem?"

"Excuse me?"

"For years I have lived here, paid my rent and been practically a model tenant. I'm quiet. I don't have parties. I don't play loud music. Why are you always looking at me like I'm something you just stepped in?"

Linda opened and closed her mouth, stunned to silence for once.

"You know what? I don't care. This is me giving notice. I'll be out by the end of the month."

Penny turned on her heel and stormed back to the front door.

Linda yelled after her, "You are a horrible girl! You don't deserve that young man. And you need to go on a diet!"

"And you need to get laid, Linda," Penny called over her shoulder, flipping her the bird.

She slammed the door after her and set her bike against the wall, where it promptly fell over, causing Penny to kick the tyre in frustration. She raked her hands through her hair, and the anger flowed out of her, leaving her feeling empty and hollow. How was this fair? Wasn't life supposed to balance itself out? She had spent her whole life playing by the rules, putting others first, didn't that give her some kind of karmic surplus on which to draw on? She went to the mirror in the bathroom to splash water on her face and stared back at her reflection, rivulets of water dripping from her chin. She would pass from this world and leave nothing behind. Who would remember her? Lloyd. Steve. Not her grandfather, silent and lost already. Not her mother, gone. Would she know? Wherever she was, would there be some maternal part of her that recognised that her child was no longer on the earth?

"Call the doctor," she told herself.

But when she picked up the phone, it was Dean that she called.

He came without asking why. That was the first thing she had been surprised about. She had stumbled over her words, and in the end, she had simply asked him to come, and he had hung up the phone and been there before she had even had a chance to change out of her work clothes. She grabbed her backpack and left without a backwards glance. The afternoon was still young, schoolchildren were walking home, and Penny leaned her head against the door and watched them.

"They look so happy," she said. "Remember when you were a kid, and you just felt invincible?"

Dean snorted, "Yep. I felt that way right up until two years ago when I tried to jump a fence and landed on the other side with a bad back."

Penny laughed despite herself.

Dean glanced over at her, "So, what are we doing this

afternoon? Hitting the road to look for elusive fields? Sitting by the ocean? Drinking sangria and listening to sad poetry?"

Penny met his eyes and looked away, "You know I think you might be my only friend. I didn't realise I didn't have any until this afternoon and I needed to talk to someone and realised the only person I can talk to is you."

"What did you want to talk about?"

Penny shook her head, "Not yet. I just... What were you going to do this afternoon? If I hadn't called?"

"Well, it's Aberdeen's birthday. So, I was planning to buy some flowers and head over there. She's having a small group of people for drinks and a grazing platter."

"Then let's do that."

CHAPTER 17

Penny woke unsure of where she was. Glancing around, she saw the sun streaming in the windows below the loft platform where she lay and was slightly disoriented at seeing the sun coming in from below her. Suddenly, the night before came back to her in fragments and she sat up quickly. Her head thumped like a heartbeat, and she promptly lay back down and closed her eyes for a moment.

"Oh god, oh god," she breathed. *What had happened?*

She had quit her job, she remembered that much. Dean, and Aberdeen's party, and too much sangria. A vague recollection of standing under the stairs and feeling the world spin and feeling as though she were spinning with it, alive. Then she briefly recalled vomiting into some bushes while Aberdeen held her hair back from her face. She had told Dean she didn't want to go home and he had looked at her with concern. Aberdeen had offered her a spare bed, but Penny had looked at Dean, and he had helped her to the car and then driven her here and... god, what happened?

She remembered taking the stairs up to the apartment, leaning on Dean for support. He had led her inside. It was an old building, used for some purpose long forgotten, the apartment almost only one big room, with wide arched windows lining one side, a loft which served as a bedroom and a small bathroom off a tiny kitchen. He had shown her the internal stairs that led up to the rooftop where the city lights had winked and sparkled in front of her, like a kaleidoscope. Then, she had come inside and... what? Had they... No. Tentatively, she reached out with her arm feeling the mattress beside her. Empty. She cracked an eyelid. No Dean. But there was a glass of water beside the bed, and she reached for it gratefully, draining it in three large gulps.

She sat up more cautiously this time and noticed Dean curled up on the couch below, a worn quilt over half his legs, his jeans still on and his chest bare. The sunlight was catching the fine blonde hairs on his arms that were thrown carelessly above his head. He stretched suddenly and opened his eyes, seeing her and smiling.

"Hey there," he said.

Penny half smiled at him, "Hey."

He got up and began making coffee, and Penny swung her legs out of bed to realise she was wearing one of Dean's shirts and nothing else. Had he undressed her? She couldn't recall.

"Your clothes are in the dryer," he called up to her, as

though reading her mind. "You changed out of them last night, and I washed them for you."

"Oh. Well... thank you."

Finding an old robe hanging over the back of a chair, she put it on and padded down the stairs feeling fragile and not a little worse for wear. Dean pushed a steaming cup of coffee in front of her as she sat down at the bench and busied himself watering a collection of plants that sat under one of the big windows.

"Did I... did I tell you..." Penny began and stopped. *Did I tell you what? Tell you about how I'm dying, according to Henry? Tell you I quit my job? Tell you that I'm living a life that I can't stand? What did I tell you, Dean?*

He looked over to her. The sunlight backlit him, bouncing off the curves of his bare shoulders in a way that was heartbreakingly beautiful. Instinctively her hands went to reach for a piece of paper and a pen before she realised she had none. *Arms*, she wrote inside her head. *Sunlight. Perfect.*

"You didn't tell me. You were upset, I could see that. But no, whatever you could have told me, you didn't. I didn't ask. But you can, Penny. If you want to."

She shook her head and stared down into the mug in front of her. *Grief. Alone. Gone.*

"I don't know where to begin," she said. But then, as she sipped at the coffee, the words began to come. The conversation with Henry, quitting her job, yelling at Linda, the day in the bridal shop when she wore the dress and knew she never wanted to put it on again. She told him things she had never even admitted to herself, fears and dreams. She cried until she felt limp and heavy. And through it all, he sat across from her quietly, not telling her she was wrong or interrupting. He made her feel like he had all the time in the world, like there was no one but her. Finally, she stopped, spent.

Dean reached over and took her empty cup and rinsed it in the sink.

"You need a bath," he announced.

"Excuse me?"

"A bath. They're soothing, and you are made of jagged edges right now."

Comfort. Kindness. Him.

Without waiting for a response, he went into the bathroom off the kitchen and shortly Penny began to hear the water running into a tub. Dean hummed to himself, padding back and forth to the kitchen for various small bottles. Penny got up and followed him in. The bathroom housed a large old clawfoot tub that had a showerhead above it, a double sink, an overstuffed armchair beside a full-length mirror, and a jungle of plants. Oddly, there was also a small bookshelf beside the mirror, housing an eclectic assortment of titles.

"Oh!" she said, surprised.

Dean glanced over at her, "These plants prefer humidity, and there is a lot of light in here from the skylight. And the books are what I've called The Bath Books. You know, small and easy to hold while in the bath."

Penny looked up, the skylight was a six-foot-wide expanse of glass that ran the length of the room.

"People could see you bathing!" she said, feeling scandalised.

Dean shrugged, "I guess. But they would have to be really keen to climb on to the roof to do it."

He turned off the taps. Steam was rising from the water, and the smell of lavender and rose floated delicately in the air. The water was a very light purple.

"On of my friends makes bath bombs," Dean said, shrugging.

Leaning forward, he tucked a strand of her hair behind her ear, his hand cupping her face for a moment. She reached up and held his hand, squeezing his fingers gently. Suddenly, she couldn't bear to be alone.

"Stay," she said.

He looked into her eyes for a moment, blue and green searching hers.

"Okay."

He busied himself by the sink, rearranging things while she shucked off the robe and shirt and stepped into the bath. She gingerly lowered herself into the water, wincing a little at the heat of it. As her skin grew used to the warmth, she lay back into the water, sliding until her whole head went under, muting the world outside, coming up only when her lungs screamed for oxygen.

Penny rested her head against the side of the bath and watched as Dean plucked a book from the shelf and pulled the armchair to the side of the tub and made himself comfortable. She should have felt awkward, lying naked in a bath with little more than a film of slightly coloured water to cover her. She knew he could see the shape of her beneath it. As she shifted, her nipples broke the surface. The swell of her breasts rising out of the water. Dean looked at her in a way that was neither leering nor completely asexual. It was more... familiar. Like he had seen her naked a hundred times and was completely at ease. As though he saw her lying in his tub every day.

He opened the book and turned to a page, reaching into his pocket he pulled out a pair of glasses and slipped them on, looking at her with mild embarrassment, "I can't read without them. I usually wear contacts."

"I'm literally naked in front of you. Your glasses don't bother me."

"Right. Well. This is from a book my friend wrote. Leif. You met him, remember? It's a collection of his poetry."

He smiled at her and leaned forward to tuck a strand of hair behind her ear.

"Why?" she asked.

"Because that's what he writes."

She had meant why was he being so kind. Why did he still want to be around her when she was so clearly messing up her whole life? Why was he so easy to talk to? Why did he make her feel like she was home?

"That's not what I meant," she said.

"I know," he said softly. Then, clearing his throat, he began.

"Click clack
    Click clack

On the empty carriage

I sit swaying in my seat
Rocking like a lullaby
Gently to my sleep
Alone inside the carriage
My thoughts are all I keep
And I shall see my beloved
And lay flowers at her feet..."

At midday, Dean dropped Penny back to her unit. She had made an appointment later that day to see Dr. Adrian, who had been Penny's doctor since she was a baby, a kindly old man who was nearing retirement age. He gave her a quick physical, ordered some routine blood tests and persuaded her to have a skin check. Penny instantly felt the weight of all the days she neglected to use sunscreen as he inched over her body with his dermatoscope. Was this how it was to be then? A tiny mole that would take away her life. One after-noon too many spent soaking in the Queensland sun?

"All good," he announced when he was done.

"I'm okay?"

"Well, we can take the blood tests, and I'll check for any abnormalities, but as far as I can tell, you're as fit as a fiddle. People with darker skin have less chance of getting skin cancer than fair-skinned people, but it's also missed more often, so it's always worth checking. I seem to recall that your mother was fair-skinned?"

She nodded dumbly and took the pathology slip he held out. Dr. Adrian tilted his head and looked at her with concern.

"Was there a reason why you felt you might not be okay?" he asked.

"No. Not really. I just wanted to check and make sure. What would it mean - medically - if someone had... say, bad blood?"

"Bad blood?"

"Yes."

He sat back in his chair, "Well, any number of things. It could be as simple as low iron, to any of the bloodborne illnesses. It could mean haemophilia. It could be leukaemia or lymphoma. What do you mean? Did you read it somewhere?"

Penny shook her head.

"Are you okay, Penny? Emotionally, I mean."

"I'm fine. Thank you. I'll go get this test done. How long before the results come in?"

"A couple of days."

"Right. Well, thank you."

She picked up her bag and left the office, leaving her doctor staring curiously after her.

CHAPTER 18

Penny found herself riding to her father's even before she realised where she was. She pushed her bike in the back gate at Lloyd's and bent down to scratch the cat before walking inside. Lloyd was in the kitchen, staring intently at the back of a coffee jar as though it contained the secrets to the universe. He was so absorbed that when she greeted him, he startled, the coffee jar jumping out of his hands and he made an almost comedic fumble to stop it from smashing on the ground.

"Hey, kid," he said. "I didn't hear you come in."

He began to ramble while pouring her a juice and Penny watched him, the greying hair at his temples, the way he had a slight limp from an old knee injury that troubled him more as he aged. *I should tell him*, she thought. *Just that I'm waiting on some results. To prepare him, just in case.*

"Dad?" she said. "Can I talk to you?"

"Of course," he said, sliding her drink in front of her and popping an umbrella in the top. "You can always talk to me, you know that."

Sitting down, he fiddled nervously with the edge of the tablecloth and wouldn't meet her eyes.

God, he is acting weird. Is he picking up on my energy?

"Dad," she began.

He looked at her with such genuine fear in his eyes and Penny faltered. How could she do this to him? She was all he had. She looked at the umbrella in her glass of juice, and her heart broke at the sight of it. Who would look after him when she was gone?

"I have to tell you something," he blurted.

Penny was startled momentarily, "Uhh, okay. I have to tell you something too."

He seemed to not hear her at all, and Penny felt slightly miffed. What happened to of course you can talk to me, Penny? She didn't want to upset him, but this wasn't exactly how she imagined her only parent would be when his only child sat him down to talk about something.

"There is no easy way to tell you this. So, I just need to come out with it."

For a moment, Penny's heart sped up. He had found her. He had found Charmaine. That's the only reason he could be acting this way. My, god. Henry was right. Instinctively she glanced around the room for some sign of her mother, barely hearing his words.

"... and she is sick. Real sick. You might be a match."

Penny jolted back into the conversation.

"I'm sorry, what?"

"My daughter."

"Yes."

"She's sick."

Penny stared at him. *He knew?* He looked at her imploringly. Sweat beaded on his forehead.

"You're going to need to start again," she said.

"I have a daughter. Her name is Alice. She had leukaemia."

"I'm your daughter," Penny said, dumbly.

"Of course you are, honey. This doesn't mean I love you any less."

He blinked at her slowly, like an owl. Penny said nothing, trying to fit all of the pieces together in her head, and none of them seemed to make any sense. It was like having a conversation with Henry, all riddles and nonsense.

"Dad," Penny said slowly. "You need to explain this from the beginning."

Lloyd took a deep breath, "It started years ago when you were about six. I met Marg at a job I was doing for her. Your mother was gone then, I can't remember how long that time, maybe eight months or so. You remember?"

"No."

"Oh. Okay. Well, Marg and I were good friends. She was on her own there at the house, smart lady, just living on her own. The house was old and needed a lot of work, so I was back and forth often. One thing led to another and... well..."

"You had an affair."

Lloyd cringed, "It wasn't like that."

"Well, what was it like, Dad?" she spat the words out, feeling bitter and embarrassed as though she were taking on the role of a scorned wife.

"We were friends. I was lonely. My wife was gone, and I was raising a kid on my own. I didn't know what I was doing. I just started opening up to Marg. She taught me how to French braid, you know. So I could do your hair."

Penny closed her eyes. *What the fuck is happening? What the actual-*

"Anyway, she got pregnant. She didn't tell me at first because Charmaine had come back then and I was busy trying to settle her back in. You weren't coping very well with her return. Real clingy, nightmares and stuff."

I think I'm getting a headache, Penny thought absently.

"Alice was born, and I wanted to support them, but I couldn't leave Charmaine. Or you. So, I just kind of... didn't tell anyone."

"So, they don't know about us?"

"Marg and Alice know about you, yes. I just didn't tell Charmaine or you. It didn't seem fair. Charmaine was so fragile. And you? You had been through enough."

"So, you told your other family but not us? What possessed you to think that was okay?" She felt betrayed and jealous, imagining him turning up at another house, with a daughter who had a mother. How much had he told them? Had they seen pictures? Did they know when she broke her arm in ninth grade?

"I'm not proud, Penny. I just needed to tell you because Alice is sick. She's been sick before, with the leukaemia, when she was young. But she beat it then. It's just now, the chemo isn't working. She needs a bone marrow transplant. The doctors have said you probably won't be a match since you're only a half-sister, but I need to ask. I'm sorry."

Alice. Alice has cancer. Her father's daughter. Fucking Henry.

"She's sick," Penny said. Her voice was hollow, coming from somewhere far away. She stared at her father, a man she thought was solid and stable. The parent she could rely on. Her constant. Her whole life was a lie.

"Yes. She is. Will you think about it, Penny? She *is* your sister."

Penny stood up, the chair screeching along the floorboards.

"Just... stop," Penny rubbed her hand over her eyes and down her face. "I hate literally every word out of your mouth right now."

"Penny-"

"Stop it! Just stop talking! Oh my god! I've been walking around thinking *I* was sick, Dad! I quit my job! I - *oh my god* - I told my landlord to get laid!"

"You're sick?"

"No! I'm not sick. Alice is fucking sick. Your *daughter* is sick."

"I don't understand. Why would you think you were sick?"

"Because Henry told me I was! Never mind. It doesn't matter. When?" she asked.

"When, what?"

"When do I need to get tested?"

"You'll do it? You'll get tested?" Lloyd sagged in relief.

"Of course I will get tested. I'm not a monster. It's not her fault you're a cheating, lying asshole."

Lloyd's mouth opened and closed as he bit back his words. He swallowed, "As soon as possible."

"Write it down. Her name, her address, and her doctor. I'll deal with them."

Lloyd jumped up from the table and grabbed an empty envelope from by the phone, scribbling down the details. He handed it to her with a shaking hand.

"Thank you, Penny."

She nodded briskly and took the paper and turned to go, stopping with her hand on the door.

"Dad?" she said, without turning around. "Don't... don't call me for a while. I don't want to speak to you. Please."

It had been years since she had heard the sound of her father crying. And it still broke her heart, even as she walked away.

Things have been moved in the house. I came in after work and the picture of Penny and I had been shifted from its spot, a line of dust where it used to sit still visible. Other things had been moved around too, books and knick-knacks rearranged. The smell of the cologne was so strong that it felt like its own physical presence. I want to tell Lloyd, but he will think I've gone crazy – and to be honest, I feel a little crazy. Just today, I was standing outside the pharmacy getting some fresh air when I saw a car go by and I swear I saw Lloyd in the driver's seat, but it wasn't his car. There was a woman in the other seat, and as they went past, she leaned over and touched him in this way that seemed so intimate that it stopped me breathing for a moment. Of course, it wasn't Lloyd, it was just someone who looked like him. And I know that. Rationally, I know it, just like I know no one breaks into someone's house to move around their books – but, my brain keeps whispering anyway.

The only upside to my days at the moment is Penny. The other week- end, I was at Lloyd's cooking breakfast in the kitchen, and she came in still wearing her nightgown and rubbing sleep from her eyes, and I realised she is nearly as tall as I am. How did that happen? It feels like not that long ago, she was still this little sprite of a creature climbing into my lap. I can't remember the last time she did that, I wish we knew when the 'last time' would be the last time. I would have savoured it. After breakfast, we sat in front of the television watching terrible shows and painting each other's nails. Penny french braided my hair. I asked her when she learnt how to do it, and she said that her dad had taught her. I didn't even know Lloyd could braid. All these years later, and he still surprises me. Who knows? Maybe he did start wearing cologne, after all.

CHAPTER 19

Steve had come home at dusk that day to find Penny sitting in the lounge room, staring at the blank television. She looked up and attempted to give him a smile, but he took his bag straight to the bedroom to begin to unpack. Steve had always been like that. The few times they had ever gone away, Penny would leave her suitcase in the corner of the room for weeks afterwards until she finally broke down and began to pull clothes out and reluctantly put them away. Unpacking felt like admitting the holiday was over. Steve would do it the moment they came home. Maybe that was a sign you had built a life you wanted, when you were happy to unpack and settle back into it. Suddenly, Penny felt desperately like being 'away'. Somewhere else, somewhere anonymous where no one knew her name, and she could be anyone she wanted to.

Penny wandered into the bedroom and sat down to watch him.

"How was your trip?" she asked.

"It was okay. How have you been?"

Their words were oddly formal, clipped, like they didn't know how to be around each other anymore. They were three feet apart, but she had never felt more distant.

"I haven't been great, actually," she swallowed, "I quit my job."

Steve froze with a shirt in his hands and looked up at her, "What?"

"It just kind of happened. And... I may have told Linda we were giving notice."

Steve slowly put down the shirt and began to pinch the bridge of his nose with his fingertips, "Penny, what the hell has happened?"

She started to fill him in, beginning with meeting Henry's nephew and the strange premonition Henry had given afterwards. She tactfully left out the part about staying at Dean's house.

"I don't think I *am* sick. Not anymore. But when I thought I was, it was like I just couldn't stand being *in* my life anymore. Like I had spent all this time doing things I thought I was supposed to be doing while waiting for my real life to start. I don't know. I guess I kind of flipped out."

Steve had closed his eyes, and when he opened them, he was looking at her like he was seeing her for the first time and was unsure who she was. She took a deep breath and began to tell him about going to see Lloyd and about Alice and Marg.

"And then it turns out there is this whole other family. He spent my whole life just lying to me."

"Like father like daughter," Steve muttered.

"What did you say to me?"

"Nothing."

"Steve! *What* did you say?"

"I'm just pointing out that the apple doesn't fall far from the tree, Penny. Lloyd was running around on your mum, and you're running around with that bartender."

"I'm not running around!"

"Whatever."

Penny suddenly felt like she'd had the wind knocked out of her. In her head, she saw herself and Dean sharing a burger, singing together in the car, her body naked in the bath. She had wanted him. Badly. Desperately, almost. She was furious with Lloyd. Unimaginably angry. And... she understood. She knew loneliness. She knew you could live with someone, brush your teeth next to them, sleep beside them and be completely and utterly alone. Steve was right. God-fucking-dammit.

"God. You're right."

"I am?"

"Yes. You are totally right."

"Well, I mean... look, Penny. We will fix this thing with Linda, okay? And the job thing? Well, whatever. And your dad! Yes. That's a mess. But you've got to stop acting so unhinged. We can-"

Penny found herself tuning out to the sound of his voice as he talked, wandering to and fro putting away shoes and placing dirty clothes in the hamper. She thought back to the afternoon she had gone to see her father after Grant had told her that she wouldn't get the editing job, her talks with Ray and his friends, and with Dean. What she had really wanted, deep down, was someone to give her permission to quit. It wasn't just the job, if it was, it would have been simple. It was everything. She wanted someone to realise that she hated her life because it was one she had been ferried along to. She needed someone to tell her that she could leave it all if she wanted because she was scared to do it herself. That was what Henry had done, really. Penny realised that Steve was still talking, while he inspected his eyebrows in the mirror, using a pair of tweezers to pluck stray hairs.

"Steve. Stop," Penny said, cutting him off. "I don't want to fix things with Linda. I hate it here. It wasn't just that I flipped out and did something crazy, I flipped out and did the things I had always wanted to do. This whole life? It's been me checking boxes that I thought I was supposed to have ticked. I don't want this."

"You don't want our life together?"

He said it like a challenge. Like he expected her to back down, smooth his ruffled feathers. Penny, who cooked spaghetti with zucchini. Penny, who hid the pop tarts. She looked at him now and realised that no, she didn't want this life with him. If she had been a different girl, they probably would have dated for a while and broken up, but she had been a girl who needed something reliable, and he had been that. Beautifully boring, perfectly predictable. Steve would never vanish without a trace. No matter when she came home, Steve would be there, drinking his green smoothies and counting his calories. She had been terrified for so long, but she wasn't scared anymore.

She swallowed hard, pushing the words from her mouth so she couldn't take them back, breathing life into them, "This isn't working. We... I think we need to break up."

She had said it. It was done. The words sat there between them, heavy with truth.

His hand that held the tweezers froze in mid-air for a moment before he continued, "You're insane. We're engaged."

She shook her head, "I can't. I can't marry you, I'm sorry. I've known for a while. I just couldn't begin to imagine what my life would look like without you. But I *do* need to be without you."

He put down the tweezers and sighed in a way that made her feel like she were a child, and he was explaining something very simple to her, "Is this about your dad? I know you've had a bit of a shock, but you can't make knee-jerk reactions right now. You don't mean this, and you would end up regretting it."

In all the years they had been together they had never fought. Not really. When Penny had heard about other people fighting with their partners, she had always felt slightly smug, as though she and Steve must have fit together so flawlessly that there was no reason to argue.

"Steve, I'm not going to change my mind. We're over. We are done. Surely you must know this too? You have to feel this if I feel it."

"Why?" he asked her. He looked genuinely shocked, and Penny realised them not being together had never crossed his mind. In spite of all the ways that they didn't fit. Or maybe because he never saw all the ways they didn't fit.

"We don't work together, Steve. We haven't for a long time."

"That's crazy, Penny. You're talking crazy."

Penny closed her eyes and held up her hand, "Steve. Please. Can you stop calling me crazy or insane every time I say something you disagree with? It's such a dismissive asshole thing to do-"

"Then tell me why!" he exploded.

Penny felt something inside her snap, "*Why?* Because you bought me a voucher for bikini waxes for my last birthday and I freaking *hate* bikini waxes. Because you ask me about what I'm eating like I'm doing something shameful. Because every time I cook, I have to make sure it's something *you* want to eat, but you never ask me what *I* would like to eat when it's your turn to cook. You cut your toenails at the kitchen table. You *never* listen when I speak and-"

"You don't hate bikini waxes," Steve interjected. "You always get them."

"I always get them because you like them! I've told you multiple times that I hate them. Why would anyone like having hot wax poured on their genitals, Steve? Why?"

"You've gone mad," he said in bewilderment.

Mad? She felt her eye twitch.

"Stop calling me crazy!"

"Then stop acting crazy! You can't just leave someone because they buy you a bikini wax!" Steve shouted.

Penny thought briefly of Linda who she imagined had a glass pressed to the wall right now so she could hear everything that was going on with the crazy woman and her lovely fiancé next door.

She lowered her voice, "It's not the wax, it's everything. It's like you are trying to shape me into the person you want me to be instead of loving the person I am. It's not just you, it's me, and how I have always just let those things happen instead of telling you that I don't like them or that I disagree."

They stared at each other for a moment, watching and waiting to see what the other would do.

"I don't know who you are anymore," he said finally, and leaving his bag half unpacked, he left the room.

A jingling of keys.

A front door slamming.

"I'm Penny," she said aloud, then lay down on the bed and cried. She cried for her mother, for her grandfather, for Lloyd, and Alice, and Marg, and for herself, and the desperate guilt she felt because the moment the door had shut, she had been filled with relief.

It was done.

She was free.

CHAPTER 20

Mae had been practically everywhere. She had visited the boss at the pharmacy where Charmaine used to work, which was insightful, but nothing glaring came up. She went to the library and touched the old librarian there. Mae could now recite the entire works of Shakespeare, but aside from knowing that Charmaine had come religiously, checking out books on everything from flowers to poetry, she had no real leads to go on. She had deliberately bumped into Charmaine's psychologist outside of his office, spilling his coffee on his jacket and managed to touch him while she apologised and handed him tissues from her handbag to wipe down his shirt front. Nothing. Well, a lot, actually. But nothing useful. Mae had taken to hanging out outside the pharmacy and brushing into customers entering, in case some of them had been customers of Charmaine's. Sometimes it was the people you least expected that yielded the most information.

. . .

One thing everyone had noticed was that in the weeks leading up to her disappearance, Charmaine had been acting strangely. Skittish, was the word in the pharmacist's head. She appeared jumpy, dark circles formed under her eyes. Privately, he had wondered if she were ill. The librarian had noticed her checking around her repeatedly as she walked the shelves. Several customers had felt slighted by her distraction. One of them had a terrible crush on her and would come in to buy cough drops every week, just to be close to her. She had crawled piece by piece through his memories to make sure there was nothing more sinister than a crush, but he was clean. In many ways, Mae felt like by now, she knew Charmaine herself, she could hear her voice, she knew the smell of her perfume. Her face was always slightly different, depending on whose mind she was in. That was the way of it. No two people ever had the same version of a person in their head. We all see what we want to see. It was why someone would always find their lover to be the most beautiful creature on earth. In their mind - they were.

Some way or another, she had to get in and see inside that woman that had lived across the road. She was the last person left. She found herself walking Drayton Street again, walking up the path to the woman's house. From the memories of the other people on her street, they had never seen her outside, Mae surveyed the overgrown yard and wondered how often - if ever - she came out here. The cat was lying under the lemon tree, lounging in a patch of sun. Mae walked up and knocked on the screen door. She had no real plan of precisely what she was going to do or say until the door opened.

"I told you before, I'm not selling," the woman said as soon as she saw Mae.

"I'm not here for that," Mae said. After years of lying and manipulating people into letting her see inside them, she decided to play it straight. "I'm not a real estate agent. I'm looking for someone, and I think you might be able to help me."

The woman narrowed her eyes but didn't shut the door. *That was progress at least*, Mae thought.

"The woman's name is Charmaine Green, she used to live across the road years ago. Real slim, blonde hair, blue eyes. She disappeared thirteen years ago, and I'm just trying to speak to anyone who might remember her from back then and see if they know anything."

"I remember her," the woman said. "But I never spoke to her. I don't know her."

"Maybe you might have seen something?" Mae prompted. "It could be anything at all. If I could just come in for a few moments and talk to you..."

That had been the wrong thing to say. As soon as the words were out of Mae's mouth, the woman began shutting the door again.

"No. I don't know anything. I didn't see anything."

"Please-"

The door shut in her face.

She was lying. Mae didn't need to touch her to know that much. It might be nothing at all, or it might be the very thing Mae needed to have some idea of where Charmaine had gone when she left the unit, there was no way to tell unless the woman told her herself or she could touch her.

She knocked again and waited a few minutes.

Finally, she called out, "Hey, the number on that card? It is a real number. Call me if you think of anything, okay?"

There was no answer, but the curtain twitched again, and Mae knew she had heard her. She walked back the path to the street and on to the station.

Penny didn't know how to call her father's other family and arrange a time to come and meet them. What would she even say? "Hi, I'm Penny, Lloyd's other daughter?"

In the end, she settled for just showing up unannounced. Marg answered the door. Penny stared at her for a moment, feeling rude but unable to stop. She didn't know what she had been expecting, maybe someone like her mother - Marg had blond hair, but that was where the resemblance stopped. Charmaine had looked almost ethereal, her hair unbleached and long, it looked straight, but the underside was full of body and curl - no one would have noticed unless they had spent time brushing her hair. She had a sudden memory of braiding her mother's hair, that was so real that for just a moment she felt that she could still feel the weight of that braid in her hand. Marg's hair was smooth and short, framing her face, with a slight tinge of strawberry blonde. Her eyes were blue too, but the colour of denim. Her skin was freckled. She looked... normal. Ordinary. Penny could have walked past her in the shops and never even noticed her, and she wondered abruptly if she ever had.

Marg's face registered surprise for a moment, but then she quickly composed herself.

"Penny," Marg said.

Penny's heart thumped, but of course, Marg would know who she was, Lloyd had told her. Penny opened her mouth but couldn't think of any words. A small breath escaped her lips and Marg seeming to sense her discomfort simply opened the door and gestured for Penny to come inside. She led Penny down the hallway and past a formal lounge room into the kitchen of the house.

Penny was oddly conscious of how she was looking around the house as though she were at an open house inspecting it. The walls were filled with dozens of photos, and from each frame, peered faces from a life that Penny had known nothing about. Penny caught sight of Lloyd in one of the images and faltered for a second. He had told her, and Penny had come to the house, but until that moment, it had still seemed vaguely impossible. There he was, her father, with his dark smiling eyes, an elfin-like toddler on his lap. She turned away and walked on.

The kitchen was bright and airy with a large farmhouse style table in the centre of it. Marg gestured for her to sit and Penny pulled out one of the chairs and perched primly on the edge. Her leg jittered up and down nervously, and she pressed her hand down on it to still it. Marg made cups of tea and put one in front of Penny, pushing a sugar jar and bottle of milk towards her before taking a seat across the table. Penny's stomach was in knots, and she was certain she wouldn't be able to drink it, but she carefully put spoons of sugar into the tea for something to do, pouring in milk with a shaking hand. She didn't sip at it but placed her hand around the warmth of the cup for strength.

Finally, Penny spoke, "I'm sorry I didn't call first - I just didn't know what to say."

Marg nodded and sipped at her tea, "I'm glad you came. Lloyd told me that he was going to tell you about Alice. I'm sure you have a thousand questions, and I'd be happy to answer anything that you want to know about us or... what happened."

"I wouldn't even know where to begin," Penny said.

"I want you to know that I always thought you should have been told, but you weren't my daughter, and it wasn't my decision. Lloyd was doing what he thought was best for you."

Penny wanted to snap at that, the casual way Marg spoke about him, as though she knew him better than Penny herself, although perhaps she did. There were sides to her father she knew nothing about. Every memory she had of him felt tainted now. Why did he get to decide what was best for her? What gave this man, who had lied to her, the right to make these decisions? She wanted to get up and walk out, but as she looked up at Marg, she saw nothing but openness in her face, and a faint trace of desperate hope. Penny was there to give her daughter a chance at survival.

"I think my mother knew," Penny said abruptly. "She wrote me emails. I haven't told... dad. I haven't really told anyone. They came late, years after she wrote them. She spoke about... well, she spoke about a lot of things, but she mentioned an affair in there. I always thought it was just her paranoia. But she was right. I think she knew."

Penny remembered the way they had begun, how Charmaine had been trying to convince herself it was only paranoia, probably not trusting her own instincts. She had been right all along. Something tugged at her, a piece of the puzzle turning around in her head, so close to fitting... if she could just...

Penny was pulled out of her thoughts, realising Marg had been talking to her, "I'm sorry?"

"I said, would you like to meet Alice?"

Penny swallowed hard and nodded.

Marg led Penny up towards the back of the house to the doorway of the bedroom. Her hand rested lightly on the door for a moment, almost reverently, before she turned the handle and pushed it gently open.

"I'll leave you to it," she murmured, disappearing back up the hall.

Penny opened the door and stepped inside.

Alice was small and fine-boned. Her head was swathed in a bandana made of a shiny peach coloured fabric with iridescent threads that caught the light streaming in from outside to the window seat where Alice sat. She had fallen asleep reading a book, which sat open on her lap. Penny peered at it, there were illustrations of birds with descriptions beside it. Looking around the room, she realised the walls were covered with books. Some were neatly lined on shelves, with others stacked on top. On the floor, there were stacks and stacks of them. Any other time, Penny's eyes would have immediately been drawn to the books when entering a room, but this time, she had only seen Alice. Framed photographs of birds covered what space was left - beautiful, professional photography of birds in the wild. Penny walked over to one of ibis's dancing in a wetland, looking ethereally beautiful, like ballerinas.

"Not bad for a bird known as a bin chicken, hey?"

Penny looked over at Alice, startled. She had a soft, shy smile on her face. Her eyes were a deep brown. *Like Lloyd's*, Penny thought. *Like mine.*

"It's not their fault, you know? That they go through bins, I mean. They are beautiful birds, really. They're just surviving in a world we built where their home used to be."

"You like birds, hey?" Penny asked a smile curling on her lips.

Alice shrugged, "I like how free they are. Delicate, but resilient. And clever, most of them."

Alice stood up and extended her hand, "You're obviously Penny. I'm Alice."

Penny took her hand and shook it awkwardly.

"I'm sorry. I don't really know what to say. I didn't... Lloyd never..." she trailed off, unsure where to begin, anger still simmering inside her for her father and the man she thought he was.

"He didn't tell you. I know. I know you didn't know."

"But you knew?" It was a statement rather than a question, but she still felt compelled to ask.

One side of Alice's mouth turned up in embarrassment, "Yes. I'm sorry."

What did it mean that one family knew, and the other was in the dark? Did he really think he was protecting them?

Or was it that he could only be honest with the ones he loved best? She hated that she felt jealousy for this girl who was dying. *Would* die, according to Henry. It made her feel petty and small.

She and Alice made small talk about the books on the shelves for a while, Penny awkward and uncomfortable at first, Alice warm and chatty. *We are nothing alike*, Penny thought. Alice was instantly charming, coaxing details of who Penny was out of her until she began to relax.

Marg stuck her head in and asked if they wanted tea.

"We'll take it in the garden, thanks Mum," Alice answered. When she left, Alice turned to Penny and whispered conspiratorially, "It's easier if you give her something to do. She fusses."

She led Penny into a garden that looked like something pulled straight from an early twentieth-century novel. Wild-flowers, fragrant herbs, ivy, hedges, and a large stone bird feeder. The lawns were actually soft underfoot, a feat for the sunburnt country where green turf turned to yellow spikes within a season. *This girl has had a completely different life to me*, Penny realised. While Penny had been eating microwave meals with Lloyd, it was clear Alice had been doted upon by Marg. Occasionally, Alice would pull a face or wave her hand in a mannerism that Penny recognised as her father's, and she would feel as though she had slipped through some strange fracture in reality to another world. Everything had a surreal feeling to it. Marg had arrived with a pot of tea and two cups, a blanket draped over her arm that she coddled

Alice into putting over her lap, despite the fact that Penny could feel trickles of sweat rolling down her back in the heat of the afternoon. As soon as Marg was out of sight, Alice had removed the blanket and given Penny an embarrassed smile as she folded it over the arm of the chair.

Suddenly, Alice had reached out and fingered a lock of Penny's hair, dark and wavy.

"I have hair like this," she said. "Well... before. We have the same eyes."

"We do," Penny agreed.

"I would have liked a sister," Alice said, before abruptly changing the subject.

Alice told Penny that she had been sick before, as a child. She downplayed it, but the way she averted her eyes, when previously she had been so candid, made Penny think it had been a long and challenging illness.

"When?" Penny asked. "How old were you?"

"Six."

Penny did the math in her head. Thirteen years ago. While Penny was dealing with her missing mother, Lloyd had been both trying to find his wife and confronting the fact he might lose his youngest daughter. She wanted to bury her head in her hands and cry at the unfairness of life.

"Oh, Alice," was all she could say.

She reached her hand out and took hold of her sister's. The skin was dry and cool, Penny could feel the bones beneath her skin, light and delicate. They reminded her of the birds on Alice's walls. Alice squeezed her hand gently and together they sat and watched the sun sink behind the trees.

Penny left Alice that night with reluctance. Marg had insisted she stay for dinner and Penny had found herself eager to accept. She watched in fascination as Marg bustled around the kitchen, pulling dishes from the oven, while simultaneously straining pots, in the practised dance of one accustomed to the kitchen. Alice hovered around, pretending to sample things and Marg swatted her away playfully. *So, this is what having a mother is like*, Penny thought and felt as though she were a scientist studying a species she hadn't seen before. Of course, she had seen other families interact, but never one that could have very nearly been her own. They ate at the table, with Marg playing easy listening music on the radio. Alice picked at the food mostly, while Marg looked at her with concern. They followed the meal with coffee and shortbread cookies. Penny thought briefly of Steve and how many calories he would have totalled the meal to be, before pushing him from her mind. Both Marg and Alice came to the door to see her out, waving as she rode down the footpath, the streetlights shining her way.

She liked them. She hadn't meant to, not really. She had meant to go and meet them, this other family that Lloyd had kept a secret for almost two decades. The family she had shared her father with without realising it. She thought she would feel resentful, maybe even dislike them. But they were so normal and nice. *Damn it*, she thought. Her phone vibrated in her pocket, and she stopped riding to read the message. Dean. Her heart skipped a beat, and Penny immediately felt ridiculous, like she was thirteen years old with a crush. *Get a grip, Penny*, she thought but smiled despite herself.

Hey there, I was thinking about our quest for the field and thought of a place that might fit the bill, Dean wrote. *Are you free tomorrow? YES! Because you quit that job you were too good for! Seriously, though, are you free?*

Penny sent a reply saying that she would go and began riding again, playing the evening over in her head. She was more than halfway to the station, and thinking about her conversation with Marg at the kitchen table, when she realised what had been nagging at her. She had been telling Marg about how Charmaine had known about the affair. I think she knew, she had said. When Charmaine had first mentioned her suspicions, she had been chasing her thoughts with doubts about what she had seen or felt. She couldn't trust her own instincts because she had lived so long with her own paranoia - but she had been right. Which meant, if Charmaine had been right about the affair, what else had she been right about? Had there really been someone following her, after all?

I keep thinking about the car with Lloyd in it, and the more I think about it, the more I'm sure it was him. Who was that woman?

CHAPTER 22

The next day found Penny sitting beside Dean in his old beat-up car, while Mae sat in the back, having come along for the ride. Penny felt vaguely put out by Mae's presence and then embarrassed that she would feel like she was disappointed not to have alone time with Dean. And Mae had been doing her a favour and was working on trying to find her mother. As they drove, Mae recounted the places she had been and the people she had read. Penny hadn't discussed that Dean had told her about Mae's strange ability, but as they were getting in the car her hand had brushed Mae's and she had looked up sharply at her and then found Dean's face. A shadow had passed across it and disappeared just as quickly. Penny wondered what she had seen, but thereafter she didn't try to hide how she was receiving her information from Penny.

"I'd really like to talk to that shut-in that lived across the road from her, but she just will not open the door. I swear she knows. Maybe she's psychic. Do you ever wonder that? How many people are walking around with random gifts or curses and we just have no idea? Like, this one time, I was having my hair cut and thinking what a jerk..."

Mae chatted on, and Dean cut eyes at Penny and winked.

"She never shuts up."

Mae snorted, "Why don't *you* shut up? It's even gluten-free. Add *that* to your diet."

An hour later, they arrived in Drummott, a small town that people mostly passed through on the way to somewhere else. They drove through the centre of town and turned on to a road that led to a boarded-up hospital.

Dean pointed out the window, "There is a field behind it and an abandoned building back there"

"How did you find this place?" Penny asked.

He shot her an embarrassed look, "Well, when we were teens we would go up here and muck around for a laugh. Not into this building, but the main hospital. I ran into a friend yesterday, and we were talking about it, and it reminded me. I thought it was worth checking out."

They drove further up the road and pulled up at the edge of a field, parked the vehicle and got out.

It sat well back from the old hospital - a smaller building, two stories in size, squat and alone in the field. Nearby, a single tree rose up, it's bare branches stretching towards the sky.

"We have been driving around and looking for an empty field with a single tree in it. But I thought it doesn't have to be a house, it could be any kind of building that someone could shelter in."

Penny gazed across the field towards the building. Multiple windows had been broken, either by vandals or by storms flinging branches off of the tree. It looked desolate. No one could live in there.

Penny, Mae and Dean got out of the car and walked towards the building, the mood sobering. The front of the building looked solidly locked up with a fat chain and padlock wrapped around the door handles.

"Let's try the back," Mae suggested.

A path of rough concrete ran beside the building, and Penny trod carefully, her feet crunching on the broken glass from the upper windows that littered the ground. As she turned the corner, she bumped hard into someone, who let out a yelp, startling Penny. Penny shrieked and jumped back, smashing up against Dean's chest, who made a winded sound and began coughing.

"Sorry!" Penny said. Dean waved his hand that he was okay and Mae hid a smile. Penny peered cautiously back around the corner and came face to face with a woman who was doing the same thing.

Rosie Parker stepped out, "Penny! God, you nearly gave me a heart attack!"

Penny stared at her, agog, "You nearly gave *me* a heart attack! What are you doing here?"

Rosie's expression went blank, her cheeks reddening, "Uhh. Nothing. Why? What are you doing here?"

It was Penny's turn to blush, "Also nothing. We were just... you know... doing nothing."

Rosie eyed her sceptically.

"Right. Who are your friends?" She glanced behind Penny. "Dean?"

"Rosie? What are you doing here?"

"What are *you* doing here? You rotten little shit! Call your mother! She's been trying to call you all week."

Dean blushed a rich scarlet, "I've been working."

Rosie gave him a look of profound scorn, "Oh yes, obviously. This looks *exactly* like working."

Penny looked from one to the other like a tennis match.

"Awesome," Mae broke in. "So, you all seem to know each other. We'll just be on our way then since you're done here."

Rosie looked at Mae and did a double-take, her mouth dropping open slightly.

Mae rolled her eyes, "Yeah, I know. I look like someone you've met before."

Rosie stepped forward, "No. you look like no one I've ever met before." She reached her hand out as though to touch Mae, who stepped back abruptly. Rosie withdrew her hand, shaking her head.

They stood there awkwardly for a few moments.

Finally, Penny spoke, "So... *are* you done here?"

"What?" Rosie asked.

"You know," Penny said. "Are you done doing your... nothing."

"Oh! Umm. Yes. I'm done. I'm leaving actually."

Mae squinted her eyes at Rosie for a moment and reached out abruptly and grabbed her by the wrist. Rosie gasped and wrenched her hand away, her eyes wide.

"What *are* you?" Rosie blurted out.

"A Scorpio," Mae answered. "Damn, girl. You have been through some shit. Seriously."

Rosie rubbed her wrist where Mae had touched her as though it had been scorched.

Mae turned to Penny, "You should tell her why we are here."

Penny stared at Mae incredulously.

Mae raised her eyebrows, "You should. She might be able to help."

"But... Rosie may not understand about our... nothing," Penny said cryptically.

Mae snorted, "Trust me. That girl has her own nothing going on. Tell her."

Penny finished telling Rosie the story, her face flushed with embarrassment. She looked up at Rosie to see if she thought they were all bonkers.

"Wow," Rosie said.

"You think your mum might have been here?"

"We don't know. We wondered if she might have been."

"I think she was."

"Why?"

Rosie sighed, "I'm going to be honest here because you have been with me. I was here to see a ghost. To move it on, actually."

Penny could not have been more shocked. She had expected Rosie to call her crazy and leave. Instead, she was talking about ghosts like it was the most natural thing in the world. She looked over to Mae, who shrugged and raised an eyebrow. Dean looked unsurprised, and Penny got the impression that he had heard this story before. She desperately wanted to know what was going on between Rosie and

Dean, but it didn't seem the right time to ask. Rosie had explained to them that she had a sixth sense, the ability to see spirits that hadn't moved on yet. There was one here, she said, that appeared to be tethered. She had heard about it from a friend whose teenager had been doing a midnight walk through the building with some friends and been scared witless by bangs and thrown objects.

"And naturally you decided to go *towards* the danger?" Dean asked. "You're such an asshole."

Rosie flipped Dean the bird, "Well, I can't leave it here. It's not it's fault it's tethered."

"I would totally leave it here," Mae put in.

"Anyway, the spirit, it was talking in riddles, which they do-"

"We have some experience with that," Dean said.

"And it mentioned a woman. One that came here and was sad. Now, again, this could be all confused. They don't always make sense. But it felt real when he told me."

"He saw someone?" Penny asked.

Rosie nodded, "But that's not all. He saw someone else. He said that a man came and took her away."

Mae let out a snort of air and Penny felt her stomach roll. Dean reached for her and took her hand, giving it a reassuring squeeze.

"Can we go in and ask him again? Maybe he could tell us some more to see if it really was my mum?"

Rosie shook her head sadly, "I'm sorry, Penny. I already moved him on. He's gone."

They creaked open the door Rosie had indicated to them

and stepped inside. The hall was unevenly lit, in some places the doors to the rooms stood open, and light streamed in from the windows, interspersed with puddles of darkness where the doors were shut. The hallway was littered with leaves and dust. Old hospital beds lay collapsed against the sides, as they walked past one room, Penny peered in to see it full of wheelchairs.

"Holy shit," Mae breathed. "I gotta say, I am not a fan of this. What the hell is it?"

"It was the old hospital," Rosie said. "The original one before they built the big building out there. I guess after that it was used for storage."

"It looks haunted," Penny commented.

Rosie shrugged, "It was."

"Right," Penny said, shuddering. She reached for Dean's hand and found it, warm and dry and comforting.

Mae, Penny and Dean tiptoed down the hall, past walls with holes in them and what appeared to be the remains of a long burnt-out fire. Rosie, by comparison, walked unbothered, confidently striding ahead, leading them to a set of internal stairs and up to the second floor where she said she had met the spirit. If possible, the second floor was in worse shape than the first. Penny was unable to see the old linoleum through the debris that covered it. Dirt and bits of broken plaster littered the floor. Old wiring hung from the ceiling. It looked like someone had been tearing this place apart, piece by piece.

"It was the Other," Rosie said, seeing their faces. "He had been here a long time. It... does something to them, when they are stuck like that."

A spirit had done this, Penny thought. She was shocked at the amount of damage.

"A sledgehammer couldn't have been much worse," Dean remarked.

Rosie shrugged, "Anyway, I found him up there in the last room. I don't know exactly where he saw the woman he was talking about though. But he was tethered to this floor. So, it had to be up here. I honestly cannot imagine why anyone would stay here with a tethered spirit. It would have been terrifying. Even shielded, as she would have been, there would have been noises and movements that would have frightened her."

"Unless someone outside frightened her more," Mae said quietly.

Penny's breath hitched in her throat.

"Stop it!" Dean said, wheeling on Mae. "The ghost said that a man took her away. That could mean anything. It could have been a friend picking her up. Just because you see monsters doesn't mean everyone is one."

He looked over at Penny and took her by the shoulders, "It doesn't mean anything, Penny. It doesn't."

She nodded and swallowed. Mae looked at her feet with a petulant expression.

"He's right," Rosie offered. "It could mean anything."

They continued on, reaching the room Rosie had pointed out and Dean began sifting through what was left of the walls that had come to rest on the ground. Leaving him to it, Rosie, Mae and Penny took a room each close by.

"You're totally sure there are no other ghosts in here that are going to kill me?" Mae asked dubiously.

"I am," Rosie said.

Penny stepped into a room with faded green walls. The windows were made with wire in the glass, she saw. All of them unbroken, but one had been stuck open slightly, and a cool breeze from the outside tickled her face. Her skin felt dust-covered and grimy, and she lifted her hair off the back of her neck and fanned herself. The walls here too had been somewhat destroyed, though not as bad as some of the other rooms. In the corner stood a small sink, with a surprisingly clean mirror above it. She went to it and looked into it. Her reflection stared back, her dark eyes bottomless and unreadable. Mae was singing loudly in the other room, an old Australian folk song, startlingly off-key.

"Mae, will you please stop?" Dean called.

"I'm scaring off the ghosts," Mae called back.

"You're scaring off me."

Penny turned around and began picking up broken pieces of plaster, checking under them for any sign that her mother may have been there. She didn't know what she was looking for. There was a bed collapsed on the floor in one of the corners, and she was tugging it towards her, hoping to leverage it up, when there was a cry from one of the other rooms. Penny dropped the bed and ran back to the hall, bumping hard into Mae as she did.

"What was it?" Dean said, breathlessly, coming up beside them.

"In here!" Rosie called.

They followed the sound of her voice to a room halfway down the hall, Rosie sitting in the middle, clutching a worn fabric satchel. Her eyes met Penny's.

Penny came to her like a sleepwalker, her feet carrying her along, though her mind was refusing to work. She knelt on the ground beside Rosie and held out her hands to take the frame Rosie had pulled from inside.

It was the photo of her and Charmaine, taken when she was twelve. Penny's head rested on Charmaine's shoulder as she leaned into her. Her mother was staring back at her with those clear blue eyes. She looked up at Rosie, Henry's words in her head.

A house in a field with one tree. And you. And she. He had looked at Rosie. *And you.*

It wasn't quite a house, and it wasn't quite her mother. But he had been right.

Penny opened the satchel and pulled out a sweater that was dirty and looked like it had been chewed by mice. There were little bits and pieces inside, parts of her mother that broke her heart. A toothbrush. A pen with a chewed lid. A library card. A prescription bottle that's label had long since faded to white, pills still rattling inside of it.

"If she had these then she was still taking her medication," Penny said. "Or, at least, she intended to."

Penny stood up and began moving more items on the floor.

"There is nothing else, Penny. I already looked over there," Rosie said.

"They're not here," Penny said, picking up an overturned wheelchair and pushing it to one side.

"What?" Mae asked.

"The journals," Penny said, wiping her hands on her jeans.

"Journals?" Rosie asked, confused.

"My mother wrote - prolifically - in journals. There were eight of them, I remember because I used to count them," she lifted a piece of plaster that fell apart into smaller pieces inside her hands.

"They'll be covered in fabric," Dean put in and began helping Penny throw the pieces of plaster into a corner.

"Wait," Rosie said.

"Oh god," Mae whispered.

"What?" Dean asked.

"She knows - we know - where they are," Mae said.

They went back to the room the spirit had been in, and Mae pushed aside the bed that was up against the wall. Only it wasn't a wall. There was a small door cut into the side of it.

"I'm sorry," Rosie said. "I didn't know. I thought they were his. He said he kept them here. I guess... he moved them. Keeping them safe, in his own way."

Dean pried the door open and inside lay a neat stack of books. The fabric was covered in a fine dust. On top lay a straight-edged razor, the edge brown with what was unmistakably old blood. Penny felt her knees go weak, and she stumbled back a bit.

"Oh, no!" Rosie said, catching her by the arm. "No, honey. That's not - that isn't your mum. No. That was his. It was the item he was tethered to. It was odd, really. He could obviously move and touch things, he could have carried his own tethered item out of here, but he never left."

Rosie smoothed Penny's hair in a comforting, motherly gesture that for some reason, left Penny wanting to cry. She took a deep breath and nodded.

Dean reached out and plucked the razor off the top with the tips of his fingers, grimacing as he did so, before dropping it back on the floor of the closet. He pulled the books out and handed them to Penny. They had been gnawed on some of the corners, by mice or moths, but were in far better shape than the other items they had found. Someone had cared for them - for whatever reason. She stroked the cover of the top one, the one made from the tablecloth that Lloyd had scorched. She flipped open the page to her mother's familiar scrawl. They smelled musty and of dust, and yet, she thought she could almost smell her mother's lavender perfume rising from the pages. Her eyes welled with tears. She sat on the floor amongst the debris, placing the journals one by one in front of her as Mae, Dean and Rosie looked on, their eyes full of sympathy. Mae coughed awkwardly. Here they were, her mother's memories, all the things she didn't want to forget. Her own snippets. Suddenly, Penny sat up straighter.

"One is missing," she said.

Dean squatted beside her, touching each one as though he were counting.

"Seven," he said.

"Maybe it's somewhere else in here," Mae said, reluctantly.

"No, these meant something to the Other," Rosie said. "If he took them, he would have taken them all."

"It's a ghost. Hardly a rational person," Mae retorted.

They searched the entire second floor, and then the first floor for good measure. But even as they looked, Penny knew they wouldn't find it. It was gone.

CHAPTER 23

Penny sat back in Dean's armchair. The items they had collected sat in a box across the room. There had been a slight disagreement between them about what to do when they found them. Rosie had wanted to call the police, but Mae had baulked at the suggestion immediately. Whatever she was up to, it was nothing she wanted the police to know about. Penny was inclined to agree with her. The case was cold. As far as the police were concerned, Charmaine had just walked away from her family. Finding the items didn't disprove that, it showed she was there at some point. Dean pointed out that there could be clues that they couldn't see, fingerprints or DNA, but Mae had scoffed at that.

"Kids have probably been coming through here, pretending it was haunted-"

"It *was* haunted," Rosie interjected.

"Whatever," Mae replied. "The point is, dozens of people could have been through here in the last decade. They're not finding jackshit."

In the end, they had decided to take the things with

them. And now, the box sat in the corner, radiating a weird energy and making Penny feel uncomfortable.

"Can we move the box... outside or something," she called out to Dean.

He peered around the corner from the pantry, "Outside?"

"Just not in here. It's staring at me."

He gave her a sceptical look, but obligingly grabbed the box and put it in a storage closet off the kitchen.

"Better?" he asked.

"Much."

Dean went back to the pantry and retrieved a large wok, before pulling a colourful assortment of vegetables from the fridge, which he began chopping up.

"I thought I would make a stir fry," he said, over the sound of onions frying in a pan. Soon the smell of garlic reached Penny and her stomach rumbled.

"Let me help," she offered.

"No need," Dean replied, "This dish takes hardly any time at all. I guess you could do the ramen?"

Penny smiled, "Actual carbs? That sounds delicious."

They worked together for a few moments and within twenty minutes were sitting up on the roof in old reclining garden chairs, watching the city lights wink on. Penny speared a piece of zucchini and bit in dubiously, but it was delicious.

"Hey," Penny asked. "What's the deal with you and Rosie?"

Dean laughed, "Rosie? Oh, man. She's horrible. The worst. You know she stuffed me in a closet, and wouldn't let me out for twenty minutes once?"

"Excuse me?"

"Well... she was eleven. And I had just cut her hair, this huge chunk right near the top. I didn't mean to, I was just pretending and she moved and the next thing I knew I was standing there with a hunk of red hair in my hand and two very angry tweens yelling at me. They bundled me into the closet and wouldn't let me out until I said I was sorry, which I was not going to do except I really had to pee."

"So, you knew each other as kids?"

"She's my sister's best friend, which by extension makes her my sister of sorts. I do like her. I just give her crap because I think it makes her feel like part of the family."

"I thought maybe you used to date or something," Penny said.

"That's disgusting!" Dean exclaimed.

Penny found herself feeling somewhat relieved. Rosie Parker was gorgeous, she could all too easily imagine Dean and her finding each other attractive.

"You knew about her gift thing, though?" Penny asked.

"Yeah, I knew. It's a long story and not really mine to tell. If you ask Rosie though, she would tell you."

They ate companionably for a few moments before Penny put down her fork.

"I broke up with Steve," Penny said.

Dean looked up from his bowl in surprise, "When?"

"The other day. The day he got back from his trip. He's been staying with his parents."

Dean took another mouthful of his food and chewed it slowly, before asking if she was okay.

"You know what?" she answered after thinking on it for a moment. "I am. I know I probably shouldn't be, we had been together a long time. But, it was like I had spent so long clinging to everything that I had because it was all I had, I never stopped to wonder if it was even something I wanted. Yes. I am okay. I feel guilty and like a shitty person, but I'm okay."

"You're not a shitty person, Penny. You're the least shittiest. You would absolutely fail at being a shitty person."

Penny smiled, "Well, thank you."

They finished their meal and lay side by side for a while, talking about the day. Dean looked over at her thoughtfully.

"Penny? Can I ask you something?"

Penny's heart sped up, "Yes."

Dean reached out and took her hand, "Do you like strawberry ice cream?"

The ice cream store was a small boutique one, not far from where Dean lived, and they were able to walk there, arriving just before closing. Dean ordered two strawberry ice creams in waffle cones, and they sat outside on the edge of a garden bed.

"There are dark chocolate chips in it, which I think really makes it," Dean said.

"Very decadent," Penny said. It was actually delicious, and she was sorely tempted to ask if they sold it by the tub.

They walked back to the apartment, Dean collecting sprigs of rosemary from one of the public garden beds along the way.

"What are you doing?" Penny hissed.

"Borrowing. I'm going to put them in water so they'll root and I can stop having to run down here every time I need rosemary."

"You're stealing it!"

"No! Well, yes. I suppose I am. But I kind of thought it would be nice. I could grow this little rosemary plant, and every time I water it, I would remember that I grew it starting from this night. Like a little plant memory." He gave her a grin that Penny supposed was intended to be charming and much to her dismay, it was.

She shot him a look in return, one side of her mouth curling up at the corner.

"What?"

"Well, now you've made it sound sweet and romantic and I kind of want one."

Dean grinned, "Go on then. I'll be your lookout."

"I couldn't!"

Dean rolled his eyes and jogged back to the plant plucking a small stem off of it, and presenting it to her with a little bow, "Your thieved goods, m'lady."

Penny laughed and playfully pushed him on the shoulder, but tucked the rosemary into her shirt pocket, where the deep earthy scent of it rose to greet her.

They watched television and made fun of the stars of a reality tv show before Dean offered to drive her home, but Penny insisted on helping him with the dishes first. Dean ran the sink, and they worked in tandem, him washing while she dried. Every now and then her arm would bump his as she took a dish, the warmth of him seeming to radiate towards her. She watched his hands as he moved a dish from the bench to the sink, it was a small domestic task, but suddenly she wanted very much to touch his hand. To have it touch her. As she took the dish from him and placed it on the rack, she turned to him. Dean glanced over at her and then looked at her again, longer this time, tilting his head at her, enquiringly.

His eyes drew her in, one green like summer grass, the other a stormy blue. He hadn't shaved today and stubble darkened his cheeks. She reached out to run her fingertips over it. Dean stood still, allowing her to trace his jawline. There was something earthy and real about him, an honesty that was unlike anyone she had ever known. He closed his eyes. Moving closer, Penny stood on tiptoe and leaned forward, brushing her lips gently against his. His hands ran the length of her sides, still wet from the washing up, sliding over her hips. He hooked his fingers into the loops of her jeans and pulled her towards him. They kissed, slowly at first, then more urgently, her tongue sliding along his, tasting like strawberry ice cream and dark chocolate. Dean lifted her on to the bench, and she wrapped her legs around him, holding him to her. Every part of her felt electrified, pulsing at his touch.

"We could take this to the loft?" he asked.

Penny pulled back, "I... I've never done this before."

Dean looked momentarily stricken, "Uhh. Sex?"

"No! No. I've obviously had sex. But just... only with... only..."

"With Steve," Dean finished.

"Yes."

"Do you want to have sex with me?"

The bluntness took Penny aback, but when she looked into his eyes, she saw only the same warmth and concern there that she had seen the first time he had touched her in the bar.

"Yes," she answered finally. "I do."
He smiled.

They moved to the loft, shedding clothes as they went, tumbling into the white sheets. It was as though someone had given him a book on all the secret parts of herself. His clever musician's hands, travelling the length of her skin, unlocking all the hidden places she had been waiting for someone to find. She felt as though she were being explored, carefully and tenderly. As though she were dissolving beneath his touch, vibrating like a string on his guitar. She would stay here forever... but she was rushing towards a cliff, tumbling over the edge, flying. Words were inadequate, she would never be able to describe this. She called out his name - and his body answered hers.

CHAPTER 24

Sunlight crept through the open window, she woke to feel the heat rising towards the loft where she lay. Beside her, Dean lay tangled in the sheets. She rolled over and fit her body into his arms, her bare skin against his chest. Since the first time she met Henry, she had felt as though her life had been spinning out of control. Like she had slowly been peeling back layers of herself until she felt as though she had been reduced to her foundations. Lying here, just now she finally felt as though things might be coming together.

Extracting herself carefully from his arms, she slid out of bed and threw on her t-shirt and a pair of Dean's boxers that had been sitting on a chair in a pile of folded clothes he had yet to put away. Padding down the stairs, she flipped the switch on the kettle and cringed as the sound of it boiling filled the apartment. They had left the windows slightly cracked open last night, and a pigeon landed on the sill, strutting across it, clearly waiting for something.

"I feed him every morning," Dean called out.

Penny looked up to see him standing by the stairs, his hair tousled from sleep.

"Did I wake you?" she asked, glancing mournfully at the kettle.

"Definitely," he caught sight of her face and laughed. "No. I was already awake when you got up. I just didn't want to move while you were in my arms."

Penny felt a rush of heat on her cheeks, "Oh."

Dean came down the stairs and went to the pantry where he extracted a handful of seed and poured it on the sill for the pigeon who began to peck at it, allowing Dean to scratch him on the top of the head with one finger.

"You're like a fairy tale princess," Penny observed.

"Excuse me?"

"With the wild birds flitting to your window in the morning."

Dean turned to her, "Well, he isn't *wild*. He's just his own man. And his name is Fat Pigeon - not to be confused with Skinny Pigeon who comes later to eat whatever Fat Pigeon has left behind."

"You're quite strange."

He shrugged and came into the kitchen to begin making coffee.

Penny had already pulled two cups from the cupboard and was surveying the bench for which of the unlabelled jars might hold the caffeine.

"It's this one," he said. "See? It's brown for coffee. The

sugar is in the white one. The green contains peppermint leaves because my sister is always trying to make me drink herbal teas, which I accept and then mix into the potting mix when I am repotting my plants. I have to keep some here though in case she shows up."

His hand brushed gently across her waist as he reached for the coffee, and Penny closed her eyes. Intimacy. That's what this was. It was something she and Steve had lost - or never had. They had been together, but separate. It was what she saw in couples as she had watched them through the window at work. There was something beautiful about the mundane day to day of good relationships. The sleep soaked scent of a lover. The coffee cooling on the bench, tendrils of steam rising from it. A hand on the waist. A kiss on the forehead. Small intimacies took for granted and forgotten. The lack of words as the salt is slid across the table. The cheeky butt-grab as they walk past. A meal set aside for the one who worked the longer day. The skin. The touches. The delight in knowing someone's body as intimately as their own. It was supernatural, ethereal and the strongest magic humans had. A soul dancing delight.

"What are you thinking about?" Dean asked her, spooning coffee into a cup.

Penny picked up the kettle and poured water into the mugs, the rich aroma swirling up. She looked up into his eyes.

"Magic," she answered.

They spent the morning in companionable quiet, sharing a breakfast of fruit and defrosted muffins Dean had pulled from his freezer and warmed in the oven.

"My sister is a baker," he explained.

"The same one who tries to make you drink herbal teas? Or a different one?"

"The same one."

"Well, these are delicious. You should drink the teas. Keep the woman happy, so she will keep providing you with baked goods."

When they had finished, Penny went to have a shower, while Dean began watering his plants in the bathroom. The water felt soothing on her skin, and she tilted her head back to the spray, closing her eyes and letting herself be cocooned by the warmth.

"So," Dean began, "what do you think the next step is? With your Mum, I mean."

Penny shook the water out of her ears and reached for his shampoo. The thing was, as much as Dean and Rosie had tried to reassure her yesterday that the man that had been seen with Charmaine might have been a friend, she knew that wasn't true. Afterwards, as they were leaving, she had glanced over at Mae. As they locked eyes, it was almost as though they had a private moment of understanding - Mae was probably the only person in the world aside from Lloyd, Teddy, and Penny herself who truly knew Charmaine. Mae knew what Penny herself knew. Charmaine would never have left those journals behind. She would never have taken just one. She would never have left behind the photo of Penny and her. When she left the unit, she hadn't taken her jewellery, her photo albums, or even the tiny portrait of her own mother who had died before Charmaine had really ever had a chance to get to know her. Instead, she had taken just those things she couldn't leave behind, an image of her daughter, and her memories, ink on paper - all the things she said she didn't want to forget. If a friend had picked her up, she would have taken those with her. No. Charmaine had not left willingly. She knew it. And so had Mae.

Penny conditioned her hair slowly. She thought Dean would repeat his question, but he allowed it to hang in the air, patiently waiting while she sorted out her thoughts.

Finally, she spoke, "I think we lost too much time."

"What do you mean?"

"Well, when she went missing, we all thought she had gone off her meds. Or she had needed a break - which, you know, she sometimes did. Mum was, well, I always thought she would have gone pretty good in Byron with a woman called Moonbeam herself. We didn't look at it from the perspective of her not leaving willingly, or that someone could have made her disappear. I had been thinking about that since I met Alice. She wrote about that - Lloyd's affair. She knew. He thought she didn't and that he was protecting her, but somewhere deep down, she knew. I was thinking, what if she was right about all of it? No one would have listened to her. Even I didn't listen to her when I got the emails years later. Hell, *she* barely listened to herself. But if she *was* right..."

"It means that someone was stalking her before she left," Dean finished.

"Exactly," Penny turned off the water and groped blindly through the shower curtain for a towel, which Dean placed into her hand.

She dried herself off and stepped out, Dean holding a robe out for her, which she shrugged into.

"I just keep thinking, if we had looked for her properly from the beginning and treated it like an actual missing person case, we might have had a chance. It's a big ask to have people remember anything from so long ago."

"Not if you're Mae," Dean said. "Memories are never really lost. It's just the filing system is messed up sometimes, and things get put in the basement. Mae can do it, Penny. She can find those memories that people don't even know they have."

Penny sighed, "Mae is... well. I just don't know if it's fair to ask her to keep pushing with this. I don't even know if it's fair to me. I thought when Henry said I would find her that she would be making pottery in the country somewhere. I would show up, and she would apologise, and I could be allowed to be angry for her leaving me. Instead, I found a haunted hospital building and all I had left was a photo and some journals - and more questions than I had in the beginning. I might never get answers to those."

They went out to the kitchen, where Dean began making another coffee and Penny went to stand by the window. Down the alley she could see people bustling to and fro on the footpath, going about their business. She used to look for her mother in crowds like that, imagining herself finding her.

"You could ask Henry again?" Dean suggested, breaking her from her thoughts.

Another pigeon flew on to the sill of the window and

began to scavenge from the remainder of the seed that Fat Pigeon left behind.

"Skinny Pigeon," Penny murmured. She turned to Dean, "No. I think Henry deserves some peace. The first time he... read me or whatever he did, it was an accident. After that? I was treating him like a crystal ball or a deck of tarot cards. Henry deserves some peace. And so do I."

CHAPTER 25

The next several weeks were spent in a blur. Mostly, she spent time with Alice, getting to know the sister she had just discovered she had. Alice dragged out family photo albums, filling Penny in on the years she had missed, showing her birthdays and trips to the beach. In some of the images, Lloyd stood there smiling, and Penny felt like the world was tilting slightly, as though she were seeing an alternate reality. She picked up a photo of Alice on Lloyd's shoulders and stared at it. It felt like she was looking at a stranger. *Where was I*, she wondered. *A friend's sleepover? At Papa's house? How could he have spent years splitting his time between the both of us? How much of what he shared with me had he also done with her?* For her part, Alice appeared both embarrassed by Lloyd's deception and also accepting of it. Having had years to get used to it, Penny supposed.

One day while she was leaving Marg and Alice's house, she saw Lloyd walking up to the door and faltered. For just a second she thought he was coming to see her, until she realised that of course, him coming here was normal for him - for them. He smiled ruefully at her.

"Penny," he began.

She walked past him without stopping.

Alice turned out to be wonderful. She was amazingly confident, well-read and had a cool, dry wit that had Penny bursting out with laughter. Marg was what Penny always imagined a mother would be like. Fussy, loving and somewhat irritating. She lacked Charmaine's wild beauty and artistic hands but made up for it in warmth and stability. And cookies. Plate after plate appeared as though by magic, Alice cutting eyes with Penny.

"She's neurotic," Alice announced.

"It's nice," Penny argued, shrugging.

"Mum has always wanted to meet you. I think she is trying to bestow twenty years of biscuits on you. We will both end up looking like dough ourselves."

Some days Dean would pick her up and drop her at Alice's, visiting friends that lived nearby. She split her time between his apartment and her own unit, slowly boxing up her old life while Steve stayed with his parents - both of them careful to avoid when the other would be home. On days that she stayed at Dean's, they slipped into a strange domesticity, a mixture of new and familiarity. In the mornings, she would wake before him and make coffee, taking hers up on to the roof. She began to wake before the sun, creeping down from the loft and shushing at the kettle as it boiled, trying not to wake Dean - a pointless endeavour since Penny had discovered he slept like the dead. Then she would sit on the roof and watch the sun rise over the city, broad strokes of yellows and pinks. At night, Dean would play the guitar, and she would curl on the couch and write. He had a habit of walking around naked, heedless of the broad, curtainless windows. Penny would watch him while pretending not to, the curve of his buttocks, and strong angles to his thighs. They spent hours lying beside each other, he would trace the lines of her body as though committing them to memory.

One night, as she lay on the cusp of sleep, she murmured, "Awhile back, my dad told me that life was a blank page and I could write whatever I wanted to on it."

Dean stilled for a moment, it was the first time she had mentioned Lloyd since the day she had told him about the affair. He ran a finger down her arm, making her skin rise in goosebumps.

"Mmm? And what are you writing on it?"

She thought for a while before she answered, "Penny. I'm writing Penny."

He pulled her close against him, the heat of his body warming hers.

"Me too," he said.

Dean took her along to arts nights, and she began to make friends with some of the other writers, who held a separate group where they shared and critiqued each other's work. She agreed to come along and swapped Leif his current work-in-progress for some of her more structured snippets.

On a recommendation from him, she applied for a job in a small used bookstore in the city and began working there three days a week. It wasn't a difficult job, her time mostly spent helping customers or shelving books, but it was quiet and peaceful, and allowed her time to think. As she unlocked the doors in the morning, she would breathe in the smell of the old paper on the shelves, row after row of little worlds created by people like her, who sent their work out into the world like messages in a bottle. Each one was a treasure. It began to feel like home.

She went to the facility to see Teddy, stopping by a few times a week, careful to avoid Henry. In his own way, Henry had been right about everything he had said, she had found her mother - or what she had left behind anyway - in a field with a single tree. And her father's daughter was sick - just not the daughter she thought he meant. Penny just wasn't so sure anymore that the future was something anyone was supposed to know ahead of time. Instead, she met her grandfather in the garden or out on the verandah, telling him about what she had been up to. As she chatted on to him about her new job, her sister, and Dean, she realised she was no longer making up stories about her life to fill in the gaps. Now, she was just Penny.

Mae was still working away in the background, calling Dean every now and then with any information she found out. Sometimes, Mae would come over and share dinner with Penny and Dean, and despite herself, Penny began to discover she liked Mae quite a bit. She was refreshingly blunt, which Dean said was a product of no one being able to lie to her. She saw no need to lie to herself. The box they had taken from the hospital in Drummott sat in the closet where Dean had stuck it, and one day, Penny had found Mae sitting on the floor of the closet, holding the photo of Penny and Charmaine. Penny hadn't been able to go through the box herself, not yet.

Mae looked sheepishly up at Penny, "I wish I could get a read off of an item. This would all be so simple then."

"You've done a great job. I appreciate it, Mae. Thank you."

Mae had shrugged it off and placed the photo back in the box, "Yeah, well. People are stupid, they never seem to remember the stuff you want them to. We are all just basically monkeys wearing clothes."

"A touching comparison," Penny smiled. "Actually, I was thinking, maybe it's time we stopped looking."

Mae looked up at her, surprised.

"It's just that, I think I've spent half my life waiting for my mother to come home, you know?" Penny continued. "And I think maybe it's time to stop waiting. If I am meant to find her, I will. But I can't keep living my life looking for her. Steve was right about that."

"Steve was a jerk about that," Mae said knowingly.

"Yeah. Well. He was right, too, though."

"I'll stop if you want me to, Penny. This is your show," Mae looked at the box, running a hand along the frame that sat inside it. "I just feel like there is just this one piece of the puzzle that I'm missing. I really hate not knowing shit."

Something about the way she said it made Penny think she was no longer talking about her mother. She was thinking about Him, the one she was trying to find. Penny went to reach out to touch Mae but stopped herself before she could make contact, her hand hovering awkwardly above her shoulder.

"Mae? You know it's not your responsibility to find him. I don't know exactly what happened but if you want to just go and live your life and be happy, then it's okay for you to do that. You're allowed to be happy."

Mae shook her head, "I can't. Not until he's gone."

Her voice held a note of steel in it that Penny had rarely heard in anyone else. She would find Him, Penny realised, and nothing would stop her. Mae held out her hand to Penny, and Penny looked at it for a moment before reaching out and helping Mae up.

Mae turned to look at her, her fingertips lightly touching Penny's forehead, as though whatever she had just read was visible on her skin, "That's frigging terrifying, Penny. Someone believing in you. It leaves me very little room to fail."

***

"Tell me about yourself," Alice had said one day while they sat in the garden. Alice was wearing a peach shirt that matched the headscarf she had wrapped around her head. She favoured bright colours, Penny had come to realise, deep blues, emerald greens, and pinks in every shade imaginable. Penny had bought her the outfit she had on now.

"There isn't anything to tell," Penny had said.

"Dad said you're engaged."

Dad, Penny thought. She still wasn't quite sure how to reconcile the dad she had with the one Alice would talk about. She let it go, Alice didn't need to deal with Penny's own issues on top of everything else. She stole a glance at Alice, who was sipping a lemonade through a straw. There were deep circles under her eyes. Sometimes, Penny felt obnoxiously healthy beside her, which filled her with a strange guilt.

"I'm not engaged. I mean, I was, but no. I'm not anymore."

"What happened?"

Penny took a deep breath, "I guess I just realised that we had stopped choosing each other. We kept finding reasons to live our own lives separately until we were just two people living in the same house. Or maybe, it was just because we were really young when we started dating."

"I've never dated anyone," Alice said.

"Really?"

She nodded, "I just never found anyone that I clicked with enough to want to be just with that person. It makes me sad sometimes that I have never been in love, and I could die and never have had someone be in love with me."

"You won't die, Alice."

Alice smiled but said nothing.

That afternoon as she left, Penny couldn't stop thinking about what Alice had said, and the careless way she had said it. *I could die and never have had someone be in love with me.* The Friday beforehand she had met with Alice's doctor to undergo testing to see if she was a match, a process that took several days to complete. When she had told Lloyd she would get tested, she had agreed because it was the right thing to do. Someone needed help, and she could help them. Now, having spent the past few weeks getting to know Alice, it was no longer a faceless person. Penny hadn't realised until that afternoon just how badly she needed to be a match. She needed Alice to live. *I love her*, she realised with a suddenness that shocked her. It muted the anger she felt at Lloyd for lying, overlaying it with gratitude that because of him, Alice existed at all.

Pulling her bike over to the shoulder of the road, she called the doctor to check if the results had come in yet, but there was no news.

"Possibly later today, or tomorrow morning," the receptionist told her.

Penny hung up the phone feeling desperate. She needed to know.

Henry felt strange. Parts of his mind were cracking open, and he was drowning in time, a great endless ocean, with him in the middle. He fought towards the surface, to sanity, to here. He was leaving. He knew that. And for the first time since he was twelve, since the pocket watch had smashed, he didn't know what was coming. Her face floated before him, anchoring him. Emma. His constant. She was his Southern Cross, always there, shining a light for him whenever he looked up. He had seen something about the girl, the one who had been coming to him. Penny. Her name was Penny.

Emma was talking to him, soft words that he couldn't make out. He reached for her hand and forced the words from his mouth. He knew they wouldn't make sense, they never did. But Emma would know, she would find a way to give them meaning. Emma pulled a pencil and old shopping list from her handbag to scribble down what he had said. He leaned back, relaxed now that he knew his message was in safe hands. She smiled at him, fixing his blankets. He wanted to tell her that he would stay if he could. He wanted to tell her that he had loved her since the moment he first saw her. But Henry was floating away, carried by the current of death. He gave himself over to it, riding along. From nowhere, a moment passed through his mind, one more gift from the curse that had been his constant companion for decades. The girl, Penny, an unfamiliar room. A book bound in fabric. A darkness in the shape of a man. The red light of danger. Henry's eyes flew open. He turned his head to Emma to tell her - to pass to her a warning. His mouth opened. And death took him.

Wordless.

CHARMAINE'S JOURNALS

I found a footprint in my room today.

CHAPTER 26

The whole ride over, Penny called herself an asshole. She had told Mae that she didn't want to look for her mother any more because if it was going to happen, then it would. She had told herself that she wouldn't go see Henry any more because knowing the future hadn't seemed to help her much at all and that Henry deserved better. Yet, here she was.

"Just like an asshole would be," Penny chastised herself as she locked up the bike. But she had lost so much already, her world was so small, and Alice! She and Alice were just getting to know each other. She couldn't stand it, she had to try. She slipped past her grandfather's room, without glancing in at him, focused on getting to Henry. She smiled at carers as she went past, feeling conspicuous and guilty.

Penny reached the door to Henry's room and pulled up short. The bed was stripped of its sheets. All the personal items were gone. It was empty.

"Penny?" a voice said behind her.

She turned to find Brooke looking at her with concern, "Are you okay?"

"Henry?" Penny asked. "Has he moved rooms?"

Brooke's eyes filled with sympathy, and she reached out and put her hand on Penny's arm, "Oh, honey. I didn't know that you... No. I'm so sorry to tell you, he passed."

"What?"

"He died. Four days ago now. It was very sudden. But his wife Emma was with him, he had family there."

Penny nodded, shocked to silence. Henry was gone. It had happened before, of course, with other residents where she would come in to volunteer or see Teddy, and there would be an empty room. It was often sudden. She just hadn't expected to feel this one so deeply. Henry, for better or worse, had tried to help her.

"The funeral is today," Brooke was saying.

Penny shook her head to clear it, "I'm sorry, what?"

"The funeral. It's at the cemetery out in Clayton Hills," Brooke looked at her watch. "In about twenty minutes, actually."

Penny took off at a run.

By the time she reached the cemetery, the service had already begun. Penny had ridden her bike as fast as she could to get there and was out of breath and covered in sweat. She stopped behind the bushes to quickly mop her face with a cloth from her backpack and take a drink of water. Taking a deep breath, she walked across the ground to near where the service was being held. She stood towards the back, away from the other mourners, dressed as she was, in more casual attire. The service was short, and to the point, no one gave a eulogy, and the priest finished quickly. An older woman stood towards the front, his wife, Penny presumed. She was dabbing her eyes with a handkerchief occasionally but appeared remarkably stoic for one so freshly bereaved.

The heat of the day was unforgivable, and the crowd shifted uncomfortably in their stiff clothes. Penny saw Jaxon standing next to Henry's wife, his eyes met hers, and he gave her a small nod of acknowledgement. Penny had never been to a funeral, her family had been so small, the only grief she wore was the lingering kind for missing mothers and lost memories. *Why did I come?* She thought to herself. It had just felt like something she needed to do, to see him laid to rest, this man who she didn't know but who had reached across the fog in his own mind to try to give her a gift. Death was what had driven her to go to him today, the thought of her sister slipping into those inky waters, Penny powerless to stop it. Somehow, she had ended up standing in front of a grave anyway. The flowers were removed from the top of the coffin, and it began being lowered into the ground by straps. Something about the sight, the finality of it, made Penny's stomach roll and she turned and walked up into the shade, trying to control her nausea.

Henry's wife, Emma, was hugging and shaking hands of departing mourners when she caught sight of Penny and began walking towards the large gum tree where Penny was standing.

"Penny? It *is* Penny, isn't it?"

Penny nodded, "I'm so sorry for your loss. I didn't know Henry well but…"

Emma smiled, "I know you met him when he was a spectre of himself, but he was a wonderful man. My best friend since I was thirteen."

Penny smiled, "You knew each other a long time."

"We did. I know you know about Henry's gift. My nephew told me he spoke to you, he said you seemed a little shaken up. It was worse, the more the dementia got on, the more the visions happened. He knew what would happen. He saw it… before."

Penny shuddered. She couldn't imagine knowing you would lose yourself. Since Teddy had been diagnosed, she lived in fear of it happening to her, every time she misplaced her house keys or couldn't remember someone's name, a little part of her mind would wonder if that was how it started. She imagined the frustration like trying to remember a word on the tip of your tongue, grasping and never finding.

"You're all… uh, very open about Henry's… gift."

Emma shrugged, "There doesn't seem to be much point in trying to hide it now."

By reflex, Penny and Emma both glanced at the grave, a gaping hole, with glaring green astroturf surrounding it, as though the funeral home were trying to sanitise the grimness of it. *Never a hole,* Penny thought, *Burn me. I don't want to be in the dark.*

"Henry gave me a message for you," Emma said, pulling Penny from her thoughts. "I translated it. I became quite good at that over the years. It always came out muddled. But the message is in there somewhere. He told me it was for the cent girl."

"Scent? Like... smell?"

"No," Emma laughed. "Cent. Like one cent. A penny. That's how it was, you see. Muddled up. I know it meant something to him, to have you get this. I'm glad you came today, so I could make sure I delivered his message. Anyway, I put together what he said and translated it as best I could. It doesn't mean much to me, I'm afraid. Hopefully, it does for you."

Opening her handbag, she pulled a slip of paper from it and handed it to Penny, before walking away, towards a car that was waiting nearby.

Penny opened the paper.

Unmatched. Alice will die. Alice will live.

Her breath caught. Henry had answered one of her questions, after all. And left her with another. How could Alice both die and live? She took a deep breath and turned her face to the sky. The future was not hers to know, and now it was closed off to her forever. The cemetery was empty now, except for the funeral home people who were removing their bits and pieces. One of them pulled a sheet of astroturf off of a mound of dirt that would be used to fill in the grave, and Penny turned away and headed back towards her bike.

As she reached the tree where she had left her bike, her phone rang, and she slipped off her backpack and dug in the depths for it.

"Hello?" She answered.

"Penny? This is Dr. Roma."

She already knew the answer. She had it in her hand, but she asked anyway.

"Am I a match?"

"I'm afraid not. I'm sorry."

She knew. She had known. But the disappointment crushed her anyway. She closed her eyes and took a deep breath, steadying herself. *Oh Alice*, she thought.

"It is probably for the best," Dr. Roma was saying. "We wouldn't be able to recommend you as a donor in your present condition. Your hCG has come back positive."

"What's that?" Penny asked. Was she sick too? Maybe Henry had it right all along.

"The pregnancy hormone. It looks early, only about six weeks along. Did you know you were pregnant?"

Penny dropped her phone and scrambled to pick it up, dirt collecting under her fingernails.

"Excuse me? Sorry. I just... I dropped the phone. What?"

"You're pregnant."

Penny hung up abruptly, cutting Dr. Roma off mid-sentence. She opened her phone to her period app, the one she had silenced the notifications for months ago because they annoyed her.

16 days late! it alerted her.

Sixteen? That can't be right. She had gotten it... no... it was... and then...

Her hand flew to her stomach.

CHAPTER 27

Penny wheeled her bike under the shade of a jacaranda in a park in Clayton Hills. She surveyed the ground for green ants before sitting on the grass and leaning back.

Should she feel different? To her surprise, she did feel vaguely different. Her breasts ached like they did before she would get her period, but she noticed that she was acutely aware of the fabric of her bra against her nipples. And there was a... heaviness in her lower abdomen, almost like a vague feeling of fullness. How was that even possible? Wasn't an embryo barely visible at this stage? She knew nothing about pregnancy. She had never even known anyone that was pregnant. Across from her, a mother pushed her little boy in a swing. She couldn't be someone's mother. She had never even really had a mother. Not to mention that she had just quit her job, her unit was full of boxes so she could move, she had nowhere to move to. And yet... this was the one thing she had always wanted. She had just imagined it would happen when she had a house, a husband, some stability and roots.

And Dean.

How could she tell him?

She wondered if it would have mismatched eyes like his. Dean said he had one from each parent. She hadn't even met his parents! She didn't know his family at all. Where was he born? Did he have a middle name? Christ. What was she thinking?

Her phone rang, and Penny jolted.

Steve's face popped up on the screen. A few months ago, her life had looked completely different. Now, it was tipped upside down. She debated not answering, but for all his faults, Steve had been there, bearing witness. For all the times he had been blunt, he had never lied. He wasn't the love of her life, but he was her family.

"Hi, Steve."

"Penny! Thank god."

Steve had asked for Penny to meet him, and she had agreed. Now, she found herself sitting across from him at a cafe in the city. He wore his work clothes, and Penny realised he must be on his lunch break. When Steve had first gotten his job, they had always planned to meet up for lunch and had never done it. It was one of the many ways that she and Steve had taken each other for granted, assuming there would always be a tomorrow for them. Steve appeared nervous, and the red rash that he would get on his neck whenever he was anxious was peeking out of his shirt collar. She knew all those tiny intimate things about him, and yet her body felt strange as though it wasn't sure how to behave. When she had arrived, he had already been waiting, he leant towards her as she reached him, automatically stretching out to kiss her on the cheek before catching himself, his head jutting forward and back like a turkey. It was oddly comforting, Penny felt, that he didn't know how to act around her either.

They ordered a drink each and sat awkwardly across from each other. Penny looked down at her hand where her engagement ring winked in the sunlight. She hadn't taken it off yet, she hadn't even really thought about it, it had become a part of her. The waiter brought out their drinks, and they sat in silence while waiting for him to leave.

"I'm sorry," Steve said. It came out in a rush, as though he needed to purge the words.

"What for?"

"All those things you said, when you told me to leave. You were right, and I'm sorry."

Penny sat there, feeling shocked. Apologies had never come easy to Steve, she wasn't sure he had ever told her he was sorry before.

"Thank you," she told him. "Actually, I should apologise to you too. I was never very good at opening up to you. I think... I don't think I ever really gave us a fair chance because of that. I kept so much of myself back, and it wasn't fair to you."

She thought of the time she had laid in the bath as Dean read to her from Leif's book. She had allowed herself to be naked, not just physically, but emotionally with him. She had stripped herself bare.

Steve looked relieved, virtually sagging into the chair, "I was wondering if I could come back? I could grab my bag from Mum and Dad's and be home around seven? I'll cook dinner, I'll even do pasta with actual fettuccini instead of zucchini."

She had not been expecting this, she thought when he asked to meet it would be to divide up the household items and talk about finding someone to take over the break lease at the unit. She wondered what she would have given to hear him say these things years ago, even months ago. Penny looked down at the ring on her finger again, tarnished now, somehow duller.

"I'm sorry, Steve. No," she said.

"No, not tonight? Or... no?"

"Just no," She smiled sadly at him and reached over to take his hand. "We've known each other for a long time. You were my best friend, and you helped me through all that stuff with my Mum when she went missing. I'll always love you for that."

He looked at her with tears in his eyes, "Then why? I love you, Penny."

"Because we aren't in love anymore, we haven't been in years. We aren't even compatible, really. Not as lovers, or partners. I do love you, I think I will always love you. You were my home when I felt like mine was falling apart. I need to be my own home now. Does that make sense?"

He nodded, and she twisted the ring off her finger and handed it to him. There was a white line where it once was, but it was a reminder that she knew would fade with time. Standing, she swung her backpack on to her back, "Goodbye, Steve."

"Wait!"

She turned back to him, "What?"

"I said I would cook you real pasta. If nothing else, we can at least end with a meal, right?"

She smiled, "Yes. We can."

"We could make it tomorrow night?"

Penny nodded in agreement.

"I'll see you at home – at the house then," he corrected himself.

"Seven o'clock?"

"Seven o'clock."

Penny rode through the streets, not really knowing where she was going, just feeling the breeze on her face. No more glimpses into the future. She wound up out the front of Dean's apartment. He was at work right now, and she felt vaguely relieved about that, not ready to talk to him until she had some time to herself. She let herself in with the key he had given her, and went up to the closet where the box that they had collected from the hospital in Drummott was kept. Tugging it out of the closet and into the light, she pulled the photo of Charmaine and her out. The glass was dusty, they hadn't cleaned it since they brought it back, Mae had been the only one of them to touch it at all. A small circle over their faces had been roughly wiped clean though, and Penny realised that Mae must have done that, imagining her rubbing at it with the tail of her shirt. The journals were also dirty, the fabric the covered them had perished on the corners, splitting to reveal the thick cardboard of the covers underneath. The pages were yellowed, and a few of them had suffered what looked like water damage, the edges warped. Her writing was the same. Her memories of her mother were disjointed. Odd pieces of her that would hit Penny suddenly, the way she had stood when she did the dishes in the kitchen, one foot propped against the other legs knee, as though she were in a yoga pose. The way she could twist her hair and tuck it up into itself, and it would stay for hours without the use of a tie or clip. And her writing. Sometimes she would put down her pen and stare into space, her fingertips moving slightly in the air like she was painting a scene with them that only she could see, and then she would pick the pen back up and continue writing, in that same scrawling script. Packing the journals into her backpack with the photo, she hoisted the heavy load on to her back and rode home to her empty apartment.

Back at her unit, Penny made a quick dinner of scrambled eggs, tomato and onion and then sat down and began to read her mother's journals. She had never read them before, even when she was younger and Charmaine had left them open on the table at Lloyd's house, abandoned mid-entry. It wasn't that Charmaine had been secretive about them. It was just this unspoken feeling Penny had that the journals were private and not something to be shared. She finished one and began another. Her phone vibrated beside her, and she looked to see who it was.

Dean.

I saw the box out of the closet. Did you decide to look through the journals? If you need anyone to hold your hand while you're reading, let me know. xx

She sent him a quick message to say she was okay and went back to reading.

. . .

Penny has been working on a story. I don't think I'm supposed to know because whenever I go into her room, she shoves it under a pile of notebooks, but I've listened at her door, and she is talking aloud to herself, muttering about goblins and fairies. She has worked so diligently on it for weeks now. She told me that they have a writer's club at school and I asked her if she was going to join, but she had shrugged. She's a bit of a wallflower, my girl. When she was little, maybe three years old, she was such a firecracker - Lloyd would put on some old rock 'n' roll music, and she would shake her whole body, dancing around to it. We would both laugh, and sometimes he would get up and hold her hands and dance with her. I couldn't believe how happy I was. I just wished I could have frozen that moment, and I can remember thinking that everything was completely right in my world. Then things got hard, and I went away for a while. It felt like every time I left, I would come back, and a little of that fire was gone from Penny. I don't know, maybe it's just what kids are like when they grow up. I wonder if she is different with Lloyd? Maybe they still dance together when I'm not there, holding her hands, whirling her around. I hope they do.

Penny shut the journal, tears stinging her eyes.

"Oh, Dad."

CHAPTER 28

The next morning, Mae was waiting outside Charmaine's psychologist's office again, letting clients brush past her in case any of them had been here at the same time as Charmaine. She'd been loitering nearby all morning, and the owner of the cafe next door was starting to give her the stink eye. She decided to go and buy something and sit down for a while to make herself blend in a little more. Browsing the menu, she realised she was starving and hadn't eaten all day, it was nearly lunchtime. Penny had told her to stop looking, but she had secretly still been checking a few places out, just in case. *A few more days can't hurt,* she had told herself, although they hadn't seemed to have helped either. She was leaving tonight, she had gotten a read off a woman at a club, her nowhere man was bailing the city - and Mae was going to follow him.

She moved forward in the line of people waiting to place their orders, careful to avoid touching anyone. The guy behind the counter greeted her and waited to take her order.

"I'll take the pulled pork burger with slaw and a side

salad," she scanned down the desserts, "And the raspberry cheesecake. An iced tea. Ooo! And the fries with aioli."

The cashier raised an eyebrow and Mae raised one back.

"I didn't eat breakfast," she said.

"Right."

Mae paid, took the stand with her table number on it and went to sit at one of the outdoor tables to wait. She had a good view of the psychologist's office from here, but no one was coming or going. *They've probably gone on lunch too*, she thought.

Mae pulled out her notebook that housed her notes for her own personal project. Dates, places, people, possible places he might go next. She had other notebooks, boxes of them, in storage down in Melbourne. That was where she had found him. In a bustling crowd and people bumping into each other as they hurried to where they were going. She was overwhelmed with information, pieces of people flashing in front of her, arguments with spouses, medical worries, job appointments that they had to remember. She had stopped still and closed her eyes tightly, a headache forming sudden and hard behind her eyes. She had been younger then, the headaches were worse. His hand had brushed the back of hers, and he had bloomed before her eyes. She had met a lot of people by that point and seen a lot of things that she shouldn't. Secrets. Abusive husbands. Cheating wives. Every fetish you could probably name. People that cheated on their taxes and stole from their jobs. People that... but nothing like him. Never. They were - blessedly - rare. A monster. Her eyes had sprung open, and she turned to find him again, but he was gone. Disappeared into the people that swirled by her. And she hadn't seen his face. In his mind, his face was always featureless, blank, like someone had taken an eraser to it. She knew people would never notice him in a crowd, he would slip in and out. Both familiar and forgettable, like she was. Because he was like her. When she thought of that moment when he had seen inside her, she felt like she couldn't get clean. The intimacy of his mind creeping through hers, dirty fingers prodding inside of her, dipping into nooks and crannies. Then later, when... no. She shut that part of her mind down.

The waiter brought over her food, startling Mae so that she knocked the glass of water on the table, the contents spilling over her notebook, which she snatched up and shook out.

"Sorry!" Mae apologised.

The waiter hurried off to collect a pile of napkins, and she dabbed at the pages to remove as much of the liquid as she could. It was wet but looked like it would dry relatively unscathed.

"Will it be okay?" The waiter asked, nodding at her book.

"Yes, thank you."

He put the plates down in front of her, and as she took the plate, her fingers knocked gently against his.

Kevin.

Twenty-eight. Lived in a share house with his girlfriend, Odette. Two cats named Jimmy and Elvis. He saw the psychologist across from his work on Friday's for his anxiety and had done since he was fourteen. Mae scrambled through the memories.

There!

Charmaine is waiting outside the office as he leaves.

There is a man sitting beside her and they are chatting, friendly. Kevin knows him, he comes to the cafe. He orders a flat white.

His name is... shit.

It's right there. On the tip of her tongue. She pushes through the memories again. Another day. Charmaine and the guy, standing outside after her appointment. Kevin gives them coffees to go. They were definitely friends, but there was no mention of him in Charmaine's letters. He lived nowhere inside of Penny's mind. The guy pays for both drinks. Kevin takes his card. S. Young. Kevin remembers because it's the same last name as Odette's cousin. What's his first name?

Oh, Kevin knows Japanese. Not what I'm looking for. C'mon.

Spring, but a hot day. Kevin comes out of the psychologists and is waiting to pay at reception. Charmaine gets up and heads into the office, she waves to her friend, "See you, Scott."

Scott. Scott Young.

And then... a promotion the cafe was running, Scott Young writing his details on a clipboard. Christ! She had an address.

Mae looked up at the waiter.

"Do you need anything else?" he asks.

"No. Thank you. You've been very helpful."

Mae ate her meal feeling remarkably chipper, a piece of the puzzle slipping into place, finally. Something tugged at her subconscious, but she pushed it away, focusing on her next steps. She logged on to her phone and booked a flight for six that night.

Mae's phone rang, and she clicked the answer button.

"Dean," she said.

"How's it going?" he asked.

"I've just enjoyed a delicious lunch. And yourself?"

"I'm good."

Mae could hear the clink of glasses in the background and muffled sounds from the bar. He was at work then.

"Actually, I was going to call you. I think I found a lead. There is a guy that Charmaine used to interact with, it seemed like they were friends. I didn't find anything on him inside Penny-"

"Can you not say 'inside Penny'? It sounds creepy. And I thought Penny said she wasn't wanting to look for her mother anymore?"

Mae rolled her eyes, "She did say she didn't want to look for her. I never said *I* didn't want to look for her. Anyway, the point is, if she wasn't open with the friendship, it's possible no one else knew. He might never have been questioned. Still, she might have told him something which could tell us where she went."

"She could have confided in him, you mean?"

"Exactly. I pulled a name from Kevin, the waiter's head, and I'm pretty sure I found him. I've got an address, so I'll head over there tonight... on my way out of town."

Dean was silent on the other end. He knew that her leaving meant she had found something she was tracking down and had voiced his disapproval of it repeatedly. He felt it was dangerous and had tried to dissuade her of it multiple times. Eventually, they had reached a point where they simply discussed it as little as possible. He always called to check in on her though, every week on a Sunday night. He was probably the only person in the world who gave a shit if she was alive or dead.

"Anyway," Mae said, breaking the silence, "I'll give you a call once I find out some more information and check him out."

They said their goodbyes and hung up the phone, Mae pulling out her notebook again. A blank-faced sketch stared up at her. She traced her finger across it, the ink smearing across the still damp page. He had seen inside her mind, so he knew what she was, just as she knew what he was. He was a hunter. But so was she. And she would find him.

CHAPTER 29

Penny woke late and stretched luxuriously for a moment before placing her hand upon her abdomen.

"Good morning," she whispered.

Then she bolted to the bathroom where she promptly threw up, barely making it to the toilet. Groaning, she lay down on the cool tiles, pressing her cheek to them. After a few moments, she was able to drag herself up and into the kitchen where she nibbled at dry toast and sipped orange juice. With something in her stomach, she felt surprisingly well.

"Well, okay then. I'll just eat constantly. Easy done."

She surveyed the living room, which was a mess of boxes that she had promised herself that she would tackle that day, plus she was supposed to go and look at a small apartment in Olive Wood that she would be able to afford on her bookstore salary. The commute would be a killer, but she had booked her first driving lesson and decided that she would go and get a license. *Maybe, in about seven years, I'll even be able to afford a car,* she mused, rolling her eyes. In the meantime, she would ride her bike to the station and take the train, it was nothing she hadn't done before.

She checked her watch, her appointment to view the apartment wasn't until one o'clock, she had time to go see Teddy if she hurried. She imagined telling him she was pregnant, and what that would have looked like if he had still been himself. He would have been thrilled, she knew. In her mind she saw Teddy, herself, and a toddler walking the garden beds in late spring, the sharp tang of a tomato bush on the air, a chubby little hand reaching for the red jewels, plucking them from the stem the way she had done as a child. There would be none of that. But there would be other moments. Grief, she was realising, was about learning to live with what you had and loving it anyway, despite what you had lost.

Penny chained her bike to the pole and walked the familiar garden path that led up to the facility. Rosie came towards her waving, a little girl with dark curly hair by her side.

"Hi Rosie," Penny greeted her, stooping down she smiled at the girl. "Hello, I'm Penny."

"I'm Lucy. I'm six."

Penny's eyes widened, "Well, six is very grown-up."

"It was her birthday last week," Rosie explained. "Everyone we have met now knows she is six."

"Completely understandable," Penny said, standing back up. "How have you been?"

"Good. How about you? Are you doing okay?"

Penny nodded, "I am. Thank you. And for your help that day. Thank you for that too."

Rosie smiled and began walking on with Lucy before turning around and calling back to Penny, "You know, you should come over to our house on Saturday. We are having a little barbecue, just me and my partner and a couple of our friends. You can bring Dean. His sister will be there. I know she would love to meet you."

Penny nodded, "That sounds nice, thank you."

"I'll text Dean the address."

They parted ways, Lucy firing off questions as they left.

Penny walked past the lounge, waving to the residents who sat on the couches watching the television. At Teddy's door, she stopped and took a deep breath. He was sleeping inside. Penny put her hand against her stomach where inside someone she didn't know yet was taking form, and watched the man she knew sleep - who didn't know her anymore. There was a strange, fragile sense of connection between the two, this child would be a part of Teddy. She pulled a slip of paper and the stub of a pencil from her pocket and wrote the word, 'immortality' on it.

The first time Penny had noticed that something was wrong with Teddy had been an ordinary afternoon. It had been several weeks since she had seen him between work and errands. She had felt guilty for not checking in, but Teddy had been the one stable thing in her life for as long as she could remember. Everyone else changed, they got new jobs, or changed their hair, or painted the house. But at Teddy's place everything was exactly where it had always been and no matter when she came to visit, she knew he would be there in the garden sitting on the same bench under the palm trees. That day she had known as soon as she came in that something was wrong. As she entered the street, she could hear fire alarms going off and the closer she got, the louder they got until it became clear they were coming from Teddy's house. She threw her bike on the ground out front and bolted up the front stairs, taking them two at a time and entered the kitchen to find the electric kettle on the stove-top, black smoke billowing as the plastic melted and dripped along the element, flames licking at the bottom of it. Swearing, she had quickly thrown it into the sink and turned off the burner, opening the windows and waving the smoke out with a tea towel. By the time the smoke had cleared, her heart was thumping in her chest, and she was terrified. Where was Teddy? Why hadn't he come at the sounds of the alarms? Why had he stuck the kettle on the stove-top?

She began searching the house and found him in the bedroom, a suitcase on his bed and him standing in the closet pulling clothing from the racks.

"Papa?" She had approached him cautiously, as though he were a stranger wearing her grandfather's face.

Teddy had turned around and looked at her blankly.

"What are you doing?" Penny had asked.

"Packing," he had answered.

"I can see that. Why?"

"Jill and I are going up to see Rob this weekend. Do you know where my clothes are? None of these are mine."

Penny's stomach had dropped. Jill, her grandmother, had

died of breast cancer when Charmaine had been three years old, and Rob, her great uncle, had passed away from a stroke ten years earlier.

"Papa, I'm sorry. Both of them... they've both passed away. A long time ago."

His face fell, and he pulled the shirts in his hands to his chest, "Both of them?"

"Yes. I'm sorry."

"How?"

"Grandma passed away when Mum was little. Remember? She had breast cancer."

Realisation seemed to hit him at that moment, "Yes. Yes, I remember that."

Slowly, as though he were coming to after a dream, he seemed to realise who she was and *when* he was.

In hindsight, Penny realised that over months he had grown quiet. From the outside, it looked meditative, the way he would sit on his chair while the cup of tea beside him grew cold. Now, Penny wondered if it were not him just sitting there with his thoughts. It was easier to say nothing when the person in front of you was talking about things you didn't understand and people you didn't remember you knew. He'd fallen away so quietly, his head silently slipping under the water. Had he known? Was there a moment when he came back from wherever he went when he realised he was forgetting? Or did that moment of confusion get forgotten too?

When Charmaine had gone missing, for months afterwards,

Papa would take the cordless phone with him into the garden while he worked. He said that he didn't want to miss the call.

"What call?" Penny had asked.

They were in the garden, pulling up the weeds and preparing the bed for a crop of sunflowers that he hoped would attract rosellas. She picked up an armful of weeds and put them in the wheelbarrow, brushing the dirt off her arms when she was done.

"Whenever she goes away, she calls me eventually. She will ask me to come and pick her up. I don't want to miss it when she calls me and asks me to come this time."

"You pick her up?"

He nodded, turning over a forkful of soil, and using the prong to break apart a clod of dirt. Penny had been furious with Charmaine at the time, tired of a mother who made her father cry and who couldn't be relied upon to help with homework or tell her what to do when she got her first period, or to listen to her questions about boys. She missed her. She hated her. She loved her.

"Why, Papa? It seems like at some point you would be better off letting her figure it out herself."

Teddy leant on the fork and squinted up at the sky, a cloudless blue like his eyes, "That's just what you do. If my daughter needs me, I'll come. I'll find her."

Penny had turned away, swallowing a lump in her throat, her vision shimmering with tears.

More than anything, Penny wished she could do the same for him. To find him. Like she would crack open a doorway and step through it to find him in his garden, planting the sunflowers. When he first went into care, she had this nagging thought she knew was impossible, that medically it would never happen, but a small part of her couldn't help but think if the phone rang and Charmaine was on the other end, he would rise from the bed to go and get her. They would find each other.

She came to him and smoothed back his hair while he slept. Fixing his blanket and quietly watering the plant that sat on his windowsill. She reached into her pocket and pulled out a piece of paper and began to read. It was a copy she had made of one of the entries from an old journal of Charmaine's they had retrieved from the hospital, one she had written when Penny was eight and Charmaine had been away for a while. When Penny had finally sat down and began to read the journals, she had ended up staying awake all night, soaking in her mother's words, her voice that Penny didn't think she remembered suddenly filling her ears. Charmaine had almost lifted off the page, becoming tangible and real in front of her. Penny's voice wavered a little as she began, her breath hitching in her throat.

"Yesterday, I was thinking about Lloyd and my wedding day and how nervous Dad was before he walked me down the aisle. I was laughing, saying that I was the one who was supposed to be nervous and joking with him about it. He was worried about people looking at him while he was walking me down. But that was just the way Dad has always been. He was always content to sit in the shadows while other people had the spotlight, he never needed recognition. He always just went about the business of loving people with a quiet

kindness. I think Penny gets that from him. I wish I could tell him how much I love him and how much of a wonderful father he is, but I know he would be embarrassed. He'd just huff about and say that's what father's do. But I think when I get back, I'll tell him anyway. I'll tell him, thank you for always coming for me."

The sound of a throat being cleared, made Penny turn around. Mae looked over at her sheepishly.

"Sorry to interrupt. Looked like you were having a moment."

"It's fine. He is sleeping anyway. I just... wanted to tell him. Even if he doesn't... well. You know what I mean."

"I do. Knowing what people mean is my thing, actually." Penny smiled.

"I came to say goodbye," Mae said. "Which is weird. I don't usually say goodbye."

"You're leaving?"

Mae nodded, "I have somewhere else to be."

"I'm glad you made an exception, then. Goodbyes are important."

Mae looked over at Teddy, "So, this is your grandfather, hey? He is different in your head."

"What do you mean? How does he look to me?" Penny asked.

"Younger. Soft but strong. Like... comfort, I guess."

"That makes sense," Penny said, smiling at Teddy.

"So, Dean loves you," Mae said abruptly. She sighed, "You know, he use to see me that way. When I touch him now, all I see is you."

She saw Penny's expression and waved her hand, "No, we were never involved. He is like a brother to me. Still... it is always nice to have someone think of you that way. Now though, it's all Penny, all the time."

Mae looked at Teddy curiously, her hand hovering over his.

"I've never touched someone with dementia before," she said. She took her hand away, tucking it into her pocket as though she didn't trust her hand to mind its own business.

"I'm pregnant," Penny blurted, surprising herself.

Mae looked up at her in surprise, "Dean's?"

Penny nodded, and Mae let out a low whistle, "Damn."

"I haven't told him yet."

"He will be a good dad, Penny. I know it."

Penny nodded.

"There is something else. I know you said that you weren't looking anymore, but just in case you change your mind, I found a name."

"A name?"

"There was a guy that your Mum was hanging around with. They had coffee together a couple of times. He seemed like a friend?"

Penny's heart picked up, "Like... an affair?"

"No. I don't think so at least. They just seemed friendly. I could check him out if you want?"

Penny looked at Teddy and then out the window where the sun was shining. Another lead. Maybe.

"No," she said finally. "Thank you. But no. If I change my mind, I can check it out myself."

"Right. Well, his name is Scott Young. I've got an address, do you have a pen?"

Penny pulled out a piece of paper and a pencil from her back pocket and jotted down the name that Mae recited.

"Scott Young," Penny said, trying to recall if the name was familiar, but it meant nothing to her. "Thank you, Mae."

Mae turned to go, "Well, I'd hug you but..."

"I know."

She walked to the door and stopped. Turning around, she looked at Penny.

"What the hell - let's do it."

Penny thought she was going to come back and hug her and began to reach out, but Mae walked past her and over to Teddy, taking his hand in hers.

Mae closed her eyes and gasped, her face went white, and her eyelids fluttered as though she were dreaming.

"Mae!" Penny exclaimed. She moved to grab her and pull her away but stopped, uncertain if touching her was the right thing, instead her hands floated uselessly in front of her, her breath caught in her throat.

After what felt like an eternity, Mae dropped Teddy's hand.

"I'm okay," she gasped. "I'm alright."

She moved to the bed and sat down heavily.

Penny scanned her face, Mae had just seen inside of her grandfather's mind, something Penny had always wished she had been able to do. But, of course, Mae would have known that - she would have seen it, every time she and Penny had touched.

"What... what was it like?" She asked.

Ever since Teddy had developed Alzheimer's, she had felt the burden of all of their shared memories. They all flew around inside her head like starlings, swirling and dancing with each other. For him, they were lost, they had drifted away beyond where Penny could follow. *Where do he and I live now?* she would wonder. *I carry the weight of our memories alone, they live only inside me, I carry them for the both of us.*

Mae looked at her, tears shining in her eyes, "Oh, Penny. I thought it would be terrifying; a nothingness, like being lost in the darkness. But it wasn't. It was like the northern lights, a rainbow. A garden, ripe tomatoes. A girl, her small hand fitting inside his. The taste of strawberries. Jazz music drifting from a record player. His arm on your mother's as he walked her down the aisle. And they were all there, floating along on the rays of colour."

Penny felt tears roll unchecked down her cheeks, "Thank you."

Mae shook herself and stood up, she pulled Penny into her arms.

"He still remembers he loves you," she said softly.

She pulled back and smiled, walking out and leaving Penny alone with her grandfather.

CHAPTER 30

Penny arrived back at the apartment late afternoon, she had signed on the lease at the place in Olive Wood. It was small and old but had original hardwood floors and sunlight that streamed through the windows, giving it a homely vibe. The yard was large and in the back corner was a neglected vegetable patch that in her mind, Penny was already weeding and planting. Very best of all, it would be hers. Something she had chosen. She had found herself discarding so many things as she packed up the apartment, furniture she had hated but Steve had liked, items they had been given because the original owners no longer wanted them. This was the time when she would begin to build a life that she wanted, she might not have much, but what she would have would be carefully chosen. Steve was coming by that evening, and they could go through the rest of the items together. Penny carefully folded a throw rug that he loved and placed it in a box she had labelled with his name. Pulling a sheet of paper from a notepad in the kitchen and sat down to make a list of things she still had to do. There was having dinner with

Steve, and going to see Alice, who would have been told by now that Penny wasn't a match. She had to mend things with her father and groaned aloud in the kitchen about that. And tell Dean.

Her phone rang, making her jump, her pen bouncing to the floor. Dean's name flashed up on her screen, and her heart hammered in her chest as she answered.

"Penny!" he said.

"Hello," Penny croaked back.

"Are you okay? You sound weird."

"I... yes. I just dropped something. How are you?"

Dean's voice sounded laden with suspicion, "I'm fine. Are you sure you're okay? I mean, you read your Mum's journals last night, and I just wanted to see..."

Penny swallowed, finding her mouth had gone dry, "I'm okay, really. Although I was thinking we could catch up later so we could talk."

"Absolutely. I could come by around seven o'clock?"

"Ahh, no. I've got something to do, can we make it eight-thirty?"

"Sure. I'll come by then."

They said their goodbyes and Penny hung up the phone.

Abandoning her list, Penny wandered through the rooms, aimlessly, restless. Finally, she went to her bed and opened her bedside table, pulling out the journal that lived there. Her snippets, carefully curated into something that resembled a story. She had been going over it recently, culling and crossing out words, highlighting certain parts. This was

Penny's story, but it was really only half of it, she realised. The other half belonged to Charmaine. She looked at her mother's journals where they sat stacked upon the dresser, where Penny had left them last night when she had finished.

They spanned years, from when Penny had been a little girl, up to around the time Charmaine had gone missing. In its pages were dozens of breakfasts shared, nights spent reading Penny stories, quotes from people she had spoken to. Her mother had liked the riverside, but she had also loved the city. Charmaine had been fascinated by the parts of life that people generally wanted to shove away. The hurts, the harsh words, the grime, the dirt. When she spoke of her mental illness, she never tried to dress it up. She spoke about it in a way that was so frank that it made Penny feel vaguely uncomfortable. She'd had bouts of depression, that was generally when she had gone away, plagued by a feeling of guilt that everyone was better off without her. Now, those times when her mother had gone, had been filled in. She *had* gone to Byron once. Another time she had travelled to Adelaide to try to meet with her maternal aunt, but they had refused to see her, shutting the door in her face. Sometimes she had stayed close by, walking past the house where Penny was inside with Lloyd, wanting to go in but not feeling ready.

So much of herself, Charmaine had kept hidden away. Penny thought of how she had done the same with Steve, writing in secret, keeping her thoughts to herself, and she realised she was her mother's daughter. All this time she had been wondering *where* her mother was, she had never thought to wonder *who* her mother was.

Penny pulled the slip of paper from her pocket that she had written Scott Young's name and address on. *Disappeared*, she thought to herself. Such a strange word, she said it aloud, tasting it on her tongue. Charmaine had never told anyone about her fears about someone following her. She thought it made sense in a way. Except... Except she had thought she *had* told Penny. If she had written the emails and sent them to Penny, she must have thought they were being received. Didn't she wonder why she hadn't been getting a response? Charmaine didn't even own a computer, she liked to hand-write. She had written Penny notes before, but always on paper in her own hand. *Why would she have emailed me?* Penny wondered.

Impulsively, Penny opened her emails on her phone again, scrolling to the folder she had created with the emails Charmaine had sent her. They were dated, at the top of each email, as though her mother had written the date. They sounded like her, the same words and phrasing. But something felt off, it was probably nothing she would ever have noticed had she not spent the night beforehand reading her mother's journals. It felt almost like a ghostwriter. A good impersonation, but an impersonation none the less. There were journal entries that echoed what was written in the emails, but everything was just slightly different. *It was in the details*, Penny thought. Searching for a number to call on the email provider website she dialled and was put through to technical support.

"Hi, I'm just calling about some emails I've received. They seem to be dated as though they were sent years ago, but I received them recently. Is that... how does that happen?"

They went back and forth, Penny explaining the situation in full. The short answer was, it couldn't happen.

"Even if by some weird technical glitch, your mother had sent these emails years ago, the dates on them would mean they would be bumped to the bottom of your inbox, not the top. The emails had to have been sent around the same time as they were received."

Hanging up the phone, Penny felt her stomach drop. Someone had sent her these emails. But it wasn't her mother.

How could they have known? They would have had to have known her well, someone who knew about Penny and Lloyd. There were so many details in those emails that it would have to have been someone who knew her well. It would have to have been Penny herself, or Lloyd or Teddy - but neither Teddy nor her father had ever used an email. *God, Lloyd still went to the post office to pay his bills instead of doing it online*, Penny thought. No, this was someone else. *Scott Young*. Mae had said he seemed like a friend, maybe someone that Charmaine had confided in. Penny looked at the clock. It was barely five. She had time.

CHAPTER 31

Mae had gone back to the hotel intending to put aside Char-maine Green and Penny and everything to do with it. She needed to shower and pack her things and get out of the city. She didn't usually get so caught up in cases, but there was something about this one that just got under her skin.

Maybe it was because Dean asked me, Mae thought.

But it wasn't that. It was Penny. So many people hid themselves, and Penny was no exception. The difference was, Penny wasn't hiding anything terrible. She was just hiding - wallflower who sat contentedly in the shadows, not realising how she shone. Mae had felt this tidal wave of grief just rolling off her for her mother. Penny deserved closure one way or another, and it made Mae want to find Char-maine for her in a way that was nearly desperate. And that... attachment... made Mae very uncomfortable. And that thing with Teddy! What was that? Reads were exhausting, uncom-fortable, and sometimes painful. It wasn't what people thought - that she just saw inside. She *was* inside. It was more of an absorption. Touching someone with dementia was risky and stupid, and she knew it. She had been lucky. It had just been something about seeing Penny's face as she read that note from her mother, the memory of Penny's snippets in her head, she had wanted to give her something since she hadn't been able to give her back her mother.

"Stupid girl," she sang under her breath while stripping off her clothes.

Mae looked over at the shower, longing to feel the hot water wash away the day, but something was nagging at her.

Just forget it, she told herself. *This isn't your problem. You don't owe anybody shit.*

She walked towards the shower and turned on the taps, letting the water get hot.

Nobody had seen this Scott guy though, not the pharmacist. Not Penny. Not Lloyd. It was like he existed nowhere but inside Kevin, the waiter's head. Where did they meet? Were they actually... together? No. It's didn't seem like that in Kevin's head. There was none of that incidental touching that happens when people are interested in each other. Maybe-

Stop it! Get in the goddamn shower.

Maybe she could just go back, see the pharmacist again, and double-check. She didn't know what she was looking for before. She might have missed it. She looked at her reflection in the mirror.

"Damn it," she said and turned off the taps.

The pharmacist had seen him. Not talking to Charmaine but walking past. Several times, in fact. Mae raced to the library just before it shut, bumping into the librarian as she locked the doors. There he was, in the stacks nearby. He wore an olive green coat. The librarian remembered because it was hot out, and she thought it was strange. Yes. This guy definitely knew something. Scott Young was the one who was going to break this wide open, she could feel it. He had been around her, they were friends. She might have told him things she wouldn't tell a boss or her child or her husband. Mae started to wonder if she had been wrong and Charmaine had been having an affair after all. *I'll go back*, Mae thought, *grab my things and go to the address. I'll just make one more stop first.*

Mae stood outside the woman's house again. The afternoon sun setting at her back. Just one little touch. That was all she needed. The cat was sitting on the path staring at her. Mae walked up the path towards it, making kissing noises.

"Come on, buddy. That's it. Don't run away now."

The cat eyed her suspiciously but stayed where it was. Bending down and scooped the cat up, its claws gouging into the flesh of her stomach through her shirt.

"I'm a fucking horrible person," she muttered to herself.

Mae walked purposefully towards the door and rapped on it sharply.

"Hey!" She called out. "I've got your cat."

The wooden door cracked open, and the woman appeared at the screen.

"Put him down."

"Nope. You're gonna have to open that door."

The woman narrowed her eyes.

This was it, the last real chance she had. Slowly, the

woman reached for the door handle and unlocked the security screen with a click. Mae wanted to snatch for her hand but held back, waiting for the door to open, the woman's hands reaching for her cat that began to writhe in Mae's arms. Her fingers slipped around the soft fur as she took her pet and grazed Mae's inner arm. Mae grabbed hold of her wrist. The woman gasped and tried to wrench her arm away, but Mae held on, she just needed a moment. She closed her eyes.

It was only a second, maybe two, but Mae saw it all. From grazed knees on the schoolyard to her wedding day. A man who would come home drunk and cover her face with bruises instead of kisses. A son who didn't talk to her anymore. Mae shuffled through the memories, pushing aside the things that made this woman who she was until she found what she was searching for.

People look different to everyone. A different version of yourself lived in everyone's head. So, when she finally found what she was looking for, she didn't realise who it was straight away. The woman across the road had spent years in her own cage, watching the street. Sifting through her mind, Mae saw him.

On the street, watching Charmaine's unit, again and again. Climbing through the side window. Leaving again, hours later, slipping out and into the bushes. She hadn't been having an affair. And they hadn't been friends, not the way

Charmaine had thought they were. Charmaine had been right about someone being in the unit. For anyone else, they might have called the police, they would have told their family. But Charmaine had lived for years inside a world where shadows weren't real, she no longer trusted herself.

In the woman's mind, the man had the face of her husband when he was young. Similar eyes, the bone structure was altered. She saw something dangerous in him that made her project her own trauma on to him. Mae knew him by his coat, a deep olive green. She dropped the woman's hand suddenly and stood staring at her, mouth agape. She had made a terrible mistake.

***

Mae took off at a run and reached the station as a train was pulling in. She bounded up the stairs two at a time and yelled at one of the guys getting on to hold the door for her. She slipped in as they were closing and collapsed on to a seat, trying Penny again and getting no answer. It was the guy. The one they thought was a friend, he was the one breaking into Charmaine's house. What the hell was his name? She had known it, it was... christ! Why couldn't she remember? She had gone to see Penny and said goodbye, and she had told her about the friend. Pushing hard through her own memories, she saw Penny's face, her hair falling softly in front of her face as she stood beside her grandfather. And Mae had done what she had a thousand times before, shuffled through someone else's memories to find the information she was looking for. She had reached into her read from the waiter at the cafe and pulled out the name of the guy. It was just that now - when she went looking for that information it was gone. Blank. Erased. And that was impossible. She stored thousands of memories that didn't belong to her, she knew French, mechanics, how to bake a soufflé'. She could always retrieve it. The train pulled up at the station, and she raced out the door, running towards the bar Dean worked at.

Mae ran past a group of tradesmen who stared at her as though she were on fire, and pushed in the door of the pub so hard that it hit the wall behind it and bounced back, glancing off Mae's shoulder, but she barely felt it. Dean looked up from behind the bar, alarm crossing his face.

"Dean! Is Penny with you?"

"No. I'm catching up with her later. Why?"

"Shit! I gave her the name of a guy earlier when I went to say goodbye. It was the last lead I had, and I handed it over and was going to go out of town. I'm worried she may have gone on her own."

Dean glanced around the bar at the few patrons who were now staring with interest at Mae, who appeared not to notice. He stepped out from behind the bar and motioned for Mae to follow him into one of the back rooms.

"Mae, sit down, tell me what is happening."

Mae ignored him and began pacing around the room, "I went to do a little last-minute digging, just in case, before I left town. I just had a feeling I was missing something. It was right there, I just hadn't put it all together. This guy."

"The one you told me about on the phone?"

"Right. I kept coming up with nothing, but then I got

a name from a waiter at a cafe, he had seen Charmaine with a guy, hanging out. They were friends - or acquaintances at least. It was the only thing I had left, so I went to see Penny to say goodbye and pass on the information, in case she changed her mind and decided she did still want to look for her mother. But then something about that kept bugging me, so I decided to call in on that woman that lived across the road again, just one more time. He wasn't her friend. Or he was, but he wasn't just her friend."

She told Dean about what the woman had seen, and his face went pale.

"You think Penny has gone there to see this guy?"

Mae nodded, "Yes. Or maybe. I don't know. I gave her the address."

Dean took out his phone and began dialling Penny's number.

"She isn't answering," Mae said.

Dean ignored her and called anyway, swearing when she didn't pick up.

"What do we do?" He asked her.

"I don't know."

"Well, who is he? We can go there and get her."

"I don't know."

"What do you mean, you don't know? You said you told Penny the name."

"I can't remember it. I can't remember anything about him. It's gone."

"How could it be gone? What does that even mean?"

He reached over and grabbed her by hand.

Fear rolled off him towards her, and she felt it overlaying her own. And Penny. Her smile, the brush of her lips against his as she left the loft. Sunlight in her hair. The way she would curl around her notebook while she wrote.

"Mae!" He said, urgently, ripping her from the read.

"What?"

"What do you mean it's gone?"

"What's gone?"

"The name of the guy climbing in Charmaine's window!"

She knew. She knew she knew that there was a guy that had climbed in Charmaine's window, but she couldn't see it anymore. It was there, but not there. Lost somehow, like when you entered a room and couldn't remember what you had come in there for. The moment Dean had touched her, it had dissolved. Her own memories were still there, she could see the cafe in her head, she could see the cat on the woman's driveway. But the borrowed memories were gone. All the reads from today had just disappeared. There were others there, further back. She could still remember reads on Dean, on Penny. She still remembered when she had touched Rosie that day in Drummott and what she had seen. It was just... she felt like...

"Oh my god."

"What?"

"I touched Teddy," Mae gasped.

"Penny's grandfather?"

"I touched him. I saw inside. I can still see it. But everything else is gone."

"You... you what? *Read* dementia?"

Mae nodded, "Oh my god. What have I done?"

"The guy, the name, did you write it anywhere?"

"No. I have never had to. I always remembered it."

Dean stared at her, aghast, the full weight of the situation hitting them both. Mae raked her hands through her

hair, feeling helpless. She had relied too much on remembering, she had never had to write things down. In her mind,
she saw Penny pull the slip of paper and the pencil from her
pocket where she always kept them so she could write down
her snippets. Penny wrote everything down, an ocean of
little notes that she would later write in her journals.

Mae looked up at Dean, "I never write things down, but
Penny might have."

CHAPTER 32

It was dark by the time Penny walked up to the small block of apartments that reminded her eerily of the ones Charmaine had lived in before she went missing. She had gotten lost along the way, getting off at the wrong station and having to backtrack up the line, before she finally gave up and decided to ride the rest of the way. She was going to be late getting back for dinner with Steve. Penny thought about sending him a text but decided to wait until afterwards. Maybe she could catch a taxi back and arrive not long after Steve.

An old woman peered out at her from the window of the unit that abutted Scott Young's and gave her a disapproving look.

"Why am I always getting dirty looks from people?" Penny muttered under her breath.

She knocked on the door for unit number two. *There was always the possibility he wouldn't be here anymore*, Penny thought. Whatever read Mae would have gotten would have come from years ago. There was no car in the carport beside it, and Penny wondered if perhaps they were out, but there were lights on inside.

There was no sound of movement from inside, and she was just about to turn around when the door opened, and a man stood in front of her. She scanned his face, trying to see if he was familiar to her, but nothing stood out. He was fairly plain, with mousey brown hair neatly cut and hazel eyes. She had thought briefly on the ride over that if he was the one who sent the emails, it was possible he could be dangerous, but Scott Young seemed normal looking. In fact, he was an almost weedy build and not much taller than Penny herself. Besides, Mae had said he seemed like a friend, and for all her faults, Mae wouldn't have given her the name of someone that might be dangerous.

"Can I help you?" he asked with a smile.

"I hope so," Penny said. "Are you Scott Young?"

The man's smile dropped, and his face became guarded, an odd flicker of recognition crossed his features, "I am. Why?"

"My name is Penny Green. I think you knew my mother. I was just wondering if I could come in for a few moments and have a chat?"

There was a beat of silence while he scanned her face, peering behind her to see if anyone else was there. *He is going to say no*, Penny thought and her heart welled with disappointment at yet another dead end. But then the door swung open fully and he unlocked the screen, opening it for her.

"Thank you," Penny sighed and stepped inside.

. . .

The apartment was as unremarkable as Scott Young himself. Sparsely furnished, with bookshelves lining the walls and a struggling pothos in an ugly concrete planter on a glass coffee table in the middle of the room. He indicated for her to take a seat and Penny sat down, placing her backpack beside her. Her palms were sweating, and she wiped her hands along her jeans.

"I don't really know where to start," she began.

He smiled encouragingly at her.

"My mother was Charmaine Green. She was... well... she went missing about thirteen years ago. She wasn't always well, mentally, I mean. My dad and I looked for her, but we couldn't find where she might have gone. I know she left her apartment, and we recently found where we think she might have gone but after that..." Penny held up her hands.

"Right," he said. "I did know Charmaine. Briefly, anyway. She used to have an appointment in a building that I was working in, and I would see her sometimes, say hello. I didn't realise she was missing though, I thought she might have just stopped having appointments. I didn't know her very well, I'm afraid. No more than to say hello. How long has she been gone?"

"Thirteen years," Penny said. "It's just, someone was also sending me emails pretending to be my mother. It would have to have been someone who knew her well, a friend maybe. I thought... I thought it might have been someone who knew something and wanted to reach out but maybe didn't want to have their name associated with it."

Penny tilted her head and scrutinised his face. Scott Young would have been excellent at poker, she thought, except when she mentioned the emails a flicker of shock came over his face for a moment before he composed himself. If she hadn't been looking for it, she probably never would have noticed. He hadn't sent the emails. It wasn't him.

He smiled ruefully, "I'm sorry. I really didn't know her that well. I only spoke to her a few times. Definitely not enough to send emails. How did you get my name, may I ask?"

Penny saw no reason to lie, but also wasn't about to give up Mae's secret, she settled for something in between, "A friend. An investigator. She has been looking into it recently for me, and your name came up from someone who saw you with my Mum near the psychologist's place. The person she spoke to said that you seemed friendly."

"That person must have an excellent memory to have recalled a couple of coffees from thirteen years ago," Scott mused.

"My friend is good at getting people to remember things."

"Hmm. She sounds... interesting. Well, I am sorry I can't help you. I will think about it and let you know if I remember anything."

Scott Young rose to his feet, clearly indicating that the meeting was over.

Penny sighed and turned to grab her backpack when a sudden wave of nausea hit her, and she felt dizzy, black spots appearing in her vision. She lurched to the side and nearly fell off the chair.

"Are you okay?" he asked, concerned.

Was this the morning sickness? Penny wondered. *Isn't it supposed to be only in the morning?*

She took a deep, steadying breath, "I... I'm not sure."

"You look very pale. I'll get you a glass of water," he said and hurried from the room.

Penny leaned back in the chair and closed her eyes, willing her stomach to calm. *Okay*, she thought. *Scott Young didn't write the emails. But he is definitely full of shit about something. Maybe I will have Mae come back if she hasn't left town yet and read him.* She rose to her feet cautiously, as though she were testing the floor for stability and found that once she was upright, she began to feel somewhat better.

In the kitchen, she could hear Scott opening cupboards and what sounded like a strange one-sided conversation. Suddenly, Penny did not want to stay here a moment longer. The polite part of her, ingrained into her by society told her that she should stay and say goodbye, while every crime documentary narrator was suddenly screaming at her to leave without a backward glance. Penny picked up her backpack and strode towards the door, preparing to wrench it open and make a break for it when she spied his bookshelf against the far wall. The rest of Scott's unit was sparse and precise. His bookshelf, however, was a mess. Volumes were stacked both vertically and horizontally, piles of them on top of the shelf in an alarmingly precarious heap. It wasn't that Penny herself was any neater, it was just so oddly out of place here where even the glass coffee table didn't have the usual fingerprints from use on it.

Drawn to it, she moved as though in a trance, her fingers

stroking the spines of the books, the same way she had seen Dean's stroke the strings on his guitar.

And there it was.

Mae and Dean had driven to Penny's as fast as they could, Dean cursing the traffic the whole time. Mae found herself barely able to concentrate. What was happening to her? Would it all go now? The reads slowly fading away until there was just her left behind? She could feel Teddy still within her, the place where the reads lived. Everything she had read today was gone, everything except the read on Teddy. That one was there, strong as ever. She could see it, those colours that swirled and mingled together, like coloured smoke, fragments of his memories drifting along on beams of light. *God, it was beautiful*, she thought. *But also, what the fuck did it do to me?* She hadn't realised until today how much she relied on her gift. Without it, how would she ever find Him? Would that read go to?

They reached Penny's unit and jumped out of the car, racing up the pathway to the unit. Linda peered at them from her window, and Mae gave her the finger. Dean reached the door first and rapidly began to bang on it.

"What are you doing?" Mae asked.

"Knocking," he answered.

"Screw knocking, there is a key under the frog over there."

Dean turned to get the key when the door swung open in front of them. Steve stood there in an apron, holding a spatula and looked at them expectantly.

"Who are you?" Dean asked.

Steve blinked, "Steve. Who are you?"

"Ugh, it's Steve," Mae groaned.

Steve looked at her in confusion, "Do we know each other?"

"No," Dean said, at the same time as Mae said yes.

"You look familiar," Steve mused.

"I look familiar to everyone," Mae snapped, "Where is Penny?"

Steve shrugged, "No idea. I told her I would be here at seven and she was supposed to be here. I guess she's late."

Dean looked at Mae in alarm.

"I don't have time for this," Mae said and grabbed Steve's hand.

He tried to wrench his hand from her grasp, smacking at the top of it with the spatula, "Hey! What are you doing?"

Mae dropped his hand and turned to Dean, "He's right. He saw her at lunch yesterday. She was supposed to be here."

"Of course I'm right," Steve blurted, "What is going on? Is Penny okay?"

Mae pushed her way into the house, "We have no idea. I need her journal."

Dean followed Mae into the house, leaving Steve with his mouth open at the front door, staring after them. The lounge was littered with moving boxes. *What if she has already packed it*, Mae wondered. *God, what if she took it with her for some reason?*

"Penny doesn't keep a journal," Steve said.

"Yes, she does," Mae replied.

The men followed Mae into the bedroom where she opened the bedside table drawer and lifted off a pile of underwear, throwing them on the bed. Lifting out a small journal, she flipped impatiently through the pages before finding the one she wanted, "This is from today, but she hasn't written the address down. Damnit!"

"What is going on!" Steve shouted. Sauce flung from the spatula as he waved his arms, hitting the wall and spraying on to the carpet.

Mae stood up and tore the page from the journal, "Penny found the man who was stalking her Mum and she's gone to see him. Only, she doesn't know he was the one doing the stalking. She's in danger. And we don't know the address of where she has gone."

Steve stood there, silently looking from Dean to Mae, "Penny's mother..."

Mae looked at Dean, "We have to go. Now!"

"Go where, Mae? We don't have the address!"

"I'll go back to the cafe where I got the read. If I read it from him once, I can read it again."

Dean stared at her helplessly, they both knew how long that would take.

"Wait!" Steve said. "You need to know where Penny is?"

He went to his phone and unlocked it, swiping through apps until he found the one he was looking for, "We share an account, so I can ping where she is. It's how I knew when she was with you."

He looked up at Dean, who stared back at him defiantly.

Steve flipped the phone around and showed them the map that had come up, and Mae snatched a piece of paper from the journal and wrote down the street the pin had dropped on.

"Let's go," she said to Dean and began jogging for the door.

"Hang on!" Steve said, "I'm coming!"

"No," Dean said, "We can handle it."

Mae looked at Dean, "Let him come. She's his family."

Someone is following me. I don't think it's safe here anymore.

CHAPTER 33

He filled the glass of water and contemplated his options. He wasn't sure how she had found him in the first place, he had no ties to Charmaine, and it had been so long. And she hadn't written about him - he had read all of her journals cover to cover. That had been a bit disappointing if he was honest. The first time he had stepped inside the unit, it had been such a rush. The place almost pulsed with her, the smell of her lingering in the bedroom, the clothing that she would wear tickling his arms as he slid them between the silks and satins in her drawers.

The journals had been an even more unexpected surprise - like she had written little love notes to him. Charmaine had written everything from what she ate for breakfast, to a tooth that had been aching and her fear of the dentist. She wrote prolifically of her daughter, and even that endeared her to him. She was a good mother, despite how delicate and fragile she was. He had hoped after they had talked for a while that she would have written about him. He knew they had a connection, why else would she talk to him? Why would she smile and touch his arm? But she hadn't written, and that was when he realised how much he must have meant to her, her feelings carefully hidden inside her - she didn't want to share them with anyone. He just needed to get her away from that husband who was cheating on her with that blonde bitch anyway, even though Charmaine was too trusting to believe it. After he had read about her suspicions, he had followed him to another house and watched him through the windows sitting at the dinner table like a happy little family and felt enraged on her behalf. He didn't deserve her. She needed better. She needed him.

The emails. Well, that was disconcerting. That had to be T. There was no one else who could have known. T. had been around then, it's possible he might have... no. There was no way. But someone knew something, that much was true.

He took a deep breath to steady himself before he went back out to her. It was fine, this girl didn't seem that bright. She bought the story about not really knowing her mother, which he'd had to come up with on the spot. Christ, he had nearly had a heart attack when he saw her on the doorstep and recognised her from the photo. Nosey Mrs. Phillips next door would have seen her too. That was bad. He would have to leave just in case. T. could help with that, he owed him. A small shudder went through him at having to explain what had happened, but no matter. All of this was an accident, really. Everything would be fine.

. . .

He made a list in his head, and that made him feel better.

Give her the glass of water.

God, she looked really sick. Was she going to vomit? He hated vomit.

Send her on her way.

Sorry, can't help, yadda, yadda.

Pack up his things.

Could be done in two days if he got straight to it.

Call his work and say he had a family emergency up north.

Fuck work, anyway.

Call T.

Christ, he wasn't looking forward to that.

Disappear.

Easy.

Picking up the glass of water, he plastered a smile on his face and walked out of the kitchen.

CHAPTER 34

If anyone else had been there, they wouldn't have noticed it, tucked away as it was. It sat unobtrusively on the bookshelf, slotted between the book, only the delicate spine visible. But Penny had always paid attention to the details.

Her hand trailed the length of it, and she slipped it out and held the notebook in her hands.

"I want to remember everything," she murmured to herself.

A journal, it's pages yellowed with age, covered in blue and yellow flowers on a cream background, salvaged from a dress that had been Penny's. It was in better condition than the ones she had found in the hospital in Drummott, but then it would be, indoors and kept carefully all these years. She opened it, tracing the same handwriting she had once before.

Penny, lashes like ...

Penny took a sharp intake of breath. She looked up. It

was here. Slid between the novels and cookbooks on the shelves. She could see them in all in her mind, the way they had lived in a stack on a table in Charmaine's bedroom.

The old tablecloth.

One in white linen from a dress Charmaine used to wear.

Flannel from a shirt Papa wore.

And this one, the one that was missing, wrapped in fabric that had come from Penny's dress.

Her hands were filled with her mother's memories.

He had them.

Scott came back into the room holding a glass of water, and his eyes travelled down to the book Penny held.

"Why do you have this? You said you didn't know her. Where did you get it from?"

He set the glass down on the table, and smiled ruefully, "Well, this is very inconvenient. I really wish you hadn't of found that, Penny."

He walked towards her.

Instinctively, Penny backed away, the backs of her knees hitting the chair she had been sitting on earlier, and she fell into it, still clutching the journal. He wrenched it from her hands.

"Why?" she asked.

"Why what?" he said irritably.

"Why did you take her? What did you do with her?"

Scott Young was pacing back and forth in front of her, raking his hands through his hair. It was like he was dissolving before her eyes, all that composure from earlier stripped away. He hit his own hand hard against the side of his head, and Penny jumped and stifled a gasp. Her mouth was dry, and she frantically tried to think of a way to get to the door and get it open before he could get to her. It was past time when people would be getting home from their jobs, but there might still be some people on the street - if she made it that far. She thought about the old woman next door who reminded her of Linda with her glass against the wall and suspicious glare every time anyone wandered past the duplex. *Please, oh please, have a glass against the wall*, Penny prayed.

She stole a glance at her backpack that sat beside the bookshelf, where she had dropped it when she had found the journal and thought longingly of her phone. There was nothing for it. She was going to have to try to run. Her hand instinctively went to her abdomen, and she thought briefly of the life within, barely there, mere cells, but the promise of the future. She braced herself against the arms of the chair and pushed up in one swift motion, bolting for the door. Her hand grasped the metal of the handle - she felt it, cool beneath her fingertips, like freedom - before she was wrenched back. His fingers dug into the soft flesh of her arm, and she wheeled around to face him. He looked at her, with eyes so empty and bleak that for a moment she felt like she was looking at a different man to the one that had opened the door.

Penny made another desperate attempt to get to the door, yanking her arm to free it, but he held fast. Scott had a surprising strength, he twisted her wrist behind her back, making her gasp at the shock and pain of it. Penny kicked out with her leg, wildly, connecting with something that made him grunt but he merely tightened his grip in response, yanking her arm higher up behind her until she felt like her shoulder was tearing free. She was almost frozen with pain, wanting to curl into a ball. His body was so close to hers that she could smell him, the rank scent of fear and fight – and the cloying smell of his cologne. And in her head, her mother's words took flight, filling Penny's ears with her voice.

Someone is here –
    Things have been moved –
    I'm being followed –
    I could smell his cologne –

He is going to kill me, Penny thought. *These hands, these hands, these hands. Mama. I haven't called her that in years. Isn't it funny how the brain does things like that? I wonder what she thought when these hands -*

"Help!" She screamed.

His hand clapped down on her mouth, pressing her lips hard into her teeth until she tasted her own blood. Wrenching her head side to side, she loosened his grasp enough for her to bite down hard on his fingers, feeling the give of his flesh, and the taste of him, sweat and soap. Scott let out a yell, and he drove her head into the bookshelf, volumes raining down on them both before they crashed into the glass coffee table. It shattered underneath them, shards of glass skittered across the hardwood. She was blinded by her hair that had come loose of its tie and something warm and wet that was running freely down her face. She tasted metal and salt.

Years of pedalling up hills and across the city had made her fit and strong. Freed of his grasp for a moment, Penny turned on her back and drew her leg back, smashing her foot into his face and feeling his nose break. Blood poured from it, and he howled, picking up one of the long shards from the glass, he lunged forward, slashing out at her, narrowly missing her face. His arm drew back to come at her again.

Oh, I'm going to die, Penny thought. *This is it.*

She closed her eyes, and raised an arm to shield her face and thought of her mother who she realised was dead - had known it was so for a long time if she was honest with herself, her father who she hadn't had the chance to forgive, of Dean who didn't know they were going to have a baby... And for just a second, just a moment, she could have sworn she smelled Charmaine's lavender perfume mixing with the smell of fear and blood.

Then the door busted inwards.

For a moment, Penny thought she was hallucinating. The old woman from next door came in, with what for all the world looked like a giant rocket launcher on her shoulder. Penny startled into silence and frozen to the spot, watched in absolute fascination and she unloaded the mechanism, and a large projectile shot from the end and hit him in the back with a solid thud. He fell forwards on to his face with a grunt. A potato rolled towards Penny.

"Come on!" The old woman yelled at her.

Penny scrabbled to her feet and ran towards the woman as he sat up and shook himself off. Glancing around wildly, Penny spied the concrete planter that the pothos had been in and picked it up. She swung it hard at his head, connecting with a sickening crunch and he fell forward again and lay still.

She grabbed the old woman by her sleeve and tugged her towards the door.

They raced outside and across the lawn into the woman's house, locking the door behind them.

"What is that?" Penny asked, nodding at the thing the woman was still holding.

"Potato gun. I bought it for my grandson but decided to keep it."

"Right. Okay."

The old woman went to her phone and began dialling the police. Listening to the phone call in the background, Penny walked numbly to the woman's kitchen and turned on the taps over the sink and dry retched. Her head was throbbing, and her eye had begun to close. It was like her whole body was blooming in pain all of a sudden. Should they wait outside? What if he got away? He had known she was Charmaine's daughter the whole time. She had been sitting in the living room with her mother's killer.

Suddenly, from outside, Penny heard someone calling her name.

"Penny!"

She opened the door and cautiously peered out.

"Dean?"

"Penny!"

"*Steve?*"

She saw both Dean and Steve running across the lawn to the unit, Mae tumbling from the car after them.

"What are you doing here?" she asked, as Dean reached her and pressed her tightly to him, making her yelp. He apologised and pulled back, gasping. Penny reached a hand up to touch her face, which until that moment, she had forgot about.

Steve reached her and pulled her into a quick hug before turning and retching on to the lawn.

"For christ's sake," Mae muttered, pushing past him and peering into Penny's face. "You'll be fine. Few cuts and bruises, but nothing permanent. Where is the asshole anyway?"

Penny motioned towards the unit as the old woman appeared at the door to tell them the police were on their way. She narrowed her eyes at Steve, who was still looking green.

"Who are you?" Mae asked rudely.

"I'm Mrs. Nancy Phillips," she said back.

"She saved me," Penny offered.

Mae nodded and started striding across the lawn towards Scott Young's unit.

"What are you doing?" Dean hissed.

"We still need answers, Dean," she said over her shoulder. "We still need to know where she is, and this might be our only chance. Once the police get here, it will be over."

"She's right," Penny said. She looked up at Dean, "I need to know. I have to know what happened."

. . .

Reluctantly, Dean followed Mae across the lawn, Penny holding tightly to his hand. Mrs. Phillips came too, which Penny found unsurprising, this was likely going to be the tale she told everyone for the rest of her life.

"And I never liked him," she was saying to Steve. "So secretive. Why would anyone be secretive unless they have something to hide?"

"I'm not sure," Steve replied.

Cautiously, they crept up to the doorway of Scott Young's unit, Mae peering around the corner of the doorframe and into the living room, to where he lay, a crumpled heap on the floor.

"He's breathing," she said finally. "Bummer."

Penny breathed a sigh of relief and felt strangely glad she hadn't killed him even after he had tried to kill her moments before. Pushing the door open wider with the toe of her boot, Mae tiptoed into the unit and whistled.

"Holy shit, it looks like a tornado went through here."

Mae's boots crunched on the glass as she walked over to Scott Young.

"You want the journal, Penny?" Mae called back to them.

She bent down to grab the journal that had fallen in the struggle, her hand brushing over Scott's. She gasped suddenly, falling over and scrambled towards him, placing her hands on his temples.

Penny was so startled by this that she found herself rooted to the spot. She hadn't known Mae long, but she knew her enough to understand that she barely touched people at all - now her hands were pressed to the sides of Scott Young's face, her own head mere inches from his, her eyes and Young's connected. It seemed beyond personal, bordering on intimate.

"What is she doing?" Steve whispered scuttling back towards Mrs. Phillips.

"I have no idea," Dean replied slowly.

They held their breath, the air seemed charged around them, as though it were filled with static electricity. Abruptly, Mae broke contact and fell back, looking shocked and shaking.

"You helped him," she whispered.

Young looked up at her, a small smirk creeping along his face and Penny looked away, nauseated.

Police sirens wailed in the distance, and Mae got to her feet, shaking herself off, "I have to go."

Dean nodded briskly, "Go. We'll stay."

"Where is she going?" Steve asked.

"Away," Penny answered. "She was never here."

CHAPTER 35

It was two days before Dean or Penny saw Mae again. When they woke on the third morning, she was sitting at the table in Dean's apartment looking like she hadn't slept the entire time. Dean had gotten up and made them all coffee, and Mae had held hers, warming her hands on it like it was the dead of winter and not nearly summer.

When they had finished their coffee, Mae asked Dean if she could be alone with Penny. He looked at Penny for confirmation, and Penny realised that he was worried she would need someone to support her when Mae told her whatever she had seen when she touched Scott Young but she felt surprisingly steady. She nodded and smiled encouragingly at him, and he went and got his shoes and wallet and disappeared out the front door, shutting it softly behind him.

Mae breathed a sigh as he left and smiled ruefully at Penny, "He thinks I'm a good person."

"You *are* a good person."

"I'm not, Penny. I'm really not. I've done terrible things. I know Dean told you some of it, but you don't know. Neither of you do. Not really."

"Do you... do you want to tell me? You can talk to me, Mae."

Penny thought afterwards that she felt like Mae had been waiting a long time to find the right person to tell it to, once she began to talk, the words poured from her like a dam overflowing, spilling into the room. Her anguish curling like tendrils until Penny herself felt like instead of Mae reading her, she was imprinting herself on to Penny.

"I think I might have been me for the first four years of my life. When I was four, my sister Bekka was born, and so I stopped being Mae and became her. After that, I was everyone else.

I don't know why I am what I am. I would touch people, and suddenly it was like watching a movie on fast forward, pieces of their life would come rushing at me, their feelings and all the things they didn't say out loud. I said things a couple of times when I was young, things I shouldn't have known, and I quickly figured out that people didn't like that. Secrets are as much a part of human nature as love is. And hate. Hate is a part of human nature too. It was just easier to be someone else, and since I already knew what the inside of other people looked like, it was easy enough to just put them on and wear them around.

I ended up leaving home at fifteen, I never found it very easy to be around anyone for any length of time. So, I would travel from place to place, get a job, be Rosa or Stacey or Jessica for a while. I'm not going to lie, I kind of hated people. Everyone was just so full of shit. I think that's why I liked Dean so much, there isn't a lot of bullshit to that guy, you know? He has his secrets, but they're kind of harmless, white lie type secrets. It was everyone else I couldn't stand. The asshole 'nice guy' in the elevator who would sleep with drunk girls who were passed out. The woman who would dress her kids nicely but hit them behind closed doors. And then I saw Him.

It was just one of those chance brushes that happen every day. This busy street in Melbourne with business people walking fast and a mother with her toddler crying and tugging on her shirtsleeve, a busker with his guitar case open in front of him. People kept brushing past me, and I had a headache, and then He brushed against me, his hand touching mine. Suddenly, it was like the whole street was empty, everyone else was gone - the busker, the crying kid - and the world was silent, and it was just Him and me. The things he had done... I thought I had seen every horrible thing a person could think or do, but he was..." Mae shuddered and Penny went to reach across the table, but stopped just short of Mae's hand. To her surprise, Mae grabbed it and cling to it like a lifeline, and Penny realised she was there now, with Him, back on that street in Melbourne.

"And he was inside me too, I could feel him there, putting his fingers inside of my mind and finding all the parts of me that I kept hidden. I couldn't breathe or move for a second. I was just frozen while he walked around inside me like he owned me. Like I was his. And he seemed proud of it. He watched me as I was forced to watch what he had done. He took me on this tour of his greatest hits. That was the words in his head. His greatest hits. I could feel him, standing behind me as I watched, like I could feel his breath on the back of my neck, and I felt him smile. And then he was gone." she released Penny's hand and shook herself as though to shake loose the monster from inside her head.

"I can't see faces, not really. What you see when you look at a lover is not what his friend would see or what his mother would see. The features are all the same, but the arrangement is different. This guy, though? He didn't have a face at all. In his mind, he was faceless. He was everyone and no one.

I just... I needed to catch him. Not only because he was a monster. Because he knew I knew. Everything I knew, anyone I had loved, my parents, Bekka, Dean - he knew about them. He knew about me. I didn't know what he looked like, but I knew other things. Eventually, I figured, the best way to catch him was to let him catch me.

. . .

There was a place he seemed to return to over and over. So, I got a job there and became his ideal victim. I became Jenna. Jenna had blonde hair and green eyes. Jenna was a runner. She ran in the mornings before work, long stretches up the mountain. It took me several months to build the stamina of the real Jenna. I drank green tea and ate kale chips. For dinner, I had grilled skinless chicken breasts. The day it happened was cool and crisp, I was running up the winding stretch of road lined by the rainforest. I had earphones in.

He took me just as I had rounded the third bend in the road. He wore a black jacket and a grey knit cap. I didn't see his face. I was the fourth slim, athletic, blonde woman he had taken. Jenna fit his profile perfectly, and on that day, I was Jenna.

He dragged me by the hair into the brush, leaving strands of bleach blonde on a pine tree we passed. My sneakers gouged tracks in the dirt. Three fingernails ripped on a rock as I grabbed for something to stop myself. I left a smear of blood from my cheek on the leaves and grass where I lay as he punched my face. Those are the things the police found. I didn't want to scream, but I couldn't help it. I just...

His breathing was heavy and jagged as we fought, my arms and legs scrambling against his. He was so heavy, I couldn't get him off me. He hit me in the face three times before I blacked out. Just before the world went black, I thought I had made a terrible mistake. I thought I had been stalking him, but just before everything went dark, I heard him say my name. He knew I was hunting him. He knew the whole time.

Then... I was in the dark.

There was a dirt floor. There was a stained thin mattress and a bucket. A bottle of water... and nothing else. The water alerted me to the fact he intended to keep me for a time, at least. And I knew he knew that I had seen what was coming. And I felt like that would have... excited him somehow. That I knew I wasn't getting out. See, people read about monsters all the time. They hear confessions, they watch documentaries. But, I knew things that their bones couldn't tell those who found them. I knew their last words. I *was* Him - for that moment when we touched. I couldn't fight him as myself. If I was going to get out of this, I needed to *be* Him.

When he came in, he had a trash bag and a knife. He didn't expect me to get up to greet him. He didn't expect my posture, the breathing, the way I loped across the ground towards him, not violently at first, but interested, like he was an experiment. I pulled on Mr. Stevens. Mr. Stevens, my biology teacher, 9th grade, quick wit, coffee black, took taekwondo at the YMCA. I think it was just the surprise that got him. He was down, hurt. And I was the one with the knife. I knew... I knew how he had done it. And I wanted to hurt him back. See, it wasn't just that I had seen inside him, whenever I touch someone I *am* them. I *am* what they are. He had made me *be* him. And I fucking hated that. Like I would never, ever be clean again.

I thought he was dead. I swear to god, I thought he was dead. I had called emergency from a payphone to let them know where to find him. Of course, I didn't give a name. And when they came, he was gone. I couldn't figure it out. I knew he must have gotten out, but I couldn't figure out how. Until I touched Scott Young.

He helped him. With the girls. He had never worked alone, they did it together. Scott had been on his way when... he must have found him not long after I left. Charmaine was the only one that Scott had ever taken himself. He wasn't like Him. Scott would just go along, help out, like a fucking apprentice or something. But he did help him escape."

"Oh god," Penny breathed. Her hands shook uncontrollably, and she gripped the table trying to still herself.

Mae reached across to Penny and took her hand, "But Penny?"

She looked up, seeing the first flicker of the Mae she knew alight on her face.

"Penny, I have a face."

· · ·

Scott Young had been different. His strange mind that saw so many things that weren't there, like Charmaine's natural politeness meaning affection, also saw faces in a way that was startlingly accurate. When she saw Penny or Mrs. Phillips in his head, she saw a nearly exact copy of what they actually looked like. She didn't have a name, in Scott's head, he thought of him only as T. But she did have a face.

Finally, Mae told Penny what had happened to her mother. To Penny's surprise, Mae pulled out a piece of paper from her jeans pocket. It was folded and creased and covered in writing. She read from it, looking up at Penny from time to time.

"He saw her at the pharmacy where she worked. He bought cough syrup, and she had smiled at him. He waited outside and followed her home. He started seeing the same psychologist, booking appointments that were next to hers. They would chat sometimes, get a coffee now and then. When she left for work one day he hopped the fence and got inside through a window she left open. He went into her room and looked through her things. In the bathroom, he found her prescriptions. And in a bookshelf in the lounge room, he found her journals. He read them all. Pieces of her, caught between the pages. She wrote all the time, I think. Even when she was off the meds. She was sick, he thought. But that made her seem even more beautiful. Delicate. Like a... I'm sorry, Penny."

Penny shook her head, "It's okay. Go on."

Mae swallowed, "Like a hothouse flower. That's the words in his head. I don't... I just see what they think."

She looked at Penny with guilt in her eyes, as though she were the one who had done this. Penny supposed when you could see things from inside the head of the person who had done it - when you could think their thoughts - that is exactly what it felt like.

"I know," she said. "It's not your fault."

Mae nodded and turned her eyes back to the paper, "He watched her go to see you and your dad and that made him feel jealous. He didn't like that she had other people. He wanted to keep her. So he began to let her catch him following her. He moved things in the house. Took things that he knew she would notice were missing. He... god, I'm so sorry."

"He was gaslighting her."

"Yes. When Charmaine left, he followed her to the hospital. He watched her there for a time. Sneaking in when she went for food or medication. Touching her things. To be... close. She came back one day early, she had forgotten her wallet. She caught him there and realised she wasn't imagining things. He was there. He had the photo in his hands. And she just... lost it. She ran at him and knocked it to the ground. He hit her, and she fell down and he... Penny, I can't."

For all her bluster and brashness, she was hurting. Mae could probably feel more empathy than anyone.

"It's okay. I don't need to know the rest."

"He buried her out west, there is a road that says Wilson's Creek. There is an abandoned house in a field and a windmill that is missing two blades. She's under that."

Mae got up to leave, brushing her hands against her

pants like they were covered in something she needed to get off. She stuffed the paper back in her pocket.

"Mae," Penny called out.

Mae turned around.

"The emails. Did Scott Young write them?"

Mae shook her head, "No."

Something about her face made Penny think she was lying about something.

"But you know who did?" she asked.

Mae took a deep breath, "I think it was Him."

"Him? You mean... but why?"

"The same reason he does anything. To hurt people." She opened the door to leave.

"Wait! Mae! Those emails, they were so... I mean, they sounded like her. They sounded like my Mum."

Mae shut the door and turned around, "He would have read her, Penny. I think... I think he knew what Scott was doing and he followed her too. Maybe just brushed against her one day and she didn't even know it. The thing was, when Scott had you in his house, he was thinking about Him. He was planning to bring you to Him. And now that's one more reason that I can't fail."

Penny felt a wave of nausea roll over her.

Mae pulled the door open again, "And I have to find him soon."

"Why?" Penny asked, her voice barely above a whisper.

Mae smiled, "Because ever since I touched your grandfather, I'm losing my memories."

And with that, she was gone.

CHAPTER 36

Dean had offered to drive her out to Wilson's Creek, but Penny asked Rosie if she would take her. There was the obvious reason - that perhaps her mother was tethered there and Rosie could talk to her and help Penny say goodbye. But more than that it was just that she felt like she needed someone who was a mother with her when she went looking for her own.

They had driven quietly, occasionally Rosie made small talk about her work as a photographer or her daughter. Finally, she began to talk about her husband.

"He died in a car accident, nearly three years ago now."

"I'm sorry," Penny said, looking over at her.

Her face stared resolutely at the road, her mouth tight with grief, but her eyes clear.

"Thank you. It was... well. You know how hard it is. Not getting that chance to say goodbye? It feels like everything is half done. The thing is, Penny, grief never really goes away, you just learn to live with it, and as you grow, you grow around it. I see Ben all the time. Not like, see him physically, but just reminders of him. Especially when I look at Lucy."

"Did you see him afterwards? With your... uh... gift?"

"No."

They were quiet for a moment, and Penny wondered if she had offended Rosie somehow.

"My grandmother did," Rosie said, finally.

"June?"

Rosie nodded, "It's a family gift. But I didn't have it then. She saw Ben with me, watching us, looking out for us. He said goodbye."

They drove for hours, past bushland and fields, and through small towns, before they saw the sign for Wilson's Creek. Rosie pulled up at a bakery and went in to enquire about an abandoned house with a windmill missing two blades, saying she was a photographer looking for a shoot location. She came out and began driving without a word. It was another thirty minutes down dirt roads before they found the place Mae had described.

Penny opened the door and stepped out, dirt crunching under her feet. The sky was dark with thunderheads, and she could smell the ozone in the air. The house itself was set far back into the property.

"The windmill is behind the house," Rosie said. "We will have to walk, the gate is padlocked."

They traipsed across the ground, mindful of snakes in the long grass. Thunder rolled in the distance, and Penny looked up at the sky as the first drops began to fall. The sky opened, and rain soaked them, the ran for the shelter of the house, Rosie dashing up the stairs to the verandah with Penny not far behind. Rosie shouted something that Penny couldn't hear over the sound of the rain hitting the tin roof.

"What?" she shouted back.

But Rosie shook her head.

They stood in silence, watching as the trees bent, submitting to the wind, leaves wrenched from branches flung themselves across the field, cartwheeling along the grass. It was sudden and fierce but short-lived, and within fifteen minutes, the rain had stopped, and the sky was clearing.

"I'm glad we weren't driving in that," Rosie remarked.

Penny nodded, and they walked back down the steps, heading towards the windmill that was at the back of the house, two blades missing, exactly as Mae said they would be.

"What's it like?" Penny asked. "When you see them? Are they just there like humans, or do they appear?"

"Both," Rosie said. "It depends. But I can't see your mother right now if that's what you mean."

It was what she had meant. Penny reached the base of the windmill, which stood atop small cylindrical concrete blocks. Nearby was an old water tank, filled with holes. Water leaked out from some of them, and the ground was sodden underfoot.

"I don't know where to look," Penny said. She looked at Rosie for guidance, who shook her head.

"It doesn't work that way. I'm not psychic."

"Right."

. . .

Penny closed her eyes and took a deep breath. *Where are you, Mum? Tell me where to look.*

She opened her eyes and walked slowly around the water tank.

Not here. Not here.

She turned east, back towards the windmill and stopped abruptly, heading towards a small stand of gum tree saplings twenty metres away.

"Here," she called over her shoulder.

"Are you sure?" Rosie asked. "It's a good way from the windmill."

"It just feels different here."

Rosie shrugged and came over. They hadn't brought any tools, but the ground was soft from the rain, and they pushed the soil away with their hands. They didn't need to work for long. Rosie's hands scooped away the dirt, and under it, the unmistakable stark white of bone showed itself. Rosie gasped and pulled back, but Penny felt calm, her hand reaching slowly out to touch the gentle curve, surprisingly cool under her fingertips.

She had found her, after all. Her mother.

CHAPTER 37

Penny stood at the doorway. The room was darkened from
the overcast sky, Alice was no more than a misshapen lump
of blankets on the bed. She waited for her eyes to adjust and
saw that she was lying with her back to the door. She barely
moved, and Penny turned to tiptoe away, leaving Alice to
sleep.

"I'm awake," Alice called.

"Sorry. I thought you were napping..." Penny hesitated,
unsure how to continue. She opened her mouth, but nothing
came out. She had been wanting to come see Alice for days
but was waiting for her cuts and bruises to fade a bit. She
tentatively touched her forehead, where there was still a
knot of swollen flesh. She had covered it as best she could
with makeup, but Marg's eyes had still bulged out of her
head when she had opened the door.

"The doctor already told us," Alice said. "If that was what
you were worried about telling me. It's okay, you know, we
always knew it was a long shot."

Penny's breath left her with a whoosh of relief. Alice

rolled on to her back and pushed herself upright, pulling a book she had been reading on to her lap.

"I'm sorry, Alice," Penny said. "I wanted it to be a match so badly."

Alice waved her hand as though she were shooing gnats, "Come sit here, beside me. I've missed your face."

Penny went over and sat on the chair beside the bed, the back was a strange angle that made her feel as though she were sitting at attention, waiting for something to happen. Close up, she could see that the book on Alice's lap was the book of birds that Alice had been reading when Penny first met her. She squinted down at the page, trying to make out the illustration in the dim light.

"It's a Regent Honeyeater," Alice said and traced her finger over the illustration. "They're mostly in the southern parts, but some people have seen them up here. I've always wanted to see one."

"Maybe you still will," Penny said. "We could take a trip down south and go hunting."

Alice laughed, but they both knew they wouldn't be taking that trip. Alice took her hand.

"I did it for Mum, you know? Looking for a match for the marrow. I'm just..." She sighed. "My first memories are of being sick, I remember a few things before that, but mostly I remember the hospitals. Even when I was well again, Mum would fuss. Every bruise or cough or sniffle, she would be rushing over. I'm just tired."

Penny felt a crushing weight on her chest at the thought of losing Alice, so newly found. They hadn't had enough time.

"It's not fair," she said softly before she realised she had spoken.

"No, it's not," Alice agreed, she looked up at Penny and gasped. Her hand touching the darkened bruise near her eye. She had tried to conceal it with makeup but clearly had failed.

"It's okay," Penny said, hurriedly.

"What happened to you?" Alice flicked on the lamp beside her bed and gasped again. "Oh my god, Penny!"

Reluctantly, Penny filled Alice in on what had happened with Scott Young, leaving out the part about Mae, the emails, and her monster.

"Mum said they had arrested someone on the news over a cold case, I had no idea that it was related to your mother. Oh, Penny, I'm so sorry."

"I knew she was gone, deep down. Somewhere, I think I knew."

"You found her, your mother?"

"We did."

They sat quietly for a while, Alice's hand light and soft in Penny's.

"Alice? Can I tell you something else?"

Alice turned to her, "Of course."

"I'm pregnant."

Alice sat so still that for a moment, Penny thought she hadn't heard, then her face split into a grin that lit her whole face, flushing her with so much vitality that for a brief second it was almost possible to forget that she was sick at all.

"I'm going to be an auntie!" She crowed.

"Shh!" Penny said, laughing, "I haven't told anyone yet. Not even the father. You're the first person I've told."

"My lips are sealed," Alice said, adding, "But Penny? You should tell Dad. He lost his wife. He is going to lose his daughter. Don't make him have to lose two of them."

———

She pedalled in the back gate the same way she always did. Lloyd had been told, of course, the police had informed him when Scott Young was arrested and that remains were found. They hadn't officially identified her of, but Penny knew it was her. Her mother had spoken to her that day. She knew that somehow, Charmaine had led her to where she needed to look. She had wanted to be found.

Lloyd was in the kitchen and looked up as she walked in, his face registering surprise, which he quickly covered.

"You want a drink, kid?" he asked.

She nodded and sat at the table, in the same seat that she had been taking across from him for as long as she could remember. He slid a glass of juice in front of her and placed an umbrella in it, taking his seat at the other end of the table. Between them sat the chair that Charmaine had always occupied, empty, untaken for years. Neither of them had ever sat there, Penny realised. Not even when it was inconvenient for them to pass things to each other across the table. It had never even occurred to her to sit there. They had both been waiting for her, leaving a space at the table, and in their lives, for the day that Charmaine would come home to them.

. . .

She wanted to say she was sorry. She wanted to say she forgave him. But as she looked at her father, she realised that nothing needed to be said. It was enough that she was there with him.

She swallowed, "Dad? I have something I want to tell you."

CHAPTER 38

Autumn.

Penny stood on the edge of the cliff, looking out at the view. The trees seemed to go on forever, but out there some-where, beyond where she could see, was the city and home. If she used her imagination, she could almost see a thin blue line that would be the ocean. Clouds made shadows on the valley below her, and the wind whipped her hair around her face. Up here in the mountains, the air already had a chill to it, but the autumn sun was still warm on her shoulders. Still, she tugged her cardigan around her tighter, pulling the sides over the swelling of her stomach, which rose beneath her shirt. Under her skin, the baby danced and swam. Penny pressed her hands to it and felt the slow, rolling movement. The baby reminded of her a humpback whale breaching the surface, the way it would turn over and settle back down.

.   .   .

Footsteps crunched on the dry grass behind her and Dean's warm hand pressed against the small of her back, supportive but unobtrusive. *I'm here*, it said, *whenever you're ready*. She wasn't sure she would ever feel ready.

For the last few months, she had spent all her free time with Alice and Marg. Lloyd would come over to Marg's house, and the four of them would sit around, sharing meals and laughing. It made Penny ache to think of all the time she had lost. Was this what it could have been like all along? A real family. Lloyd would look at her with guilt in his eyes and Penny knew that he would never forgive himself.

After they had buried Charmaine, Penny and he had stood in front of the plot of freshly turned soil, staring at it.

"I thought she would come home," he had said. His voice had sounded small and confused, as though he still couldn't quite believe she was gone, "She always came home."

For weeks, he had seemed so stoic about it, dry-eyed as he made the funeral arrangements. It was only as he watched the casket be lowered into the ground that she saw it all drop away, he crumpled inwards as she watched. All the years of grief pouring from him. Penny had looked at him, standing there in his new suit, the way it hung on his body which seemed smaller somehow. All of those years, he had been waiting for her. He had never given up hope she would come home. For Lloyd, moving on with Marg would have meant admitting Charmaine would never return. For better or worse, Charmaine had been the love of his life. It was in that moment that she had truly forgiven him.

. . .

Alice had died at home. It was a brutally hot summer day, the air con was blasting in the Marg's house, but Alice lay under a pile of blankets. She said she always felt cold. Alice reminded Penny of Teddy, the way she was curled up under them, all the fat had melted from her bones, until Penny could see the sharp ridges of her skeleton underneath. Her hair had begun to grow back, tiny dark fluff on her head. She hadn't been conscious at all that final day, just quietly going about her work of dying while Lloyd, Penny, Marg, and the nurse stood by, waiting for it to be over. Alice slipped away without fanfare, in a brief moment of time when all of them had left the room. Marg had been beside herself, they had been staggering their shifts beside Alice for three days so she was never alone, and when she finally went, no one could remember whose turn it had been to be there. Privately, Penny thought Alice had done that deliberately. She had never complained at all, except for the day before her death when she had turned to Penny with pain in her eyes and sighed.

"This is very hard work," she had said, before closing her eyes and drifting into a morphine laced sleep.

Alice had asked that Penny take her ashes and scatter them at the top of Mount Wonder.

"Do not bury me in the ground," she had commanded. "I don't want to be in a box somewhere. Mum would turn it into a shrine. Just take me up there and let me go."

She had asked that Penny go alone, without Lloyd or Marg.

"No weeping. Just fling me off and go and have lunch or something, okay?"

Penny had never been to Mount Wonder before today. She asked Dean to drive her. He had been giving her driving lessons for a couple of months, but she still didn't have her license and wasn't confident navigating the winding mountain roads in any case. She could see why Alice chose it. It was quiet, aside from the sounds of birds and bubbling of the nearby creek that wound its way down the side of the mountain. Dean handed her the box that held Alice's ashes.

"I don't know how to do this," she said to him.

"Neither do I. But I don't think there is a right or wrong way."

A bird landed on the tree beside them, and Penny looked over.

"Look," she whispered to Dean.

"What is it?" he asked.

The bird cocked its head at Penny and chirped at her, singing in its sweet warble. Its yellow plumage was striking against the muted green leaves. Alice had been right. It was beautiful.

"It's a Regent Honeyeater," Penny said.

Dean looked at it and leaned in to Penny, "It looks like a normal bird."

The bird took flight, and Penny watched it disappear into the trees.

She looked up into Dean's face, "I want to name the baby Alice."

"Alice," he placed a hand against her stomach, and the

baby kicked him in response, making both of them laugh. "I think she agrees."

Together, Penny and Dean removed the lid of the box and shook the contents out over the valley below, letting the wind take the ashes. They watched for a moment, quietly, before Dean took the box and reached out his hand to Penny.

"Ready to go?" he asked.

"Can I have a minute? Just... by myself?"

"Of course," he kissed her forehead. "I'll wait just up the trail."

Penny reached into the pocket of her maternity jeans and pulled out a piece of paper. It was crumpled and soft around the edges from wear. When Emma had handed it to her, she had said that Henry had wanted to give her a message. From wherever Henry was, deep inside his own mind, he had reached out to her.

Unmatched. Alice will die. Alice will live.

Alice *would* live. Whenever Penny called her daughter by her name. When Penny took her out to watch the birds, naming each one for her. Whenever Penny thought of her sister.

They say that love is the last thing to go. Long after you forget your children, your wife, your own name - you remember love.

People lived on in memories. A journal covered in linen. Zucchini pasta. A book being read by the bath. A paper umbrella in a glass of juice. A girl who looked familiar to everyone. A man who could reach through time. A pair of forgettable blue eyes.

Penny held the note out and let the wind catch it, taking it from her fingertips and sending it soaring over the valley.

I was telling Penny about the raven I kept seeing. I told her that one meant sorrow. She laughed and called it superstitious, and it is, but I can't help thinking that rhyme whenever I see one. Then later, we were walking back from the corner store after buying ice creams, and Penny grabbed my arm and pointed.

"What does two mean?" she asked.

I looked over to where she was pointing and on the fence was a pair of ravens, cocking their heads at us, looking like two old gentlemen tipping their hats.

"Happiness," I said. "Two means happiness."

ACKNOWLEDGMENTS

As always, I want to thank my dedicated team of beta readers who encourage and support me, and tell me when parts suck – Kelly, Sarah, Netra, and Danielle. Danielle has been my guiding light through this writing journey, I can't tell you how much easier it has been with her support. A special shout out to Netra and her husband Ákos (the bird-man), for their assistance with bird related questions. I write paranormal fiction so there is a lot of make believe, but I do know that bird people *will not* tolerate any inaccuracies. I don't know a lot about birds but I do admire them, and it made sense to me that Alice would be a bird person. The print hanging in Alice's room is a real print, Netra and Ákos take wonderful photographs of wildlife and they can be found on Facebook at 2MadPhotographers, Ákos's work can be found on Facebook at A Matter of Light - and there you can see the real photo I based the one on Alice's wall from.

I would like to thank the colourful and supportive group of writers on IG. Keep on rockin' on.

I also want to thank my husband and children for being so supportive of my writing. They all cheerlead me on when I'm feeling the writing blues, when I can't make something work, when I'm ready to pitch my laptop into the sea. They also share my excitement when the proof copy comes in and we collectively 'ooo' and 'ahh' over the book. It is a magic that I cannot explain when you hold in your hands the story you wove from nothing.

In many ways, Forgettable is about Penny's journey to discover herself and allow herself permission to be the person that *she* wanted Penny to be. For many women, myself included, we try to fit into the boxes that are given to us, knowing that we don't sit comfortably inside them. We wait for someone else to validate our feelings and dreams before we pursue them. We apologise. There is a love story of Penny and Dean woven into Forgettable, but there is a bigger love story in there – and that is of Penny with herself. When she lies beside Dean in bed and he asks her what she is 'writing' her life to be, she answers 'Penny'. Your children will grow up, your job will get by without you, your partner will never fill your whole life. There will be one person that you will be with, day in and day out, for the rest of your life, and that is yourself. Allow yourself to take up space. Write your own name on your life in big, bold letters.

Pieces of Forgettable were taken from my personal journals. They were so painfully raw that I felt I could never share them, except under the guise of fiction. Readers of my memoir will know that my grandfather had Alzheimer's Disease, and that this was difficult for my family. Like Penny, we too have gone through the strange grief that comes with mourning the loss of someone while they are still right there beside you.

So, this book, I dedicated to him. The man who always told me I was extraordinary, even when I was not, and who I know would have held this book in his hands and marvelled at the fact I had managed to create it.

After I finished writing, but before it was published, my grandfather passed away. He and my grandmother created a family that is close and loving. He was sent off with those who cared for him nearby.

My grandfather had twinkling blue eyes and a laugh like a surprise. Years ago, on his birthday, in a fit of sentimentality and uncommon foresight, I told him that he was an amazing father figure in my life. It embarrassed him a little then, and everyone else sighed at me being silly and insisting we tell each other things we are grateful for on our birthdays, but I'm glad that I did it.

As a child I loved him with something akin to hero worship. I loved him like the sun and stars. He colours my best memories with his presence, his spirit is so entwined with mine that I will carry him with me for the rest of my earthly days.

Here is to the man who rocked me to sleep, that taught me to ride a bike, that spent countless hours indulging my chatter, that cried on my first day of school.

Here is to the smell of the soap he used.

Here is to the singlet that must always be worn.

Here is to the white van with the blue stripes.

Here is to the man who once told me that he would

always come to save the day because that is what a father does.

Here is to one of the best men I have ever known, who left a hard act for any man to follow.

Here is to my grandfather.

Vale.

Peter James Brewer (Poppy)

13/09/1935 - 02/10/2020

You are unforgettable.

ABOUT THE AUTHOR

Liss Brewer lives in Brisbane, with her husband, her children, and her cats. Her first title, The Curator: A Memoir of Motherhood, was published in 2020. Liss then went on to write paranormal fiction, with both Shielded and Forgettable published in 2020.

Liss enjoys hot cups of tea, reading, playing in the garden, and daydreaming. Her books are available in paperback worldwide via selected sites, or via her website for Australian distribution. Ebooks are available worldwide.

You can find her on Facebook, Instagram, Twitter, and Pinterest.